W9-CIL-513

TEAM HUMAN

Justine Larbalestier
and
Sarah Rees Brennan

HARPER
TEEN
An Imprint of HarperCollins*Publishers*

HarperTeen is an imprint of HarperCollins Publishers.

Team Human
Copyright © 2012 by Justine Larbalestier and Sarah Rees Brennan
All rights reserved. Printed in the United States of America.
No part of this book may be used or reproduced in any manner
whatsoever without written permission except in the case of brief
quotations embodied in critical articles and reviews. For information
address HarperCollins Children's Books, a division of HarperCollins
Publishers, 10 East 53rd Street, New York, NY 10022.
www.epicreads.com

Library of Congress Cataloging-in-Publication Data
Larbalestier, Justine.
  Team Human / Justine Larbalestier and Sarah Rees Brennan. — 1st ed.
     p.   cm.
  Summary: Residing in New Whitby, Maine, a town founded by vampires
trying to escape persecution, Mel finds her negative attitudes challenged
when her best friend falls in love with a vampire, another friend's father
runs off with one, and she herself is attracted to someone who tries to pass
himself off as one.
  ISBN 978-0-06-208964-9 (trade bdg.)
  [1. Vampires—Fiction.   2. High schools—Fiction.   3. Schools—Fiction.
4. Maine—Fiction.]   I. Brennan, Sarah Rees.   II. Title.
PZ7.L32073Te 2012   2011026149
[Fic]—dc23   CIP
                                                                        AC

Typography by Carla Weise
12 13 14 15 16   LP/RRDH   10 9 8 7 6 5 4 3 2 1
❖

First Edition

Without Team Vampire,
the writers whose vampires
have inspired and delighted us,
Team Human would never have been.
This book is dedicated with thanks to
John Ajvide Lindqvist, Heather Brewer,
Rachel Caine, Suzy McKee Charnas,
Caroline B. Cooney, Jewelle Gomez,
Claudia Gray, Barbara Hambly,
Charlaine Harris, Alyxandra Harvey,
Tanya Huff, Alaya Dawn Johnson,
Stephen King, Elizabeth Knox,
Tanith Lee, J. Sheridan Le Fanu,
Robin McKinley, Richelle Mead,
Stephenie Meyer, Anne Rice,
James Malcolm Rymer, L. J. Smith,
Bram Stoker, Scott Westerfeld
. . . and all the many other talented advocates
for the undead.

CHAPTER ONE

Two Girls and a Hazmat Suit

I wasn't feeling very enthused about education the day the vampire came to school.

Usually, since we live in Maine, it's cold. This September, the sun was invading the sky, bright and fierce, and my best friend, Cathy, and I were hauling our bags up one of the steep streets and sweating.

I was also not feeling very enthused about vampires. But I never am.

Cathy is a different matter.

If there was a box for "vampirologist" on one of our career goals questionnaires—and there isn't; you can be a psychiatrist for vampires, or a donor to vampires, or an academic in vampire studies, but I just made up that word to mean "a big fan of the undead"—Cathy would check it every time.

Don't get me wrong. Cathy's not stupid. She's really smart: Without her encouraging me, I wouldn't be doing AP English and history. She's a dreamer. You know the type: reads poetry by the bucket load—Keats! Plath! Chatterton!—gets so into books she walks into walls, gets so into telling me a story she walks right into traffic and I have to grab her and yank her back to safety. She likes history more than the news and likes books better than most people. Of course she thinks vampires—since many of them are older than dirt and thus basically history books with legs and fangs—are totally fascinating.

So naturally when we looked across the street and saw the figure in the bulky black suit and helmet, like a cross between Darth Vader and an astronaut, Cathy's eyes lit right up, because broad daylight plus person in weird suit must equal vampire. This in spite of the fact that very few vampires seem inclined to go into the sun in a protective suit when a single pinprick to a sleeve would kill them. Let's put it this way: I'm a born and bred New Whitby girl, and I've seen a vampire in a suit exactly once, and it was on the news.

"Maybe he's a vampire," she said, inclining her head. Cathy's too much of a lady to point at people.

I'm not much of a lady, personally, so I stared pretty openly. I wasn't the only one.

"Or maybe there's been a chemical explosion and that's the member of the hazmat team who drew the short straw," I said.

We both looked ahead at the school. Craunston High stood there like always, red brick and very solid. No flames billowing from the bay windows.

"Alternate theory," I said as we crossed the road and headed in, a little ahead of the mystery suit. "He's the keenest scuba diver in the world."

Cathy returned her gaze to the possible scuba diver and took a little wistful breath: not quite a sigh, but sort of bracing herself for her latest daydream not to be true.

"He could be a vampire."

"Yeah, I can see it," I said. "He moves with the predatory grace of a penguin."

Cathy bit back a smile so she wouldn't hurt the scuba diver's feelings. Too nice for her own good, that girl. She even held open the door so he could penguin-shuffle his hazmat butt into the school.

He inclined his big black helmet to her as he passed by and advanced into the dark hall.

Then he slid off the helmet, and I saw he was graceful after all: The movement was the way you'd imagine a knight in a fairy tale would remove his helm.

He had the kind of looks that made normal sensible thoughts turn into stupid poetry: hair like sunlight trapped in shadows and eyes that were an insane cornflower blue. A face like a sculpture on a tomb, all clean white perfect lines.

A dead person's face.

The vampire turned those eyes on Cathy, who stood

rooted to the spot, and squinted.

"Could you possibly shut the door?" he asked in a low, cool voice. "It is rather bright."

◆

You probably have the wrong idea about where I live.

New Whitby. The vampire city.

It's really not as weird as people think. It's like Las Vegas. I'm sure people who actually live in Las Vegas hardly ever play slot machines or have Elvis impersonators perform their weddings.

Lots of other places were founded by people escaping persecution because of their religion. New Whitby was founded by people escaping persecution because they were the blood-drinking undead.

We're not all vampires. And we don't all want to be vampires.

When our career guidance teacher asked us to make lists of professions we were interested in, vampire was not on mine.

I know vampire isn't technically a profession. But, seriously, you should see the ones around here.

They're pros at it. Being a vampire is their job. Vampires have long-term investments, of course. And modeling careers. The camera loves Ludmilla von Doesn't Need Airbrushing.

That's part of what I think makes vampires so boring. Once you're a vampire, you don't ever need to be anything else.

New Whitby is not only a vampire city. It never was. Plenty of humans came too. People who had vampires in the family, and people who didn't, people who just arrived here and stayed. My mom's family came over from China to America because of the railroads, moved across America selling stuff to the gold miners, and settled here. You wind up where you wind up, and no place in the world is perfect. There's always something to cope with: too hot, too cold, no night life. In our city's case, it's way too much night life. With fangs.

But like I said, it's not such a big deal. There are blood banks and donors these days. You're more likely to be killed in a plane crash than drained by a vampire, even if you live in New Whitby.

There are a ton of restrictions on making vampires now, too, so most people living here don't have vampires in the family. Except for a few vampire ancestors some people inherited, like antique chairs or the family silver, or my biology partner Laura's crazy Aya or my friend Ty's Aunt Sabine, who only comes over to his house on the holidays.

She gives truly excellent presents.

So sure, at night you'll pass a vampire here and there. Occasionally you'll find yourself sitting next to one at the movies. You'll see vampire cops walking their beats. There's an all-vampire division, since human cops faced with vampire criminals are at a bit of a disadvantage.

As you may have noticed, I'm not crazy about

vampires. I always thought they were a bit creepy. On top of the whole blood-drinking thing, they don't have human feelings. And after what happened to my friend Anna this summer, I'm even less keen on them.

But vampires tend to keep to the Shade quarter, and the tourists have to go there to goggle at them. New Whitby is a city like any other, except this one's mine: stretching up steeply from the harbor, where the *Nightshade* came in three hundred years ago, to the high smoked-glass towers gleaming in the sun beside the spikes and slopes of Victorian buildings.

◆

The school's doors were also made of smoked glass. The antidiscrimination regulations mean that it's the same in all buildings throughout the city—vampire-killing UV rays must be kept out.

Cathy shut the door with such a loud bang I jumped. But when I turned to my best friend, I saw that she hadn't taken her eyes off the vampire. She was staring at him as if Richard the Lionheart had arrived at her house for tea. As if a miracle had happened.

"I'm sorry," she said. "For the noise, I mean."

"Think nothing of it," the vampire murmured.

"Hey! My name's Mel Duan," I announced, in an attempt to break Cathy out of her blissful vampire-induced daze. "Is there something I can do for you? Can we point you to the principal's office? I bet you want to be on your way as soon as possible, huh?"

I have never received any compliments on my subtlety.

"I am not anxious to leave," the vampire said. "In fact, I have been fortunate enough to be accepted as a student in this fine center of learning. But I thank you for your offer of assistance."

His eyes slid over me in a funny way: as if he were looking at a chair instead of a person. Mind you, he didn't seem terribly impressed with Cathy, either. He looked beautiful and bored.

He also looked like a crazy astronaut suit full of trouble.

The vampire inclined his head to both of us in a way I knew Cathy would shortly be describing as "courtly."

"Permit me to introduce myself. My name is Francis Duvarney."

"Heh, Francis," I said.

The cornflower eyes iced over.

"Not funny," I continued. "Obviously. Not a funny name. Does anyone ever call you Frank? Frankie?"

"No," he said, the word coming down like an icicle dropped on my head from a height, though he wasn't all that tall.

Pretty much everyone is taller than I am.

"I'm sorry," Cathy burst out in a rush. "I'm Cathy. Catherine. Whatever you like. I . . . I'm . . ." And poor Cathy, she stammered, and went bright red, but struggled on. "This is Mel. Um, welcome to Craunston High."

"Thank you," said Francis the vampire, and his eyes rested on her for a moment as if he'd just noticed her. "Pleasure to make your acquaintance."

That was all he said. He gave yet another tiny head bow, then turned and walked away to the principal's office or the little vampire's room or wherever. I didn't care. I had other things to worry about.

Namely Cathy, her big dark eyes open wide and glowing as if she had fireflies trapped inside her head.

"This year is going to be amazing," she said with deep conviction.

Yeah, we were in trouble.

"A vampire who wants to go to high school?" I said. "That is the most ridiculous thing I've ever heard."

CHAPTER TWO

Vampire in High School

"He could be a recent vampire," Cathy said. "Not quite used to it? So he decided to finish his education? Education is important."

"Um, no. Did you hear how he talks?"

"Oh, yes." Cathy's sigh could have floated away surrounded by fluttering love hearts. "He was so courtly."

Courtly! Score one for my psychic abilities.

I also figured that Cathy would be smitten instantly and that there would be trouble ahead. All easy picks because not only has Cathy long been fascinated by vampires, she also believes in the One.

Cathy believes that when she meets the One, she will know from a single glance that they will be together forever. She's dumped two guys summarily after about a week each, because if they weren't the One, why bother?

I knew from a single glance that Cathy was going to be ridiculous about this.

She currently had the weirdest expression on her face: eyes doubled in size, lips parted, a kind of softening all over. I swear her lips were glistening, even though I know for a fact Cathy doesn't wear lip gloss. Cathy doesn't wear makeup. Something to do with skin breathing and natural health. Straight from her mom, trust me.

I don't wear makeup either, but only because I can't be bothered.

I grabbed Cathy's arm and pulled her away from the lockers she was about to walk into.

Here's the thing. Boys really go for Cathy: they tend to believe she's helpless when she's just distracted. Cathy's not used to the sinking feeling you get when you realize the guy whose name you've been doodling in your homework margins not only hasn't been doodling your name, but doesn't even know it. But how else was it going to be with Francis the who-knows-how-old hot vampire? I kind of doubted he'd come to school to pick up chicks.

How would Cathy react if her love for the One was unrequited?

I feared the worst.

Wow. Francis-speak was contagious.

I was so occupied thinking of Cathy's potential heartbreak and how to snap her out of it before it actually happened that I almost let Cathy walk right past the door to our first class.

"Cathy? Hello?" I grabbed the back of her shirt and reeled her in. "We've got Mr. Kaplan, Cathy. AP Local History." I steered her into the classroom, into a seat at the back, and then flopped down next to her.

"Hey, Mel. Hey, Cathy," Ty, my ex-boyfriend and current second-best friend, said, plunking himself on my other side.

"Isn't he beautiful?" Cathy breathed.

"Who?" Ty asked. "Oh, never mind."

Francis Duwhosenamewhatsit glided into the room like an Olympic skater across ice. The penguin resemblance had vanished. He folded himself elegantly into a seat in the front row, and all talk ceased.

"His name is Francis," I whispered.

Ty giggled. I wasn't sure if he was giggling because of the name or if it was a hysterical reaction to Francis's beauty.

"He's a vampire," I added. You know, in case Ty thought he was a really convincing vamposeur.

"I can see that. What's he doing in Local History?"

"Correcting the many inaccuracies with which your teacher will no doubt fill your heads."

Of course, Francis had freaky vampire senses, for hunting and for eavesdropping on every word we said. Cathy blushed and looked down even though Francis had not bothered to turn.

"So," I said brightly, keeping my eyes fixed straight ahead. "First day back of senior year. How 'bout that?"

"Do you think he's English?" Cathy whispered in my ear. Then she glanced at Francis, fearing he'd overheard.

It was my turn to sigh. At least she'd regained the power of speech. He did sound English, but it was hard to tell with older vampires, because in the past lots of rich Americans sounded English. Most vampires claimed to have been royalty or one of the Astors or something equally snotty. Astonishing how few peasants and regular people got vamped back in the olden days, when it wasn't regulated.

"Welcome, seniors!" Kaplan said. "Since you're in this class, I assume that you're hoping to get into UNW to specialize in the history of New Whitby or possibly even vampire studies."

I wasn't hoping to get into the University of New Whitby. I was there to keep Cathy company and try to figure out what I wanted to do with my life after high school. I was not looking forward to my first session with my college admissions adviser. My SATs were really good. Not perfect like Cathy's, but nearly perfect. They'd help me get in most anywhere I wanted. But my family wasn't rich, nor were we poor enough for financial aid. Mostly, though, the problem was that I didn't know what I wanted to be when I grew up. Much less what to study in college.

Cathy wasn't really thinking about UNW either. She was thinking about Oxford. They also have vampire studies. Lots of English accents there, though considerably fewer vampires. Not that before today I'd had any inkling Cathy was interested in dating a vampire. Even though it seemed so obvious now.

I'd just thought she was interested in them. You know, the way I like basketball. Doesn't mean I want to date a basketball player. Actually, I don't want to date anyone. The last time did not go so well.

No, not Ty. The one after Ty.

"And this year we have a special treat. Francis Duvarney, a vampire who was turned in London, England, in 1867 and has lived in our fine city since 1901—shortly after the name change to New Whitby—has joined our class."

Francis inclined his head very slightly.

"Sorry I'm late," Anna said, coming through the door looking pale, and moving as fast as she could to the back of the room. Though Cathy, Ty, and I usually formed a bit of a quartet with Anna, we hadn't seen her much over the summer.

Not after what had happened with her dad. I wasn't surprised she looked pale. I was glad to see her in school at all.

Of course, it's harder to skip when your mom is the principal, no matter how much Anna must have wanted to, once she heard there would be a vampire in class. That would have to hurt.

"Don't make a habit of it," Kaplan said before continuing to extol the unique opportunity of a vampire in class, living history, blah blah blah.

Anna hardly flinched when she saw Francis. She slid into the empty seat by the window and smiled at Ty and me. At Cathy too, who didn't notice on account of being fixated on the back of Francis's head.

I thought Cathy could maybe have spared Anna some attention, given what Anna had been through. But Cathy has a focus like a laser: It's how she gets such good grades.

Kaplan seemed pretty focused on Francis himself. Not that he was alone. Everyone seemed to be staring at the vampire.

"Would you like to tell us why you've chosen to continue your education almost one hundred and fifty years after it was prematurely cut off?"

"No," Francis said.

Half the class made that sound that comes from breathing in quickly when you're surprised. Ty actually snorted. (One of the many reasons we broke up. What's fine in a best friend can be deeply wrong in a boyfriend.)

Perhaps Francis isn't so bad, I thought, watching Kaplan's face change color.

"Those reasons are too personal," Francis continued. "But it would be my utmost pleasure to contribute to this class in any way you may find useful, Mr. Kaplan. I thank you again for allowing me to take part."

No, he was just as bad as I'd thought. Was there enough room in this class for Francis Duvarney and his ego? Was it too late for me to switch classes?

Cathy's eyes were bigger and shinier than ever.

There would be no switching classes.

I was going to have to keep watch over Cathy. I wondered how her mom would feel about me moving in.

CHAPTER THREE

The Deadly Allure of the Vampire in the Lunchroom

I'd seen a feeding frenzy in the lunchroom before. It usually happened when there were chicken fingers on the menu, though. Not vampires.

Classes had been bad enough. For the first time in my life I wished there was a teacher to supervise us at lunch. It seemed to me like there was an urgent need for someone to yell, "Anyone who licks that vampire gets a detention!"

Not that I was close enough to see if there was any licking being done. The four of us were sitting at a table pretty far away, as we hadn't been willing to fight our way through the crowd. It seemed like everyone wanted to get as close as possible to Francis.

"Does anyone else think it's a bit ridiculous that he came to lunch when he doesn't eat?" I asked.

"To be fair, neither does half the cheerleading team," Ty said.

Like the rest of the lunchroom crowd, Ty and Cathy were staring transfixed at Francis. I glanced over once or twice. Anna kept her eyes on her lunch.

It was like a one-vampire zoo. Francis was sitting as if someone had tried to put a stake through his heart but accidentally inserted it where the sun did not shine—which I guess is anywhere for vampires, but in a place where the sun does not shine even for regular people. His hands were folded on the table, in the empty space where his tray should have been.

I couldn't see where the head cheerleader Robyn Johnson's hands were, but she was leaning pretty close to Francis, and for a brief moment his facade of beautiful indifference cracked.

I'd never seen anyone look scandalized before. It was kind of hilarious.

Robyn's boyfriend, Sam Martinson, from whom she was normally inseparable, was at another table surrounded by the rest of the football team. All of them wore identical scowls. That was hilarious too.

"I think it's nice that he wants to mingle with us," Cathy said.

It really didn't look like Francis wanted to mingle, though. Possibly this was best. You heard stuff about some vampires. A lot of Cathy's mom's magazines had cover stories like "Seven Sweet Nights in an Immortal's

Love Den." I was glad it didn't seem as if I'd have to worry about Cathy joining Francis's harem.

"Yeah, he's probably on a quest to rediscover his lost humanity," Ty chimed in. Which was another common trashy magazine headline, but I suspected Ty was serious.

If Francis did have a harem, it was starting to look like Ty would want in.

"And it's nice how he doesn't want to, you know, take advantage of girls," Cathy went on.

"I don't think he likes girls," I said. "Or boys. Look at the horror on his face. He doesn't look like a people person."

"He's probably shy. It's very overwhelming being the only new person at school."

"Or the only vampire."

"True!" Cathy said. "He must be overwhelmed. Oh, poor Francis."

This wasn't just Cathy being crazy for a nice pair of fangs. She's like that all the time, putting the best interpretation on things, thinking the best of people. I heard Cathy say, in all seriousness, "People lose telephone numbers all the time," when the gorgeous guy I met on our last family vacation at Cape Cod never called me. She believed that one of my exes, Trevor, was going out of town on a "business trip" when we, and Trevor, were fifteen years old.

"Cathy, please quit talking like *you* were born in 1867," I said. "The way he's looking so pained is kind of gross, if you ask me. Oh mercy, ladies are indicating they might like to tap this. How forward!"

Cathy grinned and ducked her head, long dark hair falling in front of her face. She gets out of a lot of trouble being able to duck and cover.

"I wish some ladies would come indicate they'd like to tap this," said Ty, gesturing at himself.

"I'd like to tap this," I said, reaching over to tap his knuckles with my spoon. "Oh. That was so good. I'd like to tap it again!"

I noticed Anna stayed quiet. I leaned against her. "Hey. You doing all right?"

Anna blinked at me a few dozen times, as if I'd nudged her awake.

"Yeah," she said finally. "Can't seem to get as excited as everyone else."

I couldn't blame her. Anna's entitled to have issues with vampires. Her dad is a psychologist who specializes in vampires. You know the type: They try to help the vampires compartmentalize all their lifetimes of memories and the grieving for generations of loved ones.

He also counsels us humans. Like those considering becoming vampires—he hits them with the scary survival rates, the horrors of zombification. He also helps those who have lost family who did not survive the process of becoming vampires. Dinner at Anna's always included at least one horror story.

I always liked Dr. Saunders. We've established I'm not

the biggest vampire fan—their whole living forever, no pulse, creeps me out a bit—but still, I thought he was a pretty noble guy. Until he ran off with a vampire patient.

Turns out sitting around holding the hands of tragic glamorous vampire ladies isn't such a great job for a family man.

And vampires don't pay much attention to the whole idea of "till death do them part." Trashy undead home wreckers.

"Francis doesn't excite me in any way," I assured Anna.

Anna blinked again, still not smiling.

"Hey." I nudged her. "He isn't really freaking you out, is he? He's just some idiot vampire who wants to go to high school. Which makes him even more idiotic than the regular kind."

"Yeah," Anna said, so low I could barely hear her. "Can I—can I talk to you, Mel? Alone."

Ty and Cathy were talking about some vampire documentary they'd seen and how accurate it was. They hadn't noticed us.

"Of course. C'mon."

Even Anna's walk was slow, hesitating a little, as if she were sleepwalking.

She and her mom had seemed like they wanted to be left alone after her dad left. I know I have a tendency to stick my nose in, so after a few unanswered calls I'd tried to take the hint.

Maybe I'd taken the hint too well, I thought as Anna stopped in the shadowy hallway and turned to face me. Maybe Anna needed a friend, and I hadn't been there for her.

"It might be nothing," Anna said abruptly. "But I thought—you're good at dealing with things. When stuff goes wrong, you always take care of it."

"That's me. Take Carer of Things. I should become a caretaker. Of . . . things."

Anna didn't smile. I couldn't blame her: I was too worried to put forward my best effort.

"If something's wrong, Anna, tell me."

"My mom's acting really weird."

"I guess that's normal—" I began, but Anna made an impatient gesture.

"Not like that. Not just grief. She disappears and she won't tell me where she's going. She has nightmares and wakes up screaming. She acts like she's got a secret."

"What kind of secret?"

Anna hesitated. "I think it's something to do with the school. She's been spending a lot of time here."

Anna's mom is our principal, so her spending a lot of time at school isn't exactly unusual. Anna must've seen the doubt on my face.

"It's dumb. It's dumb, I know it is. I shouldn't have said anything."

"No," I said. "No, it's—it makes sense that she might want to throw herself into her work, right?"

"I guess," Anna said. "Look, forget I said anything. It's cool."

She took a few steps away from me and then back.

Using my uncanny powers of observation, I could somehow sense it was not cool.

"Anna." I put out a hand and stopped her pacing. "It's not dumb. I'm glad you told me."

"It's probably nothing."

Under her thick red curls, she looked white as paper. That hair made sure she got called Annie, as in Little Orphan, for years until two things happened: She got hot, and her dad left.

"Well, let me make sure," I said. "I'll keep an eye out. I'll see what's going on."

Anna still looked uncomfortable. Being the principal's kid isn't the easiest thing. She tends to keep people at a distance.

"It's not that big of a deal. I just . . . I just wanted to let you know what's going on. That's all. Sorry I haven't been in touch lately."

"Hey. No problem." I gave her a quick hug. "You're my friend. Anything that makes you feel better is a big deal to me."

"Yeah?" Anna smiled, a tiny smile. "Thanks." After a pause, she added: "We'd better be getting back."

I nodded. "Something momentous could be happening. The beautiful Francis could have turned his head and given us a view of his amazing profile."

"How many days do you give it until someone accidentally on purpose cuts themselves to get his attention?"

"Ah, spilled blood, the vampire lover's low-cut top," I said. "Personally, I'd prefer a guy who wants to see my boobs."

"You're all class, Mel," said Anna as we went back into the lunchroom to find Francis standing at our table.

I knew I shouldn't have left Cathy unguarded in the presence of vampires!

I hurried over. If a few people got shoved, then they should have got out of my way faster. Couldn't they see I was on a mission?

"—just wanted to say welcome to the school and all," said that treacherous weasel Ty. How dare he welcome Francis! It would only keep the alluring undead presence near Cathy for longer.

Francis gave him the same sort of weird look he'd given me earlier, but after a tiny pause he said: "Thank you."

To my extreme relief, Cathy was clearly too paralyzed with nerves at Ty's daring to even give Francis an adoring look. She was staring at her plate so intently, it seemed like she was having a soul-bonding moment with the baby carrots.

"Oh, hello," said Anna behind me, making an obvious effort to be polite. "My name's Anna."

"You're welcome to sit with us if you like," Ty told Francis. It was difficult to resist smacking him.

"I'm sure F-Francis," Cathy began in a strangled whisper, which died in her throat. She continued with an effort: "Perhaps he needs to get back to his table."

Maybe it was the fact that Cathy was keeping her eyes downcast, or her painful politeness, that suited Francis's idea of how a lady should behave. Maybe it was clear to him that she was nervous, and he was being kind.

His icy voice thawed slightly, and he said: "I would be delighted to join you."

"That's awesome, Frank," I told him, and slid firmly between him and Cathy.

Francis regarded me coolly.

"So you vampires living forever," I said. "You must need a lot of hobbies to keep from going completely mad. My grandma swears by knitting. Do you knit, Francis?"

"I do not," said Francis.

"Ah," I said. "Do you crochet?"

This time he didn't bother to answer.

First day of school, and on top of college applications, community service to pad said applications, fencing for ditto (oh, okay, and because I love it), I had extra toppings on my already overloaded plate: putting Anna's mind at rest about her mom and keeping Cathy away from fanged temptation.

I like to keep busy. I was sure I could handle it.

My chair was so close to Francis's that I was practically pressed up against him. As far as I could tell—and I knew that Cathy would have questions later—he was leanly muscled all over. Not that I would tell her that. I was planning on reporting arms like undead spaghetti.

He was also cold. Not ice cold, but cool like water is at room temperature. It was wrong. People should be 98.6 degrees, not 72.

I gave creepy, cold Francis a bright smile, clapped my hands together, and said: "Can you believe summer is over? Hands up, who's going to miss the sunshine?"

✦

I don't spend all my time being obnoxious to vampires. Mostly what I'm good at is what Anna said I was: taking care of my friends. Anna and Cathy are both a lot smarter than I am, but both are really bad with people. Even Ty has confidence issues, though he tries to hide them. I'm the least brilliant one, but I've always been good at solving my friends' problems. One of Dad's proverbs is "If you want happiness for a lifetime, help somebody."

That sounds about right to me.

Only none of my friends had ever had a problem as serious as Anna's before. I didn't know how to help her.

I figured a good first step would be to spend more time with her. So that day after school I left Ty and Cathy to talk with the rest of the class about the unexpected dreaminess of the undead, and I took my bike—I'll probably be able to afford a car when I'm oh, say, twenty-five—and cycled over to Anna's house.

There was a big black new SUV in Anna's driveway. I didn't recognize the car and wondered who was there.

When I rang the doorbell, it turned out the answer was Principal Saunders.

I blinked up at her, startled to find her home this early on the first day of school, and she blinked at me as if she'd been sleeping and I'd woken her.

She was usually really well put together, but now she looked thin and pale, her hair straggling. I guessed that was normal, given her husband had left her for an undead floozy. I couldn't let what Anna had said influence me too much.

"Mel," said Principal Saunders slowly. She still sounded half asleep, but her eyes were too sharp for someone who'd been dozing.

"Uh," I said. "Hi! I was wondering if Anna could come out?"

I mercifully stopped myself from adding the words *to play* at the end of that sentence. Apparently all I have to do is feel a little uneasy, and I revert to kindergarten.

"She's doing her homework," Principal Saunders said. "She can't be disturbed."

"Oh," I said. "Oh, okay. I'll call her later."

Principal Saunders didn't respond. I gave an uncomfortable laugh. She didn't even smile.

Principal Saunders had always been distant and principal-like, but that was the thing: She was principal-like. She always smiled faintly at jokes and gave the appropriate responses.

She'd always been a pretty normal parent. She never

acted strange. Not until now. (Not like Cathy's mom, who so disliked conflict, she'd decided it didn't exist and would answer all questions with yes even when she meant no.)

"Lots of excitement at school today," I remarked brilliantly. "What with the new student and everything. Francis the fabulous."

She looked pained. I was about to apologize for bringing up vampires when she spoke.

"Don't speak to him," she said. "Don't let Anna speak to him either."

"Why not?"

"Because vampires destroy people," she said so fiercely I took a step back.

Then she gave me a brief nod and closed the door.

Anna was right: Her mom was acting weird.

CHAPTER FOUR

Of Vampires and Humans

A week later and not only had I discovered nothing new on the Anna front, but the Cathy situation was even worse. I called my sister, Kristin. Then I called her again. A billion messages later, she still hadn't called me back.

"Kristin," I said to her voice mail yet again. "The boy advice, man advice, whatever, it's not for me. It's much more serious than that. Cathy's gone all moony-eyed over a boy. Not just any boy. This one is an undead pain in the butt, and he won't go away. Help!"

The bell for the end of lunch hour sounded, and I closed my phone.

Kristin studied fashion at Parsons in New York City. Sometimes she did not surface for weeks at a time. I was sure she slept in nests of fabric samples, but she had to call me back eventually. She always did.

I was getting desperate. I knew what the lunch bell meant: study hour in the library.

Traditionally, the four of us have used this time to gossip and hang out. All you have to do is keep your voice down and sit in the group discussion area. It also helped to have some kind of map or other projectlike object in the center of the table to lean over. "What are we doing, lovely librarian? Plotting world domination! Kidding. We're working on our group project on this map thing. Clearly. And plotting world domination."

But this was not our regular foursome. Somehow Anna had been replaced by Francis, who had attached himself to our group.

I assumed this was because he thought Cathy was a properly behaved young lady. He seemed to give her fewer chilly looks than he gave the rest of us.

He certainly didn't think I was a properly behaved young lady.

Anna was sitting by herself on the other side behind a wall of leave-me-alone-I-am-actually-studying books.

I knew better than to ignore the pointed fortress of books and trespass on her space, but I missed her. Francis was a terrible substitute. Study/gossip hour had become Humans 101 hour. Actually, it seemed like every free minute we had turned into Humans 101. Francis was forever pulling out his battered notebook, asking us questions, and jotting down our responses. He didn't get many answers from me. Unless he made me angry.

It was for his journal, he told us.

"He's been keeping it since 1869," Cathy said breathlessly. "Can you imagine?"

Francis looked at us proudly, as if it were some kind of an achievement to have been scribbling things down for so long. He was a vampire. What else was he going to do? Other than drink our blood, I mean. Doing anything for a long time was easy for a vampire.

"I heard you referring to yourself as a 'total ABC,'" Francis remarked. I could hear the quotation marks around the words, as if he was picking up the phrase with tongs. "Can you tell me what that refers to in your culture?"

"My culture is American," I snapped. "And that's what it means. American-Born Chinese."

"Does it mean you can't speak Chinese?"

"I can't speak Mandarin or Cantonese or Hakka or any other Chinese language. Neither can my parents, who are also ABC," I said, and made a face at Francis.

Francis did not respond to my face making as well as he did to Cathy's damsel-in-distress glances.

"I thank you for doing me the courtesy of informing me on the subject," he said calmly. "I am most interested in the magic of other cultures."

"I'd thank you to do me the courtesy of informing yourself," I replied, doing my best Francis imitation. "Get interested in the magic of search engines."

I wished the windows were not smoked to eliminate all UV rays. Stupid city ordinances.

I was also sick of all the vampire groupies—who seemed to be about half the school population—hovering at the next table, pretending to study but mostly ogling Francis. I'd even heard some of them had tried to follow Francis home. Luckily vampires are good at disappearing into shadows and can move faster than most humans.

"Could you repeat that?" Francis was asking Ty. "A 'kegger,' did you say? Is that two g's?"

He talked the same way about keggers as he did about my being ABC, as if they were both cute human hobbies of ours.

I'd had enough. For Cathy's sake, I'd been polite all week—well, mostly polite—okay, polite by my standards—but, honestly, why should we help the vampire anthropologist?

"Yes," I answered. "Ty said, a 'kegger.' It's three g's actually and c, not k. A kegger is a place where humans gather to worship kegs, which are the totems of the original Kegger people, who landed in Iceland."

Ty snorted. He wasn't being much help in my campaign against Francis, but at least he laughed at my jokes.

"It was Iceland, wasn't it? I didn't get that wrong, did I? I was so sure that was where the spaceship landed."

"Spaceships in Iceland. That is how it went," Ty confirmed, still laughing.

Francis was not noting any of my words of wisdom.

He put down his fancy fountain pen. Cathy looked anxious.

"She doesn't mean it, Francis. Mel likes to joke around."

"She is very droll," Francis said.

I didn't roll my eyes; Francis wasn't worthy of my eye roll.

Cathy looked at Francis with such adoration I could have cried. How could she not see through him? He was studying us, and goodness only knew why. He didn't care about us as people, but as specimens of humanity. It beat me why he couldn't just watch TV and get all his questions answered that way.

I had tried to tell her he was not hanging out with us because he liked us and that he was not shy, but she was too nice to think badly of him. Mind you, it would be hard for Cathy to believe in the badness of someone pointing a gun at her and demanding money. She put Francis's note-taking down to his desire to learn how to fit it in at Craunston High.

"We all live in the same city, but how often do we interact?" Cathy had asked me earnestly. "How many conversations have you had with vampires in your life?"

Before Francis it had been none, which was exactly how I liked it. Vampires are trouble. Think about it: These days, all vampire transitions are voluntary. What kind of person would take the risk of becoming a vampire? There'd have to be something wrong with you.

Because the process can either kill you outright or turn you into a drooling, mindless monster (which would lead to you being put down almost instantly), or, if you're superlucky, you become a vampire.

Let's examine what a prize that is one more time: no more direct sunlight ever again, no more laughter. You get eternity, but you don't have the sense of humor to enjoy it! Also, vampires don't eat food. You never get to eat chocolate again. Ever.

I'd rather die.

All the vampire wannabes and vamposeurs mystify me. Who would choose the possibility of immortality over chocolate?

My eyes moved involuntarily to a poster hanging on the wall, a picture of an unsuccessful vampire transition. There were cage bars across a zombie girl's snarling face and empty eyes, and the caption read HE WON'T LOVE YOU FOR YOUR MIND THEN. VAMPIRISM. THINK TWICE.

Most PSAs drive me nuts and are kind of stupid. But the "Say 'Not Tonight' to a Bite" campaign? I was with them a hundred percent.

I heard the bell for our next class, which, sadly and once again, we all had together. Well, not Anna, apparently. She remained behind her pile of books. I wished I could join her.

Francis and Cathy walked side by side. Almost every head turned to gaze in longing at Francis and in envy at Cathy. The fact that he was asking her at what age she'd started walking and if she could remember the process would probably have undercut their envy.

I couldn't leave them alone. Kristin had not responded to my many messages, and I had to figure out how to get rid of him on my own before Anna left our group forever and Cathy got her heart broken. It felt like I didn't have much time.

Cathy and Francis's tragic farewell at the end of the day confirmed my worries.

We stood by the vampire's locker as he pulled out his astronaut suit. Just me, Cathy, Francis, and about three dozen vampire groupies.

Before he put on his helmet, he said, "I must return to my shade. *Au revoir*, my dear."

As if we didn't know where he was going. I wondered if the rest of his shade were as snooty and annoying as him. My bet was they were. Vampires band together in little fake families. So presumably they picked Francis because they liked him.

The thought of more than one Francis was appalling. Also, "my dear"? That's what your grandma calls you.

"Your shade?" I repeated innocently. I'd been playing the vampire ignoramus all week. To annoy him, you know, without being obviously rude.

"Yes, shade," Cathy said. "You know that. Like a clan, though not really," she added when Francis looked disapproving and the vampire groupies started tittering. "Coven?" There was more laughter. When Cathy is nervous, she starts to lose all her nouns. Coven? Clan? She knows no one calls a group of vampires clans or covens. "Oh, no, n-n-n-not coven. I'm not saying that vampires are witches. They're just a different kind of people and instead of living in families, like we do, they, um, they live in shades."

"I thought they were called nests," I said, enjoying the sharp intake of breath from everyone around us. Except Francis, of course.

"Mel!" Cathy exclaimed.

Yeah, now I was being deliberately rude. I know, stay classy! But Francis was so annoying. Everyone knows that *nest* is the term people who hunt vampires use. Vampires prefer to call their groups "murmurs" or "gatherings." I've even heard of some using *cemetery*, as in *a cemetery of vampires*, but here in New Whitby, where the first vampire settlers arrived on the good ship *Nightshade*, they call them "shades."

Let me make something clear: I don't agree with the nutters who want to kill all vampires. My parents voted yes on Proposition Four, and if I had the vote I would have too: Unlawfully killing vampires should be punished as harshly as killing people. Murder is murder. I don't want vampires dead. I just wanted Francis to go to a different school.

And, yes, I know using the word *nests* wasn't okay. But he was so annoying and everyone was worshipping him for it. Ugh.

Francis put on his helmet, nodded briefly, and strode toward the front door without a backward glance. The vampire groupies shot me looks clearly intended to kill and scurried after him.

The walk home was conducted in silence. Well, not the whole way. After about five blocks' worth of Cathy's disappointed silence, I choked out an apology.

If "sorry" interrupted by a coughing fit qualifies as one.

"I know you don't like him, Mel. But I do. You *know* I do. I'm not asking that you like him, merely that you be polite. He's invariably polite to you."

I decided that now was not the time to point out that she was starting to sound like Francis.

"Oh, is he?" I said. "What about all that ABC crap?" Cathy hesitated, and I pressed on. "Have you ever noticed that he looks at me and Ty differently than he looks at you or Anna? Come on, Cathy. Admit there's the tiniest possibility Francis might be a little bit racist."

Ty's not ABC: He's black. You don't want to know what I heard Francis asking him.

"Oh, no," Cathy exclaimed, shocked. "Not racist!"

I waited, because Cathy's not an idiot.

"Francis isn't racist," Cathy had to repeat, as if saying it twice made it true. "But you know, he was born a long time ago, and they thought differently then. You can't blame Francis for that."

I could, but it wouldn't do any good if Cathy wasn't

going to blame him too.

"Do you really like him?" I asked instead.

"He's been very nice to us. It's interesting getting to know a vampire."

"No, Cathy, I meant do you *like* like him?"

Cathy didn't say anything.

"He's almost two hundred years old!"

Cathy still didn't say anything.

We were only a block from home.

"You're my friend and I worry . . ." I trailed off. I'd already told her everything I didn't like about vampires in general, everything I didn't like about snotty, condescending Francis in particular. I'd told her that I thought Francis's presence was upsetting Anna, and Cathy had said that Anna shouldn't be prejudiced against all vampires because of the actions of one.

I didn't have anything new to add.

"He's just so interesting. Can you imagine being that old? Having seen so much change? And he's so polite. He opens doors for people and inclines his head in that old-fashioned way. It's like he stepped out of a Jane Austen novel."

I didn't point out that Austen's books were published before Francis was born. And not just because I knew Cathy already knew that.

"He's a gentleman. I've never met a gentleman before. But I'm not in love, Mel. I promise."

I left it at that and clutched her promise to my heart.

We had been best friends for a very long time. I hated the idea of anyone ruining that. And I certainly wasn't going to let some overly polite vampire anthropologist come between us.

CHAPTER FIVE

The Great Rat Disaster

Next day at school, I was on my best behavior. I said not a single snarky thing to, near, or about Francis.

My ability to say nothing mean to Francis was enhanced by not having many classes with him on Tuesdays.

Almost all day long I stared straight ahead and kept my mouth shut and nobly resisted the urge to go hide with Anna in the library.

Cathy looked so happy we were all getting along. Her eyes were like huge dark shining pools—a calm ocean at night.

Frankly, they made me feel a bit seasick.

Francis was still there by Cathy's side at lunchtime and still asking us an insane catalog of questions about the range of our smelling abilities, if we remembered bonding with our mothers, and what were the first stories we had learned. So many questions begging for brilliant retorts. It was painful to stay quiet. Ty even squeezed my hand to show that he could see I was trying hard. I mean, Ty. I love him, but he's not the most observant guy in the universe.

The whole thing put me off my lunch. I grabbed an apple and shoved it into my bag for later, when I would inevitably be too hungry to think.

When we were walking down the stairs toward the first floor, Francis asked me about my allergies, and I thought of so many snappy retorts that I began to feel as if he was torturing me on purpose, but I said firmly, "That's an awfully personal question, Francis, and I don't feel comfortable answering it."

"Very amusing, Melanie," Francis said, which is not my name, though people always assume that Mel is short for Melanie.

I will not tell you my full name, but I will tell you that my brother is called Lancelot.

It's so unfair that firstborn Kristin got a normal name and then our parents went all experimental on their two youngest children. We were too little and helpless to resist such atrocities. Thus as far as the rest of the world (except for Cathy) knows, my name is simply Mel.

"A true lady would never dream of discussing her health in mixed company," I told him.

"Is everything humorous to you?" Francis inquired with some asperity.

That would be Francis-speak for "snippy."

"Not everything," I said. "But it's really the only way to deal with you."

Francis's lip curled. "I deal with you, as you put it, by remaining courteous despite your ill-judged attempts at humor."

"Everyone else laughs at my jokes," I said. "Oh sorry, I forgot. You can't do that, can you?"

Cathy's breath hissed in, sharp as if she'd seen someone hurt. Ty took a step away to avoid being contaminated by me. Those were the only sounds in a dead silence.

I knew I was completely out of line. You can't say that to a vampire. It's like mocking kids with glasses for not having twenty-twenty vision.

Sure, vampires live forever. Yes, they're (mostly) beautiful, and since they can collect blood at the hospital they don't have to hurt anyone. But as I may have noted once or twice previously, there are drawbacks—did I mention no chocolate?—and the worst is that they don't feel things like we do. They don't cry and they don't laugh.

One of the few vampires who let herself be interviewed on the subject described transitioning as being reborn into a shadow world, where nothing is quite as real or could really affect her. She seemed to think that was a good thing. (See? What kind of person would want to be a vampire?)

I realize that pointing out Francis's inability to laugh makes me sound like a member of a vampire hate group. I swear I don't think it's because vampires have no souls. I believe in the scientific explanation: that it's an evolutionary protection vampires developed so they could deal with all the stress and pain of long lives. Basically, they're stretching emotions out so they will last.

I wouldn't be a vampire for ten million dollars. I'd rather live laughing for one year than live without laughing for a hundred.

But that doesn't make saying so to a vampire any less nasty.

I was opening my mouth to apologize to Francis when the stampede began. There was a crash and somebody screamed. Then many people screamed. We started hastily down the stairs and were hit with a jostling, yelling crowd of people coming up the stairs at us.

I was already standing beside the wall of the stairwell, but now I dropped my schoolbag and flattened myself against the wall so I wouldn't be trampled. The people rushing past screamed in our faces. A junior I recognized from the debate team dropped to her knees beside me. She was up as fast as if she were on the track team. I leaned back harder into the wall, barely avoiding an elbow to the face. Someone kicked my ankle with what felt like a steel-capped boot, and I dug my shoulder blades into the brick, refusing to go down.

"Run!" someone yelled.

Run! my brain said. I couldn't move. The crowd had thinned enough for me to finally see what they were running from.

Scurrying up the steps like a vast, thick, writhing gray carpet were dozens and dozens of rats.

RUN! my brain insisted.

I remained frozen, which was the only thing that kept me from screaming like Cathy and Ty. I glimpsed Cathy's face for an instant: It was the pasty white of skim milk. The same color as some of the rats' fur, though mostly they were dirty grays and browns. Their eyes were pink. Moist pink. I tried to push myself through the wall, away from rats and from the mosh pit for the Rodent Concert.

I had never seen so many rats before. For a weird moment I started counting them. It was that or faint, which was obviously unacceptable, both because I had too much pride and because the rats would walk on my face.

I could feel tiny prickling claws and scaly tails against my feet—what a day to wear sandals. I kept counting, getting up to sixty-four rats and then losing count and having to start again, refusing to look down at the ones touching my feet, brushing their fur-clad squirming bodies against my ankles.

I was so jealous of whoever had been wearing those steel-capped boots.

Finally, it was over. No more rats swarming past. They had all got up the stairs or out the doors below, and the shrieking nightmare of a crowd had got to wherever they were going.

I tried not to look at the rats who hadn't escaped the human stampede. There were an awful lot of rat bits strewn across the stairs and floor below.

"Mel," Ty said. He was getting to his feet a few steps above me with what looked like the beginnings of a nasty fat lip.

Francis and Cathy were standing on the stair railing. Francis was using all his vampire strength and agility to balance perfectly on the thin rail, as if he were a trapeze artist. Cathy stood encircled and safe in the vampire's arms. One of her hands clutched the lapel of his jacket; the other was curled at the nape of his neck.

They weren't looking at me or Ty. They were staring at each other, her eyes huge and fixed on his face with this look: I don't know how to describe it. Beseeching, imploring, adoring.

Horrifying.

It seemed like there was a bubble of silence around them, as if this was a sacred space.

I coughed. Loudly.

Francis started and drew back, just a fraction, so he was not actually touching Cathy, his fingers now hovering at the small of her back, ready to catch her if she fell.

"Are you all right?" he asked softly.

"Yes," Cathy said softly back. "Thank you."

"And we're fine down here too!" I said. "Thanks for asking, guys!"

Francis bowed at the waist, placing Cathy on the floor as if she was made of bone china and he had serious doubts about the wisdom of letting her feet touch the ground. He shouldn't have been able to keep his balance doing that, but of course he did, and the next instant he was at Cathy's side. Again, he was not quite touching her, but hovering close.

I realized that Francis wasn't looking at her like she was his favorite lab rat anymore. Cathy was staring at the floor, blushing deep painful crimson, which was—oh no—probably super hot for vampires. There was a terrible, fragile awareness in the air. It was a bit like you imagine that moment in the Bible, right after Adam and Eve ate the apple and said, "We're totally naked—how embarrassing."

The loudspeakers made their customary crackle and boom.

"This should be good," Ty said.

"DUE TO FLOODING IN THE BASEMENT, SCHOOL IS CANCELED."

The rest of the announcement was lost in the shouting, peppered with a few cheers. I imagined all those rats, fleeing a leaky pipe in the basement. I shuddered.

Principal Saunders came up the stairs. "School's canceled," she announced. "Didn't you hear?"

Her stockings were ripped, one knee was bloody,

and there was a long black stain up along her skirt. She stumbled and then nodded at me as if she'd meant to do that.

"There was a problem with the plumbing and apparently we had rats in the basement," she said in a firm and authoritative voice that was the opposite of her appearance. "There's nothing to worry about. The exterminator's coming. Go home."

"Yes, ma'am," Ty said.

"A principal's job, eh?" She smiled at me, but she was looking at a squashed rat, lying over one of the steps.

"Lucky there are cleaners," I said as cheerfully as I could manage.

Principal Saunders didn't respond.

Her gaze had shifted to Francis, his fair hair like a halo in the light filtered through the smoked-glass windows. Her eyes were wild for a second and then blank, as if she was too scared to even know how to deal.

She was terrified of him.

She knew something we didn't.

Whatever was wrong with Principal Saunders—and I was more and more convinced that Anna was right, and there was something badly wrong—Francis was involved. I just had to find out how.

Principal Saunders turned and hurried away, the sound of her footsteps uneven as if she kept stumbling.

Cathy had obviously not noticed a thing, her eyes downcast, Francis still standing too close to her.

Since it was the only thing I could do, I bent down and picked up my schoolbag. There was a faint sound inside it, the bag bulging for a moment, and then the long, furry body of a light-gray rat spilled out, hit the floor, and ran. A chewed-up apple rolled after it.

I did what I'd promised myself I wouldn't—I screamed.

I didn't lose it for long, though. Vampires might be terrorizing the principal and hypnotizing my best friend, rats might be invading my school and my bag, but hysterics weren't going to fix any of it. There was nobody around to fix things but me.

I settled my bag on my shoulders, promising myself I'd put it in bleach that night. Right after I bleached myself.

Ty was stifling a laugh. I thought about punching him.

"I can hear you trying to come up with some kind of 'let the rat out of the bag' joke, Ty," I said instead. "I have some advice for you: Don't."

CHAPTER SIX

Home on the Range

Knowing my parents wouldn't be home for a few more hours, I slammed the front door with all my strength. I was a little disappointed when it didn't break or fall off its hinges, but it was still extremely satisfying. The boom resounded through the house.

My brother, Lancelot, came thundering down the stairs, stood at the bottom, and grinned.

"What do you want, Lottie? How come you're home so early?"

Since I am his big sister, it is my job to torment him with awful nicknames.

I had been contemplating slamming the door again to get rid of the last remnants of a-vampire-is-seducing-my-best-friend rage, but teasing him would also do the trick.

"They're home," Lancelot said, seconds before Dad

came out of his study with his arms crossed and gave me his death glare. Mom was already at the top of the stairs, having presumably emerged from her study. She was also staring at me with laser eyes.

Dad moved past me to inspect the door. "Doesn't seem to be broken," he said, opening and shutting it to make sure.

"What on earth was that about, Mel?" Mom inquired.

"Bad day," I said. "Sorry."

"Then we will talk about it," Mom said. "My study," she said, starting to go back upstairs. "Now."

"How about my study?" Dad said.

"Yes," I said quickly. "I'm in too bad a mood to walk up the stairs."

Mom raised an eyebrow, clearly not buying it. She knew neither of us wanted to set foot in her domain. My mom is a slob. She hates housework. She is incapable of putting anything back where she found it. On the rare occasions when she cooks, it's like the kitchen exploded. We must be the only family in the world in which the kids yell at their mom to tidy her room.

"Fine," she said, stalking down the stairs.

Lancelot stood behind her.

"What do you think you're doing, young man?"

"Following you, Mom."

"Desist."

"Don't you want me to hear how you deal with this parent-child crisis so that I'll learn what not to do in order to continue being your best-behaved child?"

"Brat," I said under my breath.

"No," Mom said. "I do not. Go kick your soccer ball. Or clean up the kitchen. Or something." She did not suggest he do his homework, because odds were he'd already done it. Probably months ago. The little weasel is obnoxiously all-around brilliant. Just like his oldest sister, Kristin, the genius who broke her parents' hearts (well, mostly Dad's) by not going to MIT or Harvard. Not that they were opposed to her going to fashion school, but they were upset by the waste of her genius. They were slightly appeased when Kristin claimed that fashion design was all about geometry and history and chemistry and sociology.

Dad opened the study door and ushered me in.

Dad's study is like Dad, warm and old-fashioned and comfortable but also very tidy. There are three walls of bookshelves, almost all of them legal texts. Mom and Dad are both lawyers; they actually met as prosecution and defense at a trial. His desk is large and wooden and at least fifty years old, with tchotchkes on it—dragon, tiger, and phoenix figurines—arranged according to feng shui principles. Dad is very into tradition. And old stuff generally.

His battered Chesterfield sofa onto which I threw myself is probably even older than the desk, while his office chair is sleek and modern and black leather and designed by someone famous. Kristin would be able to tell me who. She's the one who picked it.

Mom sat beside me, and Dad settled on his chair, putting his feet up on the desk. Something he would not have been able to do if we were in Mom's study. There are no clear surfaces in there. Including the floor. Possibly not the ceiling, either. I couldn't be sure: It had been a while since I'd been brave enough to venture in.

"So," Mom said. "Why are you home so early and what was so bad that you tried to rend our front door from its hinges?"

"Rats," I said.

"Excuse me?" Dad said.

"There was a rat invasion at school. Hundreds of them, coming up at us from the basement. They canceled school. I'm wearing sandals."

Both my parents looked at my feet.

"Rats. Scurrying over my toes."

We all three shuddered.

"My plan coming home was: slam door, have four thousand showers."

"The rats made you angry?" Dad asked. "Me, I would have been scared."

"I was. No, Cathy made me angry."

My parents looked at each other. The last time Cathy and I had had a fight, we'd been about five. I'd given her favorite doll a haircut. Cathy had not appreciated Barbie's new mohawk.

"She's in love with a vampire."

"The new vampire student?" Dad asked, as if there

were some other vampire Cathy could have gone gaga over.

"Yes."

"But you knew that," Mom said. "You told me about it last week."

"Yes, but now it might be more than just a crush. She's got that he's-the-One look in her eye. And stupid Francis the vampire is encouraging her now. He's so much older than her. They have nothing in common. Francis is going to break Cathy's heart."

"And that's why you slammed the door?" Mom asked. I nodded.

"Oh, sweetie," she said. "That's just how love is when you're young. You get hurt. All you can do is be there for her, like she's been there for you."

Okay, so I knew from personal experience that dating a normal guy can go badly wrong as well.

I nodded reluctantly. "But he's a vampire. Don't you think that makes it a little bit different than any other guy?"

"Not really," Dad said. "Love is love. It's painful for everyone."

"Well," Mom said, "it has its upsides too." She and Dad exchanged one of their you-are-the-love-of-my-life looks. I tried not to be ill.

She gave me a brief hug. "Is that all that's bothering you?"

"Pretty much."

"It's just Cathy's love life? Not anything else?" Dad

inquired. "How's Anna doing?"

I flinched before I could stop myself. I'd been trying not to think of Anna's pale face and withdrawal from us all, of Dr. Saunders standing at her door like an avenging angel or her terrified stare at Francis today.

But I had to think about it. It was me Anna had come to for help. If Francis was involved in whatever was upsetting Principal Saunders . . .

Mom's voice went soft. "Are you that worried about her?"

"I'm handling it," I said.

I was going to handle it. I just wasn't sure how yet.

"Can we change the subject?" I continued. "Want to know what college I'm going to? What I'm going to do with my life? Wait—I can't tell you. Because I still don't know."

"Honey," Dad said, leaning forward to ruffle my hair. "As we've both told you, at seventeen it's perfectly normal not to know what you want to do with your life. I didn't decide to be a lawyer until I'd been in IT for almost five years."

I'd heard all this before. "I know, Dad. I'm not that worried," I lied.

"You shouldn't be," Mom said. "You'll do great no matter what you decide to do. Including cleaning up the kitchen, which is your punishment for assaulting the door and our ears. I made lasagna for dinner. Kitchen's a bit of a mess."

CHAPTER SEVEN

Books as Camouflage

I tried to talk to Cathy alone at school the next day, but Francis was with her at all times. Solicitously carrying her bag. Talking with her about history and philosophy and—even worse—poetry! Why couldn't he go back to interrogating Cathy about her childhood asthma? He hung about her like a bad smell—a fantastically handsome, blond bad smell.

I had to lie in wait to catch her in the one place that I knew Francis would never go.

By which I mean the girls' bathroom.

I was leaning against the bathroom sink as Cathy came out of the stalls. My whole air was extremely casual, as if to say, I like this bathroom sink. Got nowhere else to be. Could lean here all day.

Cathy went to the sink beside mine. She gave me a

little side eye as she squirted soap onto her hands. It was possible my casual lean was slightly spoiled by my fixed stare.

"So," I said. "Yesterday. Crazy, huh?"

Cathy smiled her usual faint smile. "It was."

"A plague of rats descended on us," I said. "I'm sure we all said some things, or possibly screamed some things"—or fell for some vampires—"we didn't really mean."

"I'm so sorry that those rats *touched* you," Cathy said. "So horrible."

"It was. But enough about me," I said. "Let's talk about you! And Francis."

"Wasn't he amazing?" Cathy said at once, as if she couldn't hold in her admiration a moment longer. Her eyes shone. "He lifted me as if I weighed nothing. But he was so careful. Like he was afraid he'd break me. He's such a gentleman. He saved me." She sighed.

"Yeah, so I just wanted to check on that," I said. "I mean, yes, obviously you're grateful and it's easy to confuse gratitude with something else. But we've already established that you don't like him like that, right?"

Smooth. I was so smooth.

Cathy blushed.

"Well," she said, "I did say I wasn't in love with him."

"Yes," I said. "Yes, you did!"

"I tried not to like him that way," Cathy said. "I really tried. He's older, he's a vampire, he's so handsome and charming, and he knows so much. It just seemed impossible."

I nodded my head at the impossible bit, and shook my head about the Francis being charming part. It must have looked like I was having neck spasms.

Cathy frowned for a second and then resumed washing her hands. Her cheeks were still pink.

"I'm not saying he definitely likes me back or anything," she muttered. "But yesterday I thought—I thought maybe."

"But," I began, and that was as far as I got before Cathy looked at me.

"Have you ever felt kind of . . ." She paused. "Detached from the world? As if you didn't fit in, and you weren't interested in what everyone else was interested in? As if you belonged in a whole different world?"

"Everyone feels that way sometimes," I said. "But you eat chocolate until the endorphins kick in, and the crazy thoughts go away." I grinned at her.

"I feel that way a lot," Cathy said. "I never feel that way with Francis. He's interested in the same things I'm interested in. He's seen different times, with different manners and morals. He's able to understand history as if he lived it *because* he did live some of it. He truly feels the great classics the way people in the past did. With Francis, I'm always interested. I never want to be in some other world."

"And by that you mean . . ."

"Yes," Cathy said. She looked at the floor, as if she could not look me in the face while she made her confession. "I'm in love with him."

◆

"So Cathy and Francis are in love," said Anna, from behind her book fortress.

"I didn't realize the news had reached you here in your secret lair." I stood on tippy-toes to pick up one of the books on top of her pile. *A Natural History of the Appalachias?* What class is that for?"

"I like trees," Anna told me. "A lot. The Cathy-and-Francis gossip is all over school. Everyone's seen them, drifting around, talking about eighteenth-century literature."

"Hot," I said, and sighed. "Francis hasn't even whipped it out in front of her today. And by 'it,' I mean his notebook."

Anna whistled. "His newfound love has made him forget to take notes? Sounds serious."

"Like Francis is ever anything else." I put my feet up on a chair. "So I bet you're thinking to yourself, *Why, Mel, in spite of the Ratastrophe and the fact that much of the school smells like industrial cleaners and all this vampirish romantic disaster, are you looking so cheerful?*"

"Um," Anna said. "I guess I'd be thinking that if I could see you."

I began disassembling her book fortress at the spot where her voice was loudest in order to treat her to the sight of my smiling face.

"*Underwater Acoustics Handbook*? *Songs of Poverty and Death*? Weird, Anna, very weird. Not seeing a common thread in all these books."

"I am a woman of many interests."

"Or a woman who grabbed whatever books were around to build a fort."

Anna's face was now revealed. She looked paler than usual.

"Here's my theory about your mom," I said. "I think he's threatening her or something."

I wasn't entirely clear on why Francis might be threatening Principal Saunders, or what he might want. But I really liked the idea of Francis being involved in evil goings-on.

"Why would Francis be threatening my mom?"

I told her about the look on Principal Saunders's face after the rat stampede. "Pretty suspicious, huh?"

Anna was unimpressed by my powers of deduction. "Not especially. Mom really, really doesn't like vampires. She didn't even before Dad ran away. But she's much worse now."

"Oh," I said. "That does make sense."

"You know how my parents were, Mel." She lowered her voice. "Before he left."

According to Anna, her parents had the love to end all loves. They had been together since their first year of college, and to quote Anna, every passing year only saw them more in love. To be honest, they didn't seem that much more in love than my parents. They weren't super-demonstrative around each other. I'd seen them hold hands a few times and smile at each other, but that was Mom and Dad pretty much every night of the week. But Anna was convinced it was the love of the ages.

Until her dad ran off. With a vampire.

"What if Francis caused the Ratocalypse as, I don't know, a warning? And what I witnessed was him telling her so with his steely blue eyes and her freaking out?"

Anna spluttered. I couldn't tell if it was laughter or not. "Your worry about Cathy has broken your brain, Mel. You're saying you think Francis is responsible for a plague of rats and scaring my mom," Anna said slowly. "As opposed to oh, say, the plague of rats being the thing that scared her. I hear she was not alone in being upset."

I shuddered, trying not to remember the feel of them scurrying over my toes.

My theory did sound unlikely when she put it like that.

"Don't worry about Cathy," Anna said. "Love doesn't last. Francis isn't going to stick around. He's a vampire who's a million years older than her. He'll be bored very soon."

I stared at Anna in appalled silence for what felt like hours. Anna somehow intuited that she had not entirely reassured me.

She cleared her throat. "Besides, Mom's doing what

she can to get him thrown out."

"Really?" I said too loudly. The studious freshmen at the next table over glared. The library was fuller than it usually was. Maybe because the cafeteria smelled of solvents. No rats had made it into the library.

"Mom fought the enrollment," Anna said quietly. "Said it was inappropriate to have a vampire at the school, that it put the students in danger. She hasn't given up, even though he's here. She warned me to stay away from Francis, made me promise not to have anything to do with him and not to tell him anything if he asked me questions."

"Isn't that a bit extreme?"

Why would Principal Saunders think Francis would ask Anna questions? Except that she'd warned me not to talk to him and not to let Anna talk to him as well.

She was acting like he was dangerous.

"After what Dad did? I can't think of anything that would be too extreme. He texted me his good-bye note, Mel. *Texted*. He didn't even wait till I was back from camp to say good-bye." Anna's eyes began to well.

I'd been at fencing training camp with her when Principal Saunders came to give her the news and take her home. Anna had crumpled. It had been awful. But this was the first I'd heard about the texted farewell. I didn't know what to say, so I patted her shoulder. How could he be so cruel? Why?

No wonder Anna hadn't wanted to hang much after

that. I wished again I'd tried harder to see her. I should have gone to her house, not accepted her brush-offs. My friend had needed me and I hadn't been there. She *still* needed me.

"I'm sorry," I said at last.

I was going to help her and her mom. They wanted Francis out of here and so did I. Maybe that was all that was wrong with Principal Saunders: The constant presence of a vampire in her school was making it impossible for her to put aside her personal heartbreak and concentrate on her job.

I leaned forward and spoke softly, partly because I was plotting and partly because the librarian was already giving me death glares. "But I've got a plan."

Anna gave a low moan.

"I'm going to need your help."

CHAPTER EIGHT

The Great School
After-Hours Escapade

That was how Anna and I ended up creeping through the darkened halls of the school late that night. (After we'd both finished our homework and fencing practice. What? Cathy isn't the only one who wants to get into a good college, even though I don't know which good college I want to get into yet.) I'd explained to Anna that our target was Francis's file. It could provide us with clues about him.

Anna was not entirely convinced of the genius of this plan.

The dark was almost as bad as the fact that the air still reeked of industrial-strength cleaners. A day of classes hadn't done much to weaken it. Both our eyes started watering.

To be fair, I was certain it was better than the stench of rat innards.

"I can't believe we're doing this," Anna said behind me. "I can't believe I agreed to do this."

Anna had raised a few teeny-weeny objections about us getting caught, possibly leading to jail time and, even worse, all hope of getting into a good college destroyed.

"Think of it this way," I said. "We walk through the school every day. Multiple times a day! This is practically routine. Pretty boring, if you ask me."

"Not in the dark," Anna whispered. "Not when we've broken in!"

"We used your mom's keys. That's not breaking in."

"We took her keys without her knowledge. And we're still walking around in the dark."

"Pretend it's an eclipse," I whispered back. "Just your average, everyday, really boring . . . eclipse."

"I'm here in the dark with a crazy person," Anna muttered.

In some ways, I felt like Anna was the weak link in our awesome investigating team.

On the other hand, she'd been the one who got her hands on her mother's keys. Without those, I would've had to commit the breaking part of breaking and entering.

Just *entering* couldn't possibly be a crime.

Well, maybe half a crime.

I'd never been to the school at night—except for prom

and theater and games and fencing practice and tourna-
ments. Okay, I'd been there at night many times, but now,
when there wasn't anyone else around—it was scary.

No. It wasn't scary. It was fine, and I was fine. I was
on a mission.

I gave myself a mental shake. Anna might be falling
apart, but I was going to keep it together. I was only doing
what needed to be done: saving my friends from worry
about their mothers and seduction by vampires. It just
so happened that that was one bird. And I had the two
stones. Or was it two birds with one stone?

Whatever it was. Someone had to act. That person
was me.

I opened the door to the principal's office. Anna gave
a small squeak every time the keys in my hand jangled.

Inside the office, the darkness seemed somehow
darker. On the upside, the smell of solvent was less strong
here. On the downside, I was briefly possessed by the
insane thought that Ms. Cuddy—intrepid secretary of
Principal Saunders—might be sitting behind her desk
in the dark. Waiting to pounce. I crept forward just the
same, Anna bumping into me as she scuttled behind.

Shockingly, ninja secretaries failed to leap from the
gloom.

I breathed in and out, keeping steady, inching forward until I reached my gleaming goal.

There was moonlight filtering through the blinds
onto the filing cabinets. I knelt on the floor trying to read

the label on the lowest drawer.

A loud wail shattered the silence.

Anna screamed and jumped back, hitting the wall, and I bit my tongue until two things happened.

One, I tasted blood, and two, I realized the sound was my phone ringing. I drew it out of my pocket, remembering the day when a fire-alarm ring tone had seemed the perfect solution to my constantly missing calls.

"You didn't put it on silent?" Anna demanded.

"Hey," I said, opening the phone, "I'm new to a life of crime."

"Don't answer it," Anna said. "Mel. Don't answer—"

"Hi, Kris," I said, waving a hand at Anna to calm her. She should know by now that if I didn't answer, my wonderful sister would keep calling. Kristin's very determined. "Thanks for calling me back. I'm afraid this isn't the best time—"

"I thought you needed help *urgently*," Kristin said, sounding annoyed. "With this guy."

Kristin doesn't actually like guys. She says this gives her a special insight into them, because the onlooker sees more of the game.

"Phone," Anna hissed. "Off. Now!"

"Just a sec, Anna," I mouthed, forgetting it was probably too dark for Anna to see.

"Cathy's an idiot," Kristin said. "I mean this in the nicest way possible. You know I love her. But if she's hung up on a hot vampire, you need me. Vampires are like catnip for some girls. They're girlnip."

I giggled. "Girlnip."

"Hang up," Anna ordered, low and urgent. "Mel, end that call right now!"

I nodded and waved my hand to assure her that I was in the process of ending the call.

"You don't want Cathy getting a taste for vampires," Kristin continued. "You don't want her to end up one of those idiots who hang out in the Shade wearing T-shirts that say I'M CHERRY, TAKE A BITE, do you?"

"No!" I said. Perhaps a little too loudly, but the image of Cathy in a vampire-groupie T-shirt was deeply disturbing.

Anna lunged forward, grabbed the phone from my hand, and slapped it closed.

"Sorry," she said, looking down at me and panting. "But this is not the time for a chat. We're on a mission. And it's not going to be one that ends with us both in jail."

"You're right, you're right," I said. "On task! I'll call Kristin later."

"You don't have to yell," Anna whispered.

I gave the phone in her hand a longing look, but Anna slipped it into her pocket.

"Um, Anna, could I have my phone back? I need the light to read by."

"Swear you won't call your sister?"

"I swear."

By my phone's light I found the right cabinet and then riffled through the folders, squinting at tabs. At last I found the *D*'s. Duan—my name—came right before Duvarney, but I nobly resisted the impulse to check my file. Breaking into the school to read Francis's records was completely justifiable and noble; looking at my own would be wrong.

But so tempting.

But so wrong.

I forced myself to move on to the name Francis Havelock Maurice Duvarney, scrawled on top of a folder. I yanked it out and flipped it open.

There were only a few sheets of paper inside—mine had been close to bursting its contents everywhere—which included his address (in the Shade, of course) and his date of birth, and noted that:

Francis Duvarney's former education was at Eton College, Windsor, England, in the 1860s. No record of graduation. Became a vampire aged seventeen. No criminal record before or after transition.

Then it became much more interesting.

"I knew it," I said. "I knew no vampire would ever go to high school without an ulterior motive. What a creep! How could he?"

I was becoming more heated and furious by the minute.

"Cathy thought he wanted to mingle with us," I said. "She thought he was showing interest. She thought he was being *nice*."

I spat out the word with such force that Anna made a noise. I'd almost forgotten she was there. She sat down beside me.

"What—what's he really doing?" she asked, her voice low.

I knelt there in the dark of the principal's office, clutching the folder. My suspicions had been confirmed.

"He's studying us. He's writing a book," I said. "*On Adolescent* Homo sapiens sapiens *and Love*. There is an entire section here about a previous human subject he's been studying, and how he needed a broader range of subjects for his great work. He says that part of the thesis is that if vampires study human emotions, such as love, it will help them recover their own human feelings. Francis is studying Cathy's feelings so he can teach himself how to be in love! He's faking the whole thing!"

That entire scene, with the rats and Francis and Cathy holding each other: What if Francis had set that up? What if he'd just been mirroring Cathy's reactions when he held her? How was I supposed to tell Cathy that?

"Ugh," Anna said at last. "Well, that's enough to make Cathy dump him like a ton of undead bricks. He's *using* her."

"I'll kill him," I said. Or rather, snarled, judging from

the way Anna flinched back.

"Are there any other clues?" Anna asked. "How are we going to get him to go back where he came from?"

"You don't think this is enough? Surely once I tell Cathy that he's *studying* her and she dumps him, that'll be the end of Francis. He won't want us knowing that we're his test subjects. Surely that means we'd be compromised. Scientists never want the guinea pigs to know what they're up to."

"I hope you're right," Anna said. "I don't think I'm up for any more adventures like this."

I nodded.

"Seriously, Mel, I'd really prefer if we kept things legal from now on."

"Aw, you're no fun," I told her. "But your wish is my command. Though I can't promise that what I'll do to Francis Havelock Maurice Duvarney will be entirely legal."

"Fine," Anna said decisively, prying the scrunched file out of my hands, straightening it, and using the light of my phone to return it to its correct place. "Whatever you do to him, I'm sure that vampire deserves it."

CHAPTER NINE

Farewell to Francis

"**H**e's writing a book. A scientific treatise. About us!" I told Kristin. Returning her call was my top priority after I'd climbed through the window and into my bedroom.

"Who is?" Kristin asked. She sounded annoyed. (It should be noted that my lovely older sister often sounds that way. Or at least she does when she talks to me.)

"Francis. The undead pain in my butt!"

"Why did you hang up on me?"

"Erm," I said. If I told her that I'd broken into school, there was a chance Kristin would be impressed. She loved to hear about my adventures. But there was also a big chance she'd guilt me into confessing to Mom and Dad. She did not always approve of my adventures. "I was busy. With, um, things."

"Things?"

"I was with Anna," I told her, because the truth is always best. "She's depressed. *She's* the one who hung up on you."

"Oh, that's right. Her dad ran away, didn't he?"

"Yup," I told her. "He hasn't written to her or called or anything. He told her he was leaving her mother in a text message." There was a moment of silence as we contemplated what that would be like.

"Grim."

"Very. Anyway, Francis—the undead annoying person—is writing a book, the title of which is *On Adolescent* Homo sapiens sapiens *and Love*. That's why he's at school. *Not* to complete his education. He's writing a book about us humans. It's a project to get up close and personal with us and study our mating rituals."

"With Cathy as his test subject?"

"Yes!"

"While Cathy thinks he likes her?"

"Yes!"

"But it's all for his book?"

"Yes!"

"Creep."

"Yes!"

"How deep in is Cathy?"

I thought of the expression on Cathy's face as she gazed at Francis during the Ratastrophe. "Deep."

"Hmmm. You can't tell Cathy, then; you'll have to tell him."

"Tell him what?"

"That you're on to him. That you'll spoil his pure research by telling Cathy that he's using her. He'll have to use his wiles on someone else."

I visualized informing Francis that he was completely, utterly, and irretrievably in the wrong. I visualized Francis humiliated and ashamed. I visualized myself screaming into that overly handsome face.

"That may be the most fun conversation ever."

✦

It wasn't.

For starters, it was almost impossible to get Francis alone. He was either with Cathy or surrounded by vampire groupies, or he was with Cathy *and* surrounded by vampire groupies. I arrived superearly and sat on the school steps waiting for him. But he was already surrounded as he walked up the steps. He gave me a cold, very short nod.

"Love you too, Francis," I couldn't resist calling out after him.

Robyn Johnson glared at me. A cheerleader's glare can cut you to the very bone.

For half the day, I tried and continuously failed to get him alone. Finally, I grabbed Ty just before the end of lunch. "I need you to distract Cathy so I can talk to Francis."

"Why do you want to talk to Francis?" Ty asked, with a woundingly suspicious look. "You're going to be mean, aren't you?"

"Ty!"

"You are. I know you are. I don't think I can be part of it. Cathy's really happy. Happier than I've ever seen her."

That was a complete exaggeration. Cathy was always happy. Just because she was reserved didn't mean she wasn't happy. I began to explain this, but Ty ignored me.

"Francis isn't nearly as bad as you think he is. You know he let me look at his photo album from the 1920s? It was crazy old. He owned a Fokker Trimotor! The pictures are amazing. Francis knows all about airplanes up till the 1930s, which is when he says they stopped being—what did he say?—'elegant creations of beauty' and turned into, um, something bad. Can't remember exactly what he said. Oh, yes, I can: 'Instruments of war and cattle conveyance devices'!"

I looked forward to seeing Ty realize how undeserving Francis was of his hero worship, but I didn't have the time to tell him.

"Ty, I'm sure he's wonderful on historical subjects and I'm sure he has lots of fancy ways of describing things. That's because he's really, really, really old. Do you want one of your best friends in the entire world to go out with a walking museum exhibit? It's like she's dating someone who might have been buds with her great-great-great-great-great-great-great-grandfather. That's wrong and gross and it's our duty as her friends to stop it."

"It won't last. I mean, he's bound to get bored with her, isn't he? She's seventeen and he's, um, like you said, really old. Right now they're both happy. I don't think we should interfere."

"Ty, how many favors have I done for you?"

Ty sighed. "You have done me many favors. But none of them involved making Cathy cry."

"No, but some of them involved a sketchy relationship to the law of the land."

Ty groaned. "Fine. I'll talk to Cathy, but the next favor I ask is going to be really gross. You'll be sorry."

The bell for next class rang. *Already?*

"At the end of class, Ty. Distract Cathy."

"Fine."

Ty did as promised, but Robyn Johnson jumped on Francis before I'd even grabbed my bag and stood up from my desk. And, yes, I mean *literally* jumped on him.

"Just testing your reflexes," she said, smiling at him as he put her down. "You'd be great on our squad, Francis. You're so fast and so strong." I swear she was fluttering her eyelashes. "You'd be a perfect base. Think how high you could throw me. We'd be able to choreograph the best stunts ever!"

Francis gave a small smile. "I'm flattered, Robyn. But I suspect it would be deemed illegal. You know vampires are not allowed to compete in human sports. Our enhanced prowess would give us an unfair advantage."

Robyn pouted.

"Francis," I said. "You don't mind, do you, Robyn?"

Robyn certainly did mind, but she was also a very conscientious student who did not like to be late to class. She smiled brightly at Francis, said not a word to me, and tripped down the hallway.

"I need to talk to you, Francis. It's important. Can we meet after school?" Robyn wasn't the only one who wanted to be on time for class. "Please?"

"I am not in the habit of refusing a"—Francis paused—"*lady*'s request. I will meet you at Oatmeal & Caffeine. Do you know it? The café on Chestnut and Third?"

I nodded.

"As it happens," Francis said, "I also have a request to make of you."

He nodded and strode away before I could respond. I was pretty sure he'd just made it clear that he didn't think I was a lady. Not that I cared. I mean, it's the twenty-first century, not the 1800s. We don't have ladies anymore, and if we did, I still wouldn't want to be one. I've got a lot more interesting things to be.

I turned to go in the opposite direction. What can I say? It's instinctual for me to move away from snooty vampires.

That was when I realized it was a B day. Our classes are arranged differently, blocked into A and B days, which normally I like for the variety. But I wasn't feeling too fond of the schedule when I realized that Francis and

I had the same class. AP Local History with Kaplan was in the afternoon on B days. Joy.

Lately Kaplan had been focused on New Whitby's sewerage system. A follow-up on the school's recent Rat-mageddon, which it had been announced was caused by a sewage pipe explosion in the basement. Kaplan was very into tying our lessons to current events. Actually, it was kind of interesting. And good old Frankie was able to chime in to talk about the horse-drawn wagons that used to collect the waste and how much worse the city smelled back then. I also learned that the Romans had a goddess of sewers: Cloacina. Which had me wondering if there was a goddess of farts, or of splinters, or of witty retorts.

Why yes, inventing goddesses did keep me occupied for the rest of class.

◆

Francis was already at the coffee shop by the time I got there.

I knew as soon as I walked in the door. I knew that I had made a terrible mistake. When I think coffee shop, I think of our favorite hangout, Kafeen Krank. This place was no Kafeen Krank. There wasn't a speck of graffiti anywhere.

It was very fancy. The gleaming white wooden board above the counter said *organic* on it at least nineteen times, and everyone in there except me was an adult and spoke in hushed tones over their fancy coffees.

It wasn't really the kind of place where you could

cause a scene and shout at someone that he was an undead love weasel.

Francis was drinking sparkling water, which came in a tall green Italian bottle. He rose as soon as he saw me, and held out my chair.

When I sat down, he poured me a glass.

I hate chivalry. Now how was I supposed to slap him in the face?

Instead, I found myself saying something totally unexpected.

Something horrible.

"Thank you, Francis."

"You're welcome, Mel."

I cleared my throat. My wonderful imaginary face-slapping scene might be lost forever, but I had to get the job done. I had to stop him from using Cathy for his stupid book. "I know what you're doing here."

"Drinking mineral water?"

"No, the secret thing you're doing that you don't want people to know about."

If Francis had been human, he would have changed color. As it was, he looked away briefly and took a sip of his water.

"Might I inquire who else knows?"

"You might not," I said, not entirely sure that was correct English.

"Ah," he said. "But it's a very delicate matter. Secrecy is of the utmost importance."

"I bet it is," I said. "But I'm warning you, if you don't leave Cathy alone, I will tell everyone what's up."

He did the vampire version of changing color again. "I'd really prefer you not mention anything to anyone. If anyone else knows—"

"I bet you would," I said. "So here's the deal. You keep away from Cathy. And I keep my mouth shut."

Francis was obsessed with reputation and honor and a Gentleman's Standing in Society. We'd been his society for the past month. I was sure he wouldn't relish us thinking of him as an undead love weasel.

"Ah," Francis said again, considering his perfect fingernails.

"Come on, Frankie, she's like a million years younger than you. Where's this going to lead except to breaking her heart? You're the grown-up. *Massively* grown up! You need to leave her alone. It's not right."

"I . . ." Francis trailed off. "She's rather special," he said at last.

"She is, which is why you have to leave her alone. It's not—"

"Gentlemanly?" Francis supplied.

"No, it's not," I said, though it was not the word I would have used.

Francis looked sad. Really sad. Sadder even than regular vampire sad. And sad is, in fact, the main look in the vampire's limited repertoire of expressions—that and "full of ennui."

I'd seen him wear a different look. I remembered that during the Ratastrophe, he'd looked at Cathy with the same adoring expression she'd turned on him. Much as I hated to admit it, I found myself almost believing that he really did care about her. But I knew better. He was *studying* us.

"She's human. She's a *teenager*. You're a vampire and, yes, technically *also* a teenager, but you've been one for way more than a hundred years. You should find yourself a nice vampire teenager."

"You can assure me that anyone else who knows will also be silent?"

"I can," I said, thinking of Anna, who was the most discreet person I knew.

Francis placed a twenty-dollar bill on the table and stood up. He bowed to me. "I will do as you wish. Neither you nor Cathy will ever see me again."

I almost fell out of my chair.

I had been thinking more along the lines of him transferring out of Cathy's classes.

"You're going away?" I said. "Awesome!"

Francis's chilly demeanor became even further chilled.

"Uh," I said. "I mean, it's been real, Francis. Bon voyage."

This didn't seem to please Francis either. Oh well.

"It is best for Catherine if I simply remove myself from her life forever," Francis said bleakly. "Without me, she can live a long, full life. She can be happy. I must leave her, in fact, for her own good."

I didn't much like the way Francis put that. *Parents* are always trying to make you do things for your own good. Not boyfriends. With boyfriends, the relationship is supposed to be equal. They're supposed to let you make your own decisions.

But I couldn't tell Cathy about Francis's undead love-weasel ways. Anyway, this was more proof that Francis really was too old for her.

It truly was for her own good.

Agreeing with Francis gave me a stomachache, so I sat there and made a face.

"You'll keep your promise?" Francis pursued. "Not a word to anyone? Especially not your principal."

"I promise."

He bowed again, walking away without making his own request, or leaving me with a message for Cathy. I wasn't feeling as happy as I'd thought I would.

I was also confused. Surely Principal Saunders knew about his book? It was right there in his school file.

CHAPTER TEN

Cathy in Despair

"How about we go see a movie?"

Cathy shook her head wanly. "No thanks, Mel."

"How about we go take a walk?"

A smile landed on Cathy's mouth before bouncing off, repelled by the force of her sadness. "No thanks, Mel."

I had to get Cathy out of her house. Hell, I had to get her out of her *room*. She had been sitting in here for so long, I was afraid the fossilizing process would begin soon. It was time to bring out the big guns.

"How about," I suggested, "we go get milkshakes—and it will be my treat?"

"No. But thank you anyway." Cathy wasn't even tempted.

"You drive a hard bargain. Milkshakes with sprinkles it is."

Cathy had not moved from her chair since I'd come in. She had not shifted from her piteous, curled-up position. She wasn't even looking at me. Her big dark eyes were fixed on the dirty windows, as if their grimy state was upsetting her.

Since Cathy and her mom have lived in the old Beauvier house all their lives, and it's always been falling down around their ears, I didn't think it was the windows upsetting her. I knew the house was the other really old thing that Cathy mysteriously loved. (Though I had to admit Francis was better preserved.)

In a way, Cathy's misery was all my fault.

"Oh, Cathy," I said. "I know you're sad. Francis is a complete jackass."

"Francis is not a jackass!"

"He left school without even sending you a text message saying 'I hope you enjoy the beautiful scenery on your trip through Dumpslandia.'"

"Francis hates text messages," Cathy said. "And voice mail. And the internet. He—he thinks that relying on soulless machines for communication is destroying the delicate interplay of social intercourse!"

Cathy said the words as if they carried real meaning for her. I barely managed to stop myself from sniggering at the idea of Francis saying *intercourse*.

"I'm sure he left for a good reason," Cathy continued.

"Or—or he realized that he no longer—felt anything for me, that he'd made a mistake."

"Or consider again my theory: He's a jackass!"

"He's beautiful, and he's intelligent, and when he comes into a room, nobody can help but look at him," Cathy said. "I'm ordinary. It's perfectly understandable—"

"You are *not* ordinary!"

"Compared to him—"

"He told me you were special," I burst out.

Besides vampire, another career I should probably not go in for is spy.

Luckily for me, Cathy is a trusting soul.

Her eyes shone for a moment, and I thought she was pleased to hear what Francis had said. Until I saw that her eyes were bright with tears.

"With him, I felt special," she whispered. "But I don't—I don't feel special anymore."

"You still are!" I told her fiercely. "You're brilliant in school, and you're going to Oxford, and your friends all love you. You're awesome and your life is awesome. Your life without that vampire jackass is going to be more awesome."

"It's just that nothing seems to matter much anymore," Cathy said in that low, wounded voice. "I can't even write in my diary. Francis and I promised each other that we would both write in our journals every day, for years and years, and learn about each other by reading the entries."

"Sounds like sexy good times," I said. "When did you, uh, start this diary?"

"Last Tuesday," Cathy told me. "But it's become really important to me in a short space of time. It was going to contain years of memories."

I knelt down by Cathy's chair and took her hand.

"Everything else still matters," I told her. "Except possibly the diary with its five minutes' worth of memory. Cathy, this was not your life. This was some guy."

"Yes, I know," said Cathy. She kept staring out the stupid window. "But he was a life-changing kind of guy."

I hadn't known Cathy wanted her life to change so much.

"What if," I asked tentatively, "what if Francis had to go because—because he'd done something wrong, and he couldn't face you? Maybe he, ah—cheated on his geography quiz."

"Francis has traveled all over the world! He's been to countries I'd never even heard of. Abyssinia! Champa! Prussia! Sikkim! Zanzibar! When he was seventeen, he went on a Grand Tour of Europe. Why would he cheat on his geography quiz?"

I stared at the carpet, wondering if he'd made those countries up. "You know what I mean, Cathy. What if Francis wasn't the guy you thought he was?"

"Mel," Cathy said, "Francis is gone. He can't defend himself. I really don't want to hear anything against him. I'm sure he left for a good reason. I just wish—I wish he could have told me what it was."

But we'd both decided, me and Francis, that she didn't get to know.

For her own good.

✦

"I feel like I should tell her the truth," I told Kristin. "She's really upset. She hasn't left her room in three days. I'm not sure she's left her *chair* in three days. She can't sleep."

"No wonder, if she's trying to sleep in a chair," Kristin said, her voice echoing for a second.

I lay stretched out on my bed, in tracksuit bottoms and a holey T-shirt with a picture of a saber-toothed tiger that said SABERS: BETTER THAN YOURS that I'd bought at a fencing tournament a couple years back. I didn't feel like sleeping any more than Cathy did.

I hadn't realized that guilt caused insomnia. Mind you, I hadn't realized that pining for vampires did either.

I'd thought that I was sparing Cathy heartbreak: that sending Francis away before she could get really attached was the best thing for her. But apparently when it was fated eternal love, you only needed two weeks to get attached.

I thumped my head back against the pillow and considered getting NyQuil for both of us. Except, knowing my luck, Cathy would refuse to take it because Francis thought NyQuil was dangerously modern, like texting, television, and jokes that were actually funny.

"I can't believe that even when he's gone, Francis

is tormenting us," I said. "In very, very different ways. Cathy dreams longingly of being locked in his ardent below–room temperature embrace; I dream longingly of beating his head in with a deck chair."

"*Ardent*'s a good word," Kristin observed. "Was it on your SATs?"

"I wish it had been," I growled.

Damn you, Francis, get out of my head!

"You okay, Mel?" Kristin asked.

"I'm frustrated about Cathy. She's torturing herself over this guy, and he's not worth it. I should tell her the truth. I really should."

"Doesn't sound like she'd listen," Kristin said. "There are none so deaf as those listening to 'All by Myself' over and over and over again."

I thumped my head back against the pillows over and over and over again.

Kristin may have sensed she was being less than helpful. "You knew she was going to be upset, right?"

"I guess," I said.

But I'd thought she would be upset in the same way I'd been upset when I'd broken up with Ryan. I'd been expecting Cathy to get angry, eat ice cream with me, and call him names. I'd expected to be able to comfort her.

I had not expected her to stop sleeping or eating. I hadn't expected that because it was crazy.

"It's only been a few days. Give it a few weeks before you start panicking. All Cathy needs is time."

"Yeah." I sighed. "You're right. Thanks, Kris."

I know that "all she needs is time" is a total cliché, but I hung up on Kris feeling slightly better. It was true—it hadn't been that long. Cathy hadn't even *known* Francis that long. She could sit in her chair and mope for a while, and then she'd be over it.

My phone rang. It was Cathy. An excellent sign!

"Hi," I began, not knowing what to say. I didn't want to sound too happy. Should I ask if she was feeling better? Or if she'd changed her mind about milkshakes?

"Hi, Mel," said the gentle, lilting voice of Cathy's mom.

Cathy's mom was calling me. She had never called me before. Not even once.

I sat bolt upright.

"May I talk to Cathy, please? She's not answering her cell phone."

"Wh—" I began, and then cut off the "What are you talking about, Cathy's not here" before it was born.

Think, Mel, think.

Fact: If Cathy's mother thought Cathy was here, then Cathy must have told her she was here. Fact: Cathy hated lying, so Cathy must think she was doing something really important.

Fact: All Cathy thought was really important right now was an undead love weasel.

"Wh-wh-whhhy no," I said. "Cathy can't come to the phone right now. Because! Because she's in the bathroom.

That's where she is. And I can't go in there and give her the phone. Cathy and I are close, but we're not that close. Besides, you know Cathy! She's so shy. About peeing. And just generally."

There was a long pause.

"I wondered if she was feeling better," Ms. Beauvier said.

"She's having a great time!" I told her. "Well, not right now. Right now she's in the bathroom."

"Mel," Ms. Beauvier asked, "you girls haven't been drinking, have you?"

"Just high on life!" I said. "And chocolate ice cream. You know, the classic breakup dessert. Which, speaking of, it's melting, so I gotta go. I'll tell Cathy to charge her phone and that you called!"

I hung up.

Cathy's voice echoed in my head, the way it had been that afternoon, quiet and sad and with a hint of speculation that I hadn't caught.

I'm sure he left for a good reason. I just wish—I wish he could have told me what it was.

That was how much good all this "for her own good" stuff had done. Now Cathy was off to get the answers Francis and I had kept from her.

She'd gone after Francis.

She'd gone into the Shade.

No matter how much I blamed myself for not telling Cathy the whole truth, there was one thing I was congratulating myself on right now. I was so glad I'd read Francis's file.

His address had been on it.

Presuming that Francis had told Cathy where he lived, and she hadn't—oh please no, but surely, surely Cathy could never be that dumb—gone off to comb the whole Shade for Francis, which would be like looking for one particularly snotty piece of hay in a haystack, I knew where she was going.

Who says crime doesn't pay?

CHAPTER ELEVEN

Cathy in the Shade

I'd been in the Shade before. You know how it is: Relatives come from out of town, you do the tourist thing, hop on a bus with them, and endure the withering contempt of the vampire tour guide who hates tourists for invading her neighborhood and gawking at her and her home and hates herself for making a living as a tour guide. Though your relatives don't realize it's contempt. They think the tour guide is scary, and that they're being superdaring being on a bus with a vampire who could EAT THEM ALL! They shudder with delight and point at all the scary vampire houses and ooh and aah over the lack of lighting in the Shade and at how fast the locals move.

And every single time some tourist on the bus will shout, "Oh my, did you see that bat!" At which point the bored tour guide will inform the tourists—as they have informed every busload of tourists that has ever gone into the Shade—that there is no relationship between vampires and bats or any other animal for that matter. Which is when the astute tourists will peer out the window again and notice that there aren't any animals. Animals don't like vampires, and the feeling is mutual. But the tourists will assume that there are no animals because the vampires ate them all. They will shudder again. Your tourist uncle will glance at you and notice you're not shuddering, so you pretend to be scared as well. It's sad. And when you've done it more than once, it's also deadly dull.

Being in the Shade alone was different. It's one thing when one or two of the vampires are mingling with humans but another thing entirely when there's one of you and many of them. Everything about the Shade says No Humans Wanted (Except as a Snack).

There are no apartment blocks or office blocks or malls. No buildings that had to be slapped up in a hurry because the neighborhood needed a day-care center or a supermarket. Vampires are never in a hurry, they don't eat food or have children, and they have strong views on aesthetics.

Plus they mostly like really old stuff. The couple of times someone has gotten planning permission in the Shade, the vampires have either bribed, terrorized, or once, according to rumor, killed the offending person.

Mind you, that developer had wanted to build a McDonald's for the tourists.

I rode in on my bicycle, figuring that if a vampire did go rogue and attack, the bike gave me a slightly better chance of escape. I was grateful the moon was almost full. Even so, my eyes had to adjust to the lack of lighting.

The Georgian, Gothic revival, and art deco buildings, and others whose styles I couldn't identify (neo-federalist-Transylvanian–Gone with the Wind–Greek-Explosionist?), loomed like monsters' castles against a backdrop of darkness. At every huge, black window I thought I saw someone watching.

There were no tricycles in any of the driveways, no dogs barking, no raccoons getting into the trash or cats fighting. There were no children. No laughter or crying or yelling emanating from the houses. All I heard was the occasional noise from a television and, of course, the street traffic. Vampires like to promenade.

The Shade was a dark other world, with pale-faced creatures walking a little faster and more fluidly than they would have outside the Shade. I felt like every single one of them looked me over and calculated their odds of draining me without getting caught. Every time a vampire police patrol (always in pairs like human cops) strode by in their distinctive shiny uniforms—much cooler than human cop uniforms—I had a strong urge to hug them.

The Shade was colder and darker and smelled different than human neighborhoods. It made my skin crawl.

Thinking about Cathy out here in the dark somewhere, equally alone, made me pedal faster.

If something happened to her, I was never going to forgive myself.

And I really was going to beat Francis's head in with a deck chair.

It was almost anticlimactic when I turned the corner on Francis's street and saw Cathy standing uncertainly in front of his house.

Her long hair was blowing in the breeze, her face tilted up to gaze at the windows, not with suspicion like me, but with longing. The house was a pointy-turreted affair with columns on the porch. Together, Cathy and the house looked like the cover of a romance novel.

Until I barreled forward, dropped my bike, grabbed Cathy, and shook her by the shoulders.

"Are you totally crazy?"

Cathy gave a startled yip. "Mel! What are you doing here?"

"I— What are *you* doing here?" I demanded. "As if I didn't know. What *I'm* doing here is bringing you back home. Your mom called. She was looking for you, so I said you were at my place. By the way, you're welcome. Let's go back to my place."

Cathy shook her head.

"Come on, Cathy. You don't even know if he's here. That's a vampire house. You're not going to knock on the door and ask a stranger—a strange vampire—if Francis can come out and play, are you?"

It was wrong to use Cathy's shyness against her. I knew that. As soon as I had Cathy home safe, I was planning on feeling very guilty indeed.

"No," Cathy said, looking even paler.

I felt a small glow of triumph, which disappeared instantly when Cathy said, "I'll go around the back," and headed determinedly around the building.

I charged after her. Right through some vampire's carefully tended bed of petunias, but I'd worry about undead gardeners coming after me later.

To my horror, I found Cathy prying up what seemed to be a trap door. She was trying to break into the *vampires' house*.

"Cathy," I said, in a very quiet, calm voice, "what do you think you're doing?"

"I know which room is Francis's," Cathy announced. "He described it in his journal. All I need to do is get in and make my way up to him."

I wondered if I had seemed this insane to Anna when we were breaking into the school. If so, then it was no wonder she'd been alarmed.

I was still trying to articulate my many, many objections to Cathy's plan when she gave a final heave to the trapdoor and disappeared inside.

"Cathy!" I called, scrambling after her, falling a little way until my shoes hit packed earth, and I stood around blinking in the moonlight that streamed in, revealing crates and barrels of . . .

"A vampire wine cellar? I thought they didn't drink . . . wine."

Cathy smiled at me faintly, so I knew that the real Cathy was still there somewhere under the piles and piles of crazy that love for Francis had spontaneously generated.

As far as I could tell from the limited light, the vampires' cellar was on the small side. I could make out a big wooden staircase leading up to the rest of the house. Below it, the moonlight illuminated a spiderweb. When the spiderweb trembled, so did I.

"Cathy," I said, "we have to get out of here. We're going to get caught. This is not safe."

Cathy hesitated.

"Cathy, please," I begged. "This is all my fault, I'll explain everything, but we have to get out of here. Now!"

The silver strands of the web shivered once more.

That was all the warning we got.

A blur moving with lethal intent came down those tall wooden stairs and over the railing. It coalesced into a woman, black hair flying, leaping right at us with her fangs bared.

I seized Cathy and pulled her behind me, my fists clenched. Not that I had a chance against that speed and those teeth.

"Mom!" someone shouted. "Mom, *chill*!"

◆

The vampire stopped like a bird hitting a window. Her lip stayed curled. Her fangs glittered at me.

"What are you doing in my home?" she whispered, and the harmonics of her voice made the hair stand up on the back of my neck.

Behind me, I felt Cathy shiver.

"Cathy, don't you dare move," I said in a low voice.

"Cathy?" the vampire asked, with less threat of grisly death and more surprise in her voice.

She had a faint French accent, and I finally noticed what she was wearing. (Fear for my life makes my fashion sense fly right out of my head.) Collar open at her throat, badge glinting—she was wearing the dark uniform of the vampire division of the police force.

We had broken into a vampire cop's house. We were so smart.

"Cathy?" echoed a guy around my age, who was standing on the stairs peering down at us. A perfectly ordinary guy, with a mop of curly hair and a rock band T-shirt on. He moved down the stairs at an ordinary human pace. "Cathy of the sonnets? Cathy of the love ballad?"

A visible shudder went through the vampire cop. As if that old story about vampires fearing crosses was true, and she was shying away from one.

"Please do not speak of the love ballad," she begged.

The guy sat down on the bottom step and propped his chin up on one fist. "Cathy," he said. "Great."

Since the human guy and the vampire cop had linked

up something as incredibly dumb as love ballads with Cathy, I did have an idea who might have written them: Francis.

At least we'd definitely got the right house.

"So, yeah," I said, knowing Cathy wouldn't open her mouth in a million years. "This is Cathy."

"This is a most unorthodox method of paying us a visit," the vampire observed, and sounded more French than ever. "You did not notice the front door? But I suppose you had better come upstairs. We have a kitchen and a wide variety of food suitable for humans," she added with what seemed to be pride. "Kit goes grocery shopping every week. Though I could wish he bought more vegetables."

"Nag, nag, nag," grumbled the guy, as if his presence in their shade was not completely weird and inexplicable. He got to his feet.

"This way," said the vampire.

Her tone brooked no argument. Not to mention that we had, um, broken into her home and thus put ourselves in the wrong.

With Cathy holding my elbow in a death grip, we followed the vampire up the wooden stairs and into the heart of Francis's shade.

CHAPTER TWELVE

Kitchen of the Undead

The first thing I noticed was that this vampire home had artificial lighting even though all vampires can see perfectly in the dark and, as the vampire cop had promised, a kitchen too. I had to assume both were for the benefit of the guy, who was currently sitting on the kitchen counter staring at Cathy with a great deal of curiosity.

"Francis isn't here," he observed as his vampire mom—he'd really called her that, presuming we hadn't misheard—asked us, "Tea?"

"No, thank you," I said as Cathy whispered the same thing to the floor.

"I am Camille," the vampire said. "This is my son, Kit."

We hadn't misheard, and now she was agreeing

with him. How was that possible? Forget the fact that they didn't look the least bit alike. Camille was small, bird-boned, her hair a sheet of midnight black (very appropriate for a vampire). Kit was tall and lanky, his hair an explosion of brown curls.

It made sense that vampires would still take an interest in kids they'd had before turning, but I didn't think that was what was going on. The older vampires are, the less human they look and behave. Camille's skin looked like white stone and she moved like water.

"Hi, Camille. Hi, Kit," I ventured, sitting in the chair Camille had indicated. Cathy cautiously lowered herself onto the chair next to mine, careful not to look either one in the eyes. Instead of asking the obvious: "How on earth are you his mom?" I said, "I'm Mel and this is—"

"The famous Cathy," Kit finished.

Cathy blushed and lowered her gaze even further, studying her own feet. At least she'd believe me now that Francis did think she was special. That was the only positive I could think of.

"Who makes Francis so very happy. That's a line from the aforementioned ballad," he explained. "In case you've been fortunate enough not to hear it. It's probably the best line in the whole thing, which I think speaks volumes as to how very bad it is."

I giggled. Kit immediately turned to me and smiled brilliantly.

He had a great smile, bright and a little wicked.

Though it was weird to smile like that at a complete stranger trespassing in your home.

Of course, everything about this situation was weird.

"Francis wrote a love ballad about Cathy?"

Cathy blushed even deeper. I wondered how it would feel to learn that the love of your life had written a ballad about you? Probably very different from learning that he was using you as a test subject for his book on humans and love.

Kit nodded. "For the last few days he's been singing it nonstop while accompanying himself on the lute. I offered to burn the lute during the day, but Mom won't let me."

"An officer of the law cannot sanction destruction of personal property, no matter how tempting," said Camille, who was making tea despite the fact we had refused it. "I do admit, however, that it is *very* tempting."

Cathy looked up, clearly torn between protesting the aspersions cast against Francis's lute and her shyness in front of strangers. She looked down again.

"I liked Francis a lot better before he was crossed in love," Kit remarked.

"No, you didn't," said Camille, leaning over Kit's shoulder and presenting him with a brimming teacup. He grinned.

It was creepy. Camille sounded like a mom, exasperated and fond, but she looked too young to be Kit's mom and, well, too like a vampire to be anybody's mom.

When Kit grinned at her, there was no answering grin on Camille's face. It made my skin crawl, seeing her smooth, statuelike face next to his, and their hands touching.

I looked away. Maybe that's why he'd smiled like that at me. Nobody in this house full of the quiet undead would ever have laughed at one of his jokes.

When I looked back, Camille was seated at the table, her face wearing the same nonexpression as before, but Kit was looking at me. He had one eyebrow raised, and he was scowling slightly.

I raised both eyebrows back at him. (I can't raise just one, however much I practice in front of the mirror.)

Kit's face, which was extremely expressive, possibly as some sort of compensation for living among vampires, moved from a scowl to a smirk and then back to a smile.

"To be clear. It's not that I don't like Francis," he said. "It's that . . . you know how Francis has an opinion on everything? On account of how he knows everything?"

I nodded. "I am aware of this aspect of Francis's personality. Yes."

Cathy made a small sound.

"He loves to impart his knowledge. And since he deems me to be the least wise of our shade and quite possibly of the entire world, I'm the lucky recipient of the majority of his pearls of wisdom." Kit shuddered. "And his bons mots."

Kit referring to himself so casually as part of a shade

was like hearing a fish saying they belonged to a flock of parrots. Yet it seemed rude to point out that he wasn't a vampire. Like telling a crazy person that they're not Napoleon.

"No, darling," Camille drawled, "it's that the rest of us heard them long before you were born."

"He also likes to study me." Kit mimed Francis holding a magnifying glass. I laughed again. The resemblance to Francis was uncanny.

Kit looked utterly delighted, and again it made me shiver to see him respond like that, a born class clown in a house of vampires.

"I was his human in captivity," Kit continued, trying to get me to laugh again. "I was questioned. Measured. Examined. Probed."

I thought about the human subject Francis had mentioned in his file. Was this why Kit was kept here?

It didn't sound funny at all.

"Kit!" said Camille.

"Okay, not *literally* probed."

"You're not in captivity!" Camille protested.

Kit's attention went from me to her. He frowned in concern.

"Sorry, Mom. Just being dramatic."

"He was studying us, too," I volunteered helpfully, trying not to show how uneasy they were making me. If they'd captured Kit to study him, what would stop them from keeping me and Cathy? "But I think he gave up on us," I added firmly. "We were useless to him. That's us. Totally useless."

"I think he only enrolled at your school because he decided I was too small a sample size for his magnum opus," said Kit.

Cathy shook her head but didn't say anything. Maybe she was still so focused on the Francis-writes-love-ballads revelation to think too deeply about what Francis's magnum opus could be.

"That's a big burden for you to carry," I said to Kit. "Being a representative of all humanity."

"That's what *I* said! I also told him if he was so interested in humanity, he could start watching TV. A week's worth of *Real Schoolkids of Chicago* or *Celebrity Janitor* would satisfy his curiosity forever. But Francis doesn't hold with TV."

"Or texting. Or voice mail. Or the internet. They're all soulless machines for communication that are—"

"Destroying the delicate interplay of social intercourse," Kit and Camille finished for me, in unison.

Apparently Camille joining in was the last straw. Cathy let out a low moan.

"I love him," she said, "and all you can do is laugh at him!"

Which was the moment Francis chose to return home.

He stood on the threshold of the house, holding a bouquet of dead roses, staring at Cathy. She rose from her chair. Neither of them said a word. They were too busy staring at one another.

"You have a visitor," Camille remarked dryly.

"We think she might be that Cathy you've mentioned once or twice," Kit said.

I laughed. Kit beamed. Cathy swooned.

CHAPTER THIRTEEN

Lovers' Meeting.
Plus Tea.

"**D**oes she do that a lot?" Camille asked as Francis held Cathy's supine body in his arms and gently splashed water in her face.

"She hasn't been eating," I replied. "Because of her broken heart." I really wanted Francis to put her down, but he was holding her so gently and looked so concerned.

"Make her food," Camille commanded Kit. "Something reviving. I shall make more tea."

Tea making seemed to be Camille's favorite domestic task.

I hovered uselessly next to Cathy, wondering if I should call her mother and realizing that this would all be very difficult to explain. Please be okay, I begged her silently. I'd never seen Cathy faint before. She hardly ever got sick. She didn't look it, but she was tough.

She'd always been tough. Until she'd met Francis.

Her eyelids fluttered. "Francis," she murmured.

"Cathy," he murmured back.

"Heathcliff," muttered Kit, as he set about making sandwiches. I couldn't help giggling again. Kit turned to me with a huge grin on his face. "She'll be okay," he whispered.

Kit seemed to be recovering. He'd looked badly startled when Cathy went down. I suppose if you're used to living with invulnerable vampires, seeing someone topple would be pretty disconcerting.

Francis helped Cathy sit up. "Oh," she said, putting her hand to her forehead. Then she seemed to realize that she was in Francis's arms, and she blushed. "Oh," she said again.

"You fainted," I informed her.

"You caught me," Cathy said, gazing up at Francis with admiration.

I wished that I could say he hadn't. But he had. Francis had moved faster than I'd ever seen a vampire move before. He was holding her before she was halfway to the ground. It had been most impressive.

Kit held out a cheese-and-tomato sandwich on a chipped plate.

"You should eat, my darling," Francis said, lifting her up effortlessly and depositing her on a chair.

"Oh, I couldn't," Cathy protested.

"We think that's why you fainted," I said. "How much

have you eaten in the last few days?"

Cathy blushed.

"Have one bite," I begged. "You'll feel better."

Kit held the plate closer to Cathy, waggling it encouragingly.

"Oh, no," Cathy began.

"Please eat, darling," Francis urged, taking the plate from Kit and placing it in front of Cathy. "For me?"

Cathy picked up the sandwich and took a bite. I tried not to feel wounded that she would eat for him but not for her best friend.

"It's a very good sandwich," she said, presumably to Kit, who had made it, though she was looking at Francis. She took another bite, and then another, and then ate the whole thing faster than I'd ever seen her eat before. Kit made her another sandwich, and Camille gave her a cup of tea.

"Thank you," she said. "I'm sorry to be such a bother."

"You could never be a bother," Francis assured her.

"Yes, you could," I protested. "When you weren't eating or moving from your chair, you bothered me. I was bothered. Very."

Cathy wasn't listening. She was too busy eating her sandwich, sipping her tea, and staring at Francis.

They looked lost in each other's eyes. Like I would need to make a tiny eye map for each of them to be able to find their way out, and even then they wouldn't want to.

It was even worse than I'd thought. If Francis was also clinging to this delusion of being star-crossed lovers, and by the sound of things—love ballads!—he was, this whole thing was going to get even more drawn out and messy and painful for Cathy when it ended. I leaned back against the kitchen counter, very close to tears. I blinked and dug my fingernails into my palm. I was not going to cry.

"You'll come back to school, won't you?" Cathy asked.

"I—" Francis began.

"Yes, he will," Camille interjected.

I felt so betrayed. Camille was a creepy vampire, who had leaped upon us with a jugular-tearing glint in her eye, but at least she had seemed sensible. A sensible vampire cop who made tea!

I guess she couldn't take any more of the love ballads. But it seemed cruel to inflict Francis on us instead.

"I will," Francis said.

"I'm glad," Cathy murmured. She looked down at the floor and blushed.

Francis took Cathy's hands into his. They resumed gazing into each other's eyes.

"Really?" I said to Camille. "You want him to go back to school. Don't you think that's a bad idea?"

"Yes, Mom, I thought you wanted to, um"—Kit lowered his voice—"not encourage this madness. Your words, not mine."

"Too late now," Camille said, waving in the direction

of the lovebirds. "Besides, I think the human school has been good for Francis. It got him out of our hair."

"No, it didn't. He was away during the day, when you're all resting."

"Yes, but he rested more at night. Not to mention that it got him out of your hair, Kit. Don't you enjoy him not following you about asking questions all day?"

Kit, grabbing Cathy's plate and their mugs, conceded that he did.

I tried to intervene at this point. As an uninvited guest, I felt the least I could do was wash the dishes. But Kit had plenty of reach on me, and he held the plate well over my head as I followed him over to the sink. I watched him carefully and managed to seize the plate out of his hands as soon as it was clean. His wet fingers slid against mine as I grabbed at it, and he started and then looked at me, eyes shocked-wide and blue.

He never had a chance of keeping his grip.

I dried the plate and put it back in the cupboard, which was about the emptiest kitchen cupboard I'd ever seen. I guess they didn't have many dinner parties, what with only one person in the house eating.

"Hasn't he been unbearable since he was separated from 'star-kissed Cathy'?" Camille continued from the table.

"Star-kissed Cathy?"

Kit grimaced. "The ballad."

"He only recovered from his last broken heart a few

decades ago. And that was the girl he loved before he turned. Romantics," Camille said, able to convey her derision with the faintest movement of one eyebrow.

Francis and Cathy seemed to have been rendered deaf by love.

I realized Cathy was never going to say it, even though she was always the polite one, so I offered belatedly, "Sorry about the break-in."

"Not to worry," Camille said, with another glance at the happy couple. "I can see that it wasn't your idea."

"Mom's probably glad you broke in," Kit said in a low voice, even though I was fairly certain Camille could still hear us. "She's always going on about wanting me to hang out with other humans."

I laughed again, but it wasn't even a good fake laugh. All I could think of to say was "Moms, huh? And their crazy mom insistence that you interact with your own species! By the way, how exactly is she your mom?"

I didn't say it.

At least he did know he wasn't a vampire. Phew.

Kit could tell the laugh was fake. He did not beam. His eyebrow went up in a silent question as he washed Cathy's teacup.

I didn't answer the question. I wasn't the mystery here.

CHAPTER FOURTEEN

Vampire Promenade

"**P**ermit me to accompany you home," Francis said.

"We're cool," I said.

"You're so kind," said Cathy.

Guess who Francis the Selectively Deaf paid attention to?

I cast an imploring look at Kit and Camille.

"I'm sure Francis has things to do around the house," I said. "Like his chores? Maybe somebody needs to scrub the toilet?"

"Vampires don't go to the bathroom," Kit said gloomily. "So guess whose turn it always is to scrub the toilet."

I was freaked out by the long-suffering way he said *vampires*, as if he was saying *adults*.

"The Shade is not entirely safe for human strangers at

night," Camille said, with an unreadable look at me that could have been an apology. "Better overcautious than missing a jugular vein, as the saying goes."

That was a very morbid saying. Maybe only vampires said it.

Maybe only French vampires said it.

"I'll walk with you guys and Uncle Francis," Kit offered.

Cathy heard that. Possibly it was hearing someone name Francis so familiarly that woke her from her reverie. She gave Francis an inquiring look.

"Sometimes I call him that," Kit said. "Because he's an old person."

"He has never called me that before in his life," Francis remarked in a frozen voice.

"You probably don't remember," Kit told him. "That's why it's best that I go with you, Uncle Francis. You could have one of your senile fits and end up forgetting your way home. Think how we'd miss you. Think how we'd miss the lute playing."

Kit's eyes slid back to me to see if I was smiling.

I wasn't. Kit might be making fun of Francis, an activity I approved of and enjoyed, but I didn't do it in that easy, affectionate way. Inexplicable though it was, Kit was obviously fond of Francis.

Why were all the people I met drawn to vampires? You'd think they really did have hypnotic powers.

Francis, naturally, responded with all the warmth

of an offended iceberg. "Kit, I beg of you not to display your usual insolence before guests. I dread to think what impressions Catherine has formed of our shade."

"Oh no," Cathy said. "Everyone's been lovely."

"I offered to walk them home," Kit put in. "Always the perfect little gentleman, yours truly."

"You are too kind," Francis murmured to Cathy. "Shall we, my dear?"

Cathy glowed, slipping her hand into the proffered crook of his arm, and he led her out the front door. Camille stood at the threshold, still and dignified, the lady of the house.

"Thank you for having us," I heard Cathy tell Camille earnestly.

"Come back anytime. Either of you." It was sweet of her not mention the fact that we had broken in.

I hoped we wouldn't be back. But given the way Cathy and Francis were looking at each other, it was a forlorn hope. I had a vision of incredibly awkward dinner parties, with half the table not eating. Of Ty and me chatting with Camille the vampire cop while Francis and Cathy sat on a sofa gazing into each other's eyes. Francis's feelings for her were obviously real. Sonnets? Ballads?

He couldn't have known that she would ever hear about them. I couldn't think of any reason for him to write them and torment his shade with lute playing unless he felt something for her.

Though who knew what vampires actually felt.

Even if it was real, it was still creepy.

"I need to get my bike," I said, stomping down the front steps.

Kit kissed his mom on the cheek and then came down the porch steps to join me.

"Sorry about the petunia bed," I mumbled as I picked up my bike and tried not to tread on the already trampled flowers.

"No problem," he said. "Minty changes the whole garden every few months. Some vampires"—and he said the word that way again, as if they were the grown-ups—"get very bored. Landscape gardening. Redecorating. She's probably ready for something new anyway."

I wondered how it was possible to garden only at night. Or maybe she had a suit like Francis.

"Minty?" I repeated.

Kit grinned at me. When I grinned back, he looked startled. His smile spread wider.

"Her name's Araminta. She hates it when I call her Minty. If you meet her, you probably shouldn't call her that."

"I probably won't meet her."

Kit stopped smiling.

Cathy and Francis were walking on up ahead, having, I imagined, a dreamy conversation about very little. "Oh, how I love you!" "Not so much as I love *you*!" I was glad I couldn't hear it.

"Let me take your bike."

"I'm fine," I said firmly.

I didn't know if the offer was Francis-trained chivalry or Kit reflecting on how puny human girls must be, but either way I didn't like it.

There were a lot of vampires gliding past. I suppose after midnight was the ideal time for vampires to take an afternoon stroll.

Some of them were wearing what I assumed were the height of fashion when they turned. I saw bustles and crinolines, parasols, flapper dresses, and formal shorts. (Vampires don't feel the cold.) Others were in more regular clothes, but somehow they still looked like they should be holding parasols and, indeed, some of them were. Added to that, they were strolling, but their stroll was almost as fast as I could run.

It was too, too weird. How could Kit stand it? Yet he seemed to *like* it.

Compared to the vampire women practically floating along on their escorts' arms, Cathy looked like she was stumbling. I was almost grateful to Francis for matching his speed to hers.

On the other hand, if it wasn't for Francis, neither of us would be here. I wouldn't be walking beside the oddest guy I'd ever met, wheeling my bike, while moonlight reflected off the still faces of vampires passing by. It was quite easily the strangest night of my life.

A vampire girl sailed down the sidewalk and inclined her head as she did so.

"Hello, Kit," she said, her voice very cultured and adult.

"Hello, Mrs. Appleby," Kit said, and smiled at her.

She didn't smile back, just kept sailing on.

"Mrs. Appleby?" I repeated. "She looks younger than us."

"People got married at fourteen in the Middle Ages," Kit answered. "She's a nice old thing. She used to bring me candy when I was a kid."

"Oh."

I stared at Francis's and Cathy's backs and resolved not to be rude and ask about Kit's strange life even though I was so curious I was about to burst.

"So you've lived in the Shade since you were little?" I asked, shamelessly breaking my resolution in under a second.

"I've lived here all my life," Kit said, with a sidelong glance.

"I know I'm prying," I said. "But a human, living with vampires! I'm dying to know."

"You're dying every minute, but you won't die yet," Kit said. I gave him a look and he muttered: "Something my mom says."

I was silent. So was the world of the Shade. A vampire in jogging clothes zipped by, so fast his tracksuit was a blur, his running shoes barely stirring the grass.

"Vampires jog?" I couldn't help asking. "They need to stay fit?"

"No," Kit said. "He's new. It's a human habit. It will leave him soon enough."

I tried not to shudder. How did Kit cope, living in this place?

"Someone left me on their doorstep, the day I was born," Kit said abruptly.

"Someone—" I started. "But why would—"

It wasn't like leaving a baby on the doorstep of a church or an orphanage. It was a *vampires' house*. In the Shade.

"It's something people do sometimes," Kit said, his voice gentle. "If you have a baby you don't want anyone to know about. Vampires can disappear it without a trace."

"Oh." I felt ill. He was talking about babies being *murdered*.

"Kind of like getting Chinese food delivered," Kit said. "Except getting Chinese food delivered to the Shade is actually a huge pain. When I was six, I wouldn't eat anything but potstickers for like two months, and Mom had to tip the delivery guy quadruple."

I laughed and made a horrified face at the same time.

"But they chose the wrong doorstep for me," Kit continued cheerfully. "Mom's a cop. She wasn't going to let anybody make me a delicious illegal snack. She said we had to hand me over to the human authorities, but Minty and Albert and June thought I was adorable and wanted to keep me, and Francis wanted to study me. He said I was a symbol of innocence they could all contemplate, and I think Marie-Therese was hoping that once the novelty wore off, they'd let her munch on me after all. They took a vote, and so I stayed."

"Democracy at work," I murmured, wondering how big a margin Kit's fate had been decided by. And yet I'd still grinned at Kit's eye roll when he mentioned Francis's contribution to the baby debate.

How could someone leave a baby on a doorstep for monsters to feed on? How could someone do that, and consider themselves human afterward?

CHAPTER FIFTEEN

Kit, Short for . . .

We were finally out of the Shade and I was glad. Still in the old part of town, but there were neon lights flickering on some buildings and an all-night convenience store with one or two human customers. We were in the real world, bright with colors and life. A few more blocks and we'd be in more familiar surroundings, walking past my favorite coffee shop.

The relief of it had me volunteering: "So they obviously didn't get tired of you."

"Oh, they were sick to the fangs of me by the time I was a year old," Kit said, still sounding amused. "But my mom doesn't quit once she's taken on a responsibility. And I was a smart kid. They still tell stories about how I used to stagger around holding on to her leg. The others had phases when they fussed over me, but even though Mom thought I was a nuisance—she wanted to get out and do her job—she was the responsible one. She made sure I was fed and cared for. She wore one of those dumb suits and woke me up for walks during the day so I wouldn't get rickets. Poor Mom, she took me on enough walks that I knew my way home, so it was no good leaving me on someone else's doorstep. I bet she was tempted, though."

"Bet she wasn't." I bumped Kit in the hip with my bike, a bit harder than I'd meant to.

"Ow," he said, but he looked pleased.

We'd drawn level with Cathy and Francis at last—we were at Cathy's house. I was almost disappointed. I had lots more to ask Kit.

Cathy and Francis were bidding each other a drawn-out farewell on the porch. I saw Francis touch her face.

"This whole Cathy and Francis thing is horrible," I announced.

"You don't know anything about horrible," Kit said. "You haven't heard the ballad."

It was more support than I'd received from anyone else except Kristin, so I opened my mouth to say something else when Cathy called out, "Good-bye, Mel! See you in the morning."

It seemed so normal. I waved back at her. "See you!"

"Now we will escort you home, Melanie," Francis said, before noticing something and looking scandalized. "Good heavens, Christopher, take the lady's bicycle!"

"Er," Kit said.

"I told him I had it."

"She wouldn't let me, Francis."

Francis looked disapproving and went to stand beside Kit. I was pleased to see that Kit was a head taller. Mind you, quite a few guys were taller than Francis. He'd been born in England in the 1800s. They weren't big on nutritious bone-building food back then. Francis had probably grown up on gruel and boar fat.

"In which direction do we proceed?" Francis asked.

"It's close," I said. "I can go the rest of the way by myself."

"I wouldn't hear of it," Francis said firmly.

I sighed and headed home. Maybe I could dissuade him from taking me to my front door. I had, once again, taken off without my parents' knowledge.

"You'll find Melanie is quite a character," Francis told Kit.

I decided not to point out that I was right here.

"Will I?" asked Kit. "How will I find Cathy? Aside from star-kissed. And still my age."

"Cathy is extremely mature for her age—"

"She'd have to be, wouldn't she?"

"While you, I regret to say, despite the advantage of your upbringing, are not."

"Aw, Uncle Francis," Kit said.

I snorted. Francis looked vexed.

"About Cathy," I said. "My objections are unaltered."

(How's that for Francis-speak?) "As Kit says, she's much, much younger than you. Then there's the matter of the book you're writing about her."

Francis looked, to all appearances, honestly scandalized. I'd seen scandalized on Francis a lot by now—I seemed to bring it out in him—and I was sure it was genuine.

"My book is not about Cathy."

"*On Adolescent* Homo sapiens sapiens *and Love* is not about the human girl you're pretending to be in love with for the sake of your research?"

"*Pretending?* What kind of a blackguard do you think I am? I'll have you know my love is sincere. Furthermore—"

"It's true," Kit said loudly, cutting him off. "He's really in love with her."

After tonight's display I had to admit that might be true. "But what about your book?"

"My *book*, as you so crudely put it, is not merely about adolescent humans in love. That is but one chapter of the whole. My magnum opus, which has already run to several volumes, is a history of human and vampire emotions. For far too long there have been claims that we vampires have none or that they are muted compared to those of humans. Pure human prejudice. Some of our emotions are different, I will concede, but different is not the same as lesser. I am writing the monumental work that will refute those claims for all eternity and enable humans and vampires to communicate in a spirit of mutual understanding and goodwill. In order to prove my thesis, it was necessary to study both human and vampire emotions. To compare and contrast. I have found that . . ."

"Now you've done it," Kit whispered. "He won't stop for months."

I giggled.

"I will desist," Francis said icily. "I am sorry that one of the great works of all time is so tedious to you, Christopher. And a source of mirth to you, Melanie."

"My name's not Melanie," I said, exasperated.

"Mine's not Christopher," Kit said.

"Yes, it is," said Francis, addressing me. "He's named after Christopher Marlowe. The poet and playwright. If not for his tragically early death, I feel it likely that he, and not Shakespeare, would have been remembered as the preeminent genius of his—"

"Cathy's been my best friend since birth," I interrupted. "I know who Kit Marlowe is."

"Yes, of course, you would. She is remarkably learned for one so young."

I tried not to make a face.

"May I have a word with you, Melan—Mel?"

I nodded. Francis gestured for Kit to step away.

"With regard to our arrangement, are you still determined to prevent me from attending your school?"

I stared at Francis.

"I know I agreed not to see Cathy again. But as you can see . . ." He waved his hand in the direction of Cathy's house.

"The deal's off," I said. "You can come back to school. I won't tell anyone."

I could see that telling Cathy about his book would have zero effect.

"Thank you," Francis said. "I will not soon forget this. She means everything to me."

"Uh, sure," I said. I was still wondering why he specifically didn't want Principal Saunders to know about the book that was listed in his file. It made no sense.

And, of course, if Principal Saunders didn't know about the book, why was she acting so weird? Why did she hate him? Solely because he was a vampire?

I needed answers. Anna needed answers, and I didn't know how to get them.

Francis drifted into a romantic trance, i.e., he forgot to keep pace with us mere mortals. That gave Kit a chance to cough, and bump against my bike.

"Not really," he said.

"What?" I asked. We were almost home, and I was thinking about what my parents would say if they saw me with a vampire. Not that they're prejudiced, but they'd be a bit surprised. Plus they didn't know I wasn't in my room.

"I'm not really named after Christopher Marlowe," Kit said. "Mom and Francis pretend that I am. But I remember what the others used to call me when I was really little."

He leaned in and told me with a small smile.

As they walked away, I stood in the darkness, thinking about the world my best friend had got herself mixed up in.

A world of darkness and silence—except for the occasional lute playing. A world of monsters, where humans abandoned their babies knowing they would never be heard from again.

Or if the monsters on a whim took in the baby, they would carelessly let the child know exactly what he was to them. Not a son, but a pet.

They would call him Kitten.

CHAPTER SIXTEEN

Caught in a Really Bad Romance

Cathy and I walked to school the next morning. Cathy couldn't stop smiling and exclaiming on the beauty of everything. You'd think she was on drugs. Maybe she was. Lots of people are convinced that love is a drug.

If so, Cathy was mainlining.

It turned out she knew all about Francis's book—oh, sorry, his magnum opus—and had known from almost the beginning. She was quite happy to tell me more than I ever wanted to know about it.

Which begged the question: What had Francis thought I meant when I'd told him I knew what he was up to?

What didn't he want Principal Saunders to know? And what was going on with Principal Saunders anyway?

As if thinking about Francis and Principal Saunders had conjured them up, I saw them.

Francis was waiting for Cathy on the school steps. As we approached, he stood up, bowed, and lifted Cathy's hand to his visor as if to kiss it. I can't speak for his expression, given that he was in his hazmat suit, but I imagine it was as beatific as Cathy's.

In the parking lot, Principal Saunders was locking her fancy new SUV. Her expression was the opposite of beatific. She went pale when she saw us. I thought she was going to pass out on the spot when the four of us walked into the hall together and Francis eased his helmet off and turned his cool blue gaze to her.

I swear Principal Saunders shuddered.

"Are you okay, ma'am?" I asked. She was looking thin, and the circles around her eyes were so deep and dark, I wouldn't have been surprised if bats had taken up residence.

"Fine, thank you," she said crisply. "Have you recovered, Cathy? Your mother said you were ill."

Cathy blushed. "Yes, Principal Saunders."

"Good, good. We hate to see our valedictorian away for any length of time. Hurts morale." Principal Saunders attempted a smile. It looked more like a death rictus. At the same time she looked lost.

It was the strangest thing, but something about her expression made me think of how Cathy had looked when she'd thought Francis was gone forever.

Francis's expression was unaltered. What was going on between those two? Why was the principal afraid of him? What was he up to that he didn't want her to know about?

Most important of all, how was I going to find out?

✦

I didn't see much of Cathy or Francis for the rest of the day—they were too lost in their own glittery little world, as if they were trapped in a snow globe of vampire love—but they might as well have been sitting in my lap, given that they were the constant topic of conversation. Apparently Principal Saunders wasn't the only one who had noted Cathy's absence. Many had noted that both she and Francis had been away.

Though everyone seemed to have forgotten that Francis had been absent for a few days before Cathy. They also seemed incapable of asking Cathy or Francis how they were. No, they all asked me.

"Is Cathy all right?" Ty inquired while gobbling down meatballs and rigatoni. "Was she sick? Did she and Francis go somewhere together? Are they married now?"

"She's fine. They're fine. Everything is fine," I said, even though it wasn't. "They're not married."

"What happened, exactly? Are you sure she's okay?" Anna asked, joining us because Cathy and Francis were elsewhere. Under a tree reciting poetry at each other, I imagined. Or maybe he was reading to her from the magnum opus?

I recited the touching story in a monotone. "She

thought she'd lost Francis forever. Now she has him back. She is, and I quote, 'in a blissful delirium.' So yes. I think that means she is okay."

"Oh," Anna said. She seemed taken aback, possibly because of the "blissful delirium" part.

"Well, that's good," Ty said.

"No, Ty, it's not. In case you haven't noticed, he's a vampire!"

Ty looked distressed. Francis's beauty and airplane expertise had obviously dazzled all the brains right out of his head.

"Francis is a really nice vampire," he protested. "And, you know, some human-vampire relationships work out great."

"Oh, really?" I asked. "How many people do you know involved in happy relationships with the undead?"

Ty and Anna both took this opportunity to be significantly silent.

"Aside from Francis and Cathy, I mean!"

"Well, none," Ty said. "But we know it happens. There are books about it. There are stories in the paper all the time. Did you see that one about the vampire guy who kept dating all the girl descendants in this one family? Can you imagine being like 'Granny's ex sure is hot'?"

"How is that an argument in favor of dating vampires?" I asked, wondering if Ty had lost his mind.

He ignored me. "And then there's Gina Lyons and Zac Rider."

"Their relationship is a stunt for the movie," Anna put in. "Almost all celebrity hookups are."

"Well, I think their love is real," said Ty, who seemed determined in Cathy's absence to be the romantic of the group. He hesitated, then added: "And how about Rob Lin and Aaron Zuckermann? They've been together ten years!"

"In which time Aaron Zuckermann has had like fifteen plastic surgeries," said Anna. "That we know of."

"That's because looking good is important to him. He feels he owes it to the fans and that it expresses his dedication to the job," Ty said. "It's not because he's insecure about their love."

"Uh-huh," said Anna. "Plastic surgery does not make you look good. He's freakish."

I took a deep breath. "Stop talking about celebrities! So they date vampires, so what? I assume we all agree Cathy shouldn't get extensive cosmetic surgery! And please, Ty, don't bring up any of your romance novels. They're fictional."

"Some of them are based on true stories."

"This isn't a story!" I said. "Cathy's not a celebrity! She's got herself all tangled up with this stupid vampire and her own dreams, and I'm worried sick about her!" My voice might have risen a tiny bit. Ty and Anna were staring at me.

"Oh, is that the time?" Ty exclaimed unconvincingly. "I have an appointment with, um, the counselor. I've been feeling very troubled lately!"

"Uh-huh," I said as he scampered away from the lunch table as fast as he could, abandoning meatballs, pasta, and his soda. "That or he has to go rearrange his sock drawer."

"You were a bit fierce," Anna said. She looked almost as tired as her mother. What had I been thinking, going on about love affairs with the undead, letting Ty talk about vampires and celebrities dating? This whole Francis and Cathy thing must be unbearable for Anna, considering her dad had gone off with some undead home wrecker.

"I feel fierce," I said, lowering my voice and moving closer to Anna. "I had to go rescue Cathy from Francis's house last night."

I was still talking about vampires, but at least Anna looked more awake. "You didn't! You went into the Shade? By yourself?"

"I did. It was terrifying. He lives with a vampire cop who almost killed us both!"

Anna shuddered, and I thought of her mother's shudder this morning.

"I'm sorry. I shouldn't be telling you about this when . . ." The words *your dad* hung between us, all the louder for not being spoken.

Anna bowed her head. "No, that's okay. I want to hear about it. Was the house dark and cold?"

She spoke as if she'd spent some time imagining a vampire's house, imagining it being dank and dark and refrigerator cold where her father had chosen to go.

"It was cold, but not dark." I cast about for a way to distract Anna. "You're not going to believe this, but there's a human who lives in Francis's shade."

"Actually, it's quite common," Anna said in a brittle voice. "Vampire-human cohabitation. For a brief time, at least. I imagine my dad is living in a vampire shade right now."

"Oh! I'm sorry. I didn't mean . . . I just . . . Argh. Sorry." Apparently it was foot-in-mouth day. "There's this boy who lives there called Kit. Well, not a little kid, he's our age. But he calls the vampire cop his mom and Francis his uncle. He grew up with vampires."

Anna's mouth dropped open. "Okay, you were right, I don't believe it. How on earth did that happen?"

I told her.

"He's really strange, Anna," I said, thinking of Kit cheerfully telling me his name was actually Kitten because he was a vampire pet.

"He thinks vampires are . . ." I paused, not entirely sure what he thought they were. "Grown-ups? How people are? He seems to think he doesn't quite measure up. It's awful. I got the impression he doesn't know any humans. Poor Kit. He doesn't even know that vampires and humans don't mix."

"They shouldn't," Anna said bleakly. "I'm with you. Ty's wrong about that." She twisted her hands together for a moment, then burst out: "Sometimes I think this city shouldn't exist. I mean, yes, we can mostly stay out of one another's way. But not always. Then there's people like my dad, who work with them every day, who bring them into your life even if you don't want them. It's wrong. It leads to . . . bad things."

She closed her eyes for a second. I hoped she wouldn't cry.

"One time Dad's vampire came to our house. I never told you, did I?"

"No," I said.

Anna had told me almost nothing about what had happened. Unusually for me, I hadn't really asked. I hadn't known where to start.

"Well, she did. She was pounding on our front door for hours. At least it felt like hours. Mom called the cops immediately. The vampire vanished when they showed up, which I'm sure didn't take that long, but for those moments or minutes or hours when we were waiting? It was hell. Dad was away at a conference, so it was Mom and me, holding each other in the closet, knowing that if she broke down the door, or threw herself in through one of our windows, there was nothing we could do.

"I have never been so scared in my life. She didn't just bang on the door. She howled. That noise was the worst I've ever heard. It took us a while to recognize what she was saying. But once I did?"

Anna was shaking.

"She was saying Dad's name. Over and over."

I shook my head. Anna's eyes were wet, but she kept talking, as if all these words had been building up in my quiet friend for too long and now they simply had to come out.

"The next morning there were all these gouges on our door. I think she used her nails. We had to get it replaced.

"I never saw her. But I imagined what she looked like: more zombie than vampire, huge empty eyes, hair everywhere, covered in blood. A monster. Why would my dad run away with someone, some *thing*, like that? But he did. He loved a screaming monster more than he loved us."

The tears started to roll down her cheeks.

"I'm sorry," I whispered.

"Mom's a wreck. How could he do that to her? How could he do that to me?"

I put my arms around her. "I don't know."

"I don't even see how he could love her," Anna said. "He talked to me about her afterward. He couldn't say much, because she was his patient, but he did say that you could only be sorry for her. That's not love. I keep thinking about that night, Mel. My dad felt sorry for her, but I don't think he could have loved someone like that. And if he didn't love her, why would he go with her?"

I swallowed. My mouth felt dry. "Do you think he didn't want to go with her? Do—do you think she made him?"

"I don't know," said Anna. "My mom told me he loved

that monster. She told me he looked her in the eye and said he was leaving, because he wanted to be with her and not us. My mom has no reason to lie. I can't believe she would. But I can't believe Dad could love something like that vampire, so I don't know what to believe. I don't know anything except how much I hate her!"

Anna leaned her face against my shoulder and sobbed. I patted her on the back and hated the vampire woman as well: I couldn't help but hate her, even if she was crazy. Anna was in so much pain.

This was what vampires did. They ruined lives.

I would not allow any vampire to ruin Cathy's.

CHAPTER SEVENTEEN

A Modest Proposal from Francis

What with one of my best friends breaking down in the cafeteria and all, it was a pretty crappy day. I was not exactly in the mood to see Cathy float down the school steps at the end of it, looking as if her day had been nothing but rose petals, soft music, and light gleaming debonairly off Francis's fangs.

"Hi, Mel," she said, beaming as if I was the best-friend cherry on her sundae of love. She about swooped me off my feet in a hug. "How was your day?"

"Not so good," I replied in a voice muffled against Cathy's sweater. "Anna's pretty down."

"Oh no!" said Cathy. "What's wrong?"

"She was talking about her dad at lunch today," I told her. I didn't know how much of what Anna had told me was in confidence, so I left it at that. "I was thinking that after fencing practice I could drag her to Kafeen Krank tonight. Dose her with hot chocolate. Wanna come?"

Cathy bit her lip. "Oh, Mel, I wish I could, but I have plans with Francis."

She'd stepped back from me by then, so she saw the look on my face.

"I swear I'm not going to be one of those awful people who get into a couple and start ignoring their friends! Things aren't going to be about Francis, Francis, Francis"—her voice lingered over his name—"all the time. Tomorrow I'll go over to Anna's with you. I'll make cupcakes. We can plan a whole girls' day on the weekend."

Normally I'm easily bribed by cupcakes. But not this time. I kept my arms folded and my lips pressed together.

"Francis asked me to meet him in a fancy restaurant tonight," Cathy said. She could barely contain her excitement.

I frowned. "Francis doesn't eat. Won't it be awkward?"

"No," said Cathy.

"I'd worry he'd judge the way I chewed or my table manners."

"Mel, it's going to be romantic! It's a big deal. Our first official date. And he said he had something important to ask me."

I immediately stopped thinking about how awkward romantic dinners with vampires must be. In fact, I stopped thinking at all. My brain was paralyzed with horror.

"What?" I managed at last.

Cathy wrung her hands, apparently out of joy since she was smiling. "I don't know. He hasn't asked me yet!"

What if he was going to ask if he could move to England with her, so he could stalk her vampirically around Oxford, casting a big undead shadow over her whole college life? She would be all alone. Except for him. She'd become totally dependent on him. It would be a nightmare!

"You should cancel," I squeaked, panic turning the air into helium. "You should come with me and Anna!"

"Mel," Cathy said, in a voice I could tell she was only keeping level with an effort. "I've already made plans. You would understand that if it was any other guy. I know you don't like Francis, even if I don't understand why."

I opened my mouth to tell her. In some detail.

"I didn't like Ryan, either," she said, silencing me. "But it was your decision to go out with him, and I respected that."

You may recall that I mentioned having another boy-friend, after Ty and I had our deeply amicable breakup? One who put me off dating for a while?

The thing was, Ty decided we didn't have much chemistry, which was true, but he was the one to say it, which hurt, and then I met Ryan at a fencing tournament and we had so much chemistry, I was blinded to certain things.

Such as the fact he was a jerk.

He hit on Cathy at a party. It was a mess.

"Ryan was a big mistake."

"He was your mistake to make."

"And Francis is a bigger one!"

Cathy drew close to me, so close I had to tip my head back to meet her eyes. Stupid tall people.

"Mel," she said, "you know I love you. I know you love me. I know that you only want the best for me. But Francis is wonderful to me. Francis is wonderful *for* me. Be happy for me."

"But, Cathy, he—"

"I am happy. Maybe it won't work out," she said, as if that was the world's most ridiculous idea. "You can say whatever it is then. Right now I need you to drop this."

"Cathy," I began.

She looked into my eyes. Her voice was cold, as cold as Francis's or Camille's.

"Mel," she said. "Drop it. Now."

✦

It was already dark when Ty met us after fencing, bouncing up and down on his toes. He hovered around Anna, aware she was upset, trying to make her feel better in his clumsy boy way, which involved almost tripping her up and repeatedly proffering gum. It was kind of sweet.

"Sorry about losing my license," he said. "Not that Mom would necessarily have lent me her car."

"After you crashed it?" I inquired.

"I didn't crash it," Ty protested. "It was just that if you wanted to read the license plate, you had to climb under the car. It was more of a crumpling than a crashing."

Anna gave him a half smile, which was kind, because we'd heard the story before. Ty had managed to crash the car and lose his license in the first week of summer. It had been a major drag. It was still a drag. Cathy's mom didn't own a car, so despite Cathy passing driver's ed with flying colors, she hadn't been able to get a license yet because she hadn't been able to get enough driving hours. Ditto for me: My parents shared the one car, in which I'd had precisely two lessons with Dad. Besides which, as I may have already mentioned, it would take me years to save up for a car.

Ty continued the puppy-dog-like goofiness during the entire walk to our regular coffee place, Kafeen Krank. There were many things to love about the place. They put giant marshmallows in the hot chocolate; the staff are either amusingly cranky (sorry, Kranky) or full of amazing gossip they'll share with anyone. The chairs are comfy, though dilapidated, and unlike the ones in stupid Francis's café of choice, they don't match. There's graffiti in lurid colors on every flat surface: walls, tables, floor. They even leave markers around so you can add more of your own. Much more my style. Not just the comfortable grunginess but almost everyone there was young and broke like us, including the staff.

Ty and I were talking a lot, in a manic attempt to take the wretched look off Anna's face. Ty recounted his soccer team's latest adventures. (They'd won four games in the last two seasons.) I talked about a fencing competition we had coming up. (I don't like to boast, but our team is approaching top ten in the state. Don't ask how many girls' saber teams there are in our state.) I also shared a few saber-related mishaps that may or may not have been true. (I was trying to make Anna laugh. Is that so wrong?)

That led to discussions about the haplessness of New Whitby's hockey team—the Penguins—of whom Anna used to be a big fan. Despite my and Ty's most valiant efforts, Anna did not smile.

In desperation, we talked about homework. Unsurprisingly, given all her time in the library, Anna tersely indicated she was up-to-date on everything. Had written her New Whitby sewage system essay. I too admitted that I was on top of everything, including aforementioned sewer essay. (What can I say? In everything other than love, Cathy's a great example. One I've been following since kindergarten. I shudder to think what I would have achieved left to my own devices.) Ty was doing as well as Ty ever does. He had at least found sewer maps online, though he hadn't figured out what to say about them.

In even more desperation, I talked about Cathy.

"I suck, don't I? If even Cathy's lost patience with me, I suck. I should butt out. Just briefly, until the bloom's off the rose or whatever. Then when Cathy's less starry-eyed about her walking corpse, I pounce!"

Ty looked alarmed. "You pounce?"

"With cunning arguments," I said.

"I think you're doing the right thing," Anna said quietly.

We looked at her. It was the most she'd said in an hour. She offered us both a wry smile.

"I'm just saying," she said. "Nobody knows this better than me, right? Vampires have a lot of glamour—because they're older and more experienced and strong and pretty—oh, just because they're vampires. I don't think it's a bad idea to keep reminding Cathy to be sensible. I think you're being a good friend."

Anna reached out and squeezed my hand, which was lying beside my giant brownie.

"Aw," I said. "Anna. Thank you for that touching tribute. You still can't have any of my brownie, though."

Anna shrugged. "Worth a shot."

I broke a bit of it off and handed it to her because it was nice to see her smile. Ty made a low moaning sound that was meant to indicate his imminent death by starvation.

"Forget it, get your own."

"I left all my money in—" Ty thought this over. "Well, in the vending machines at school."

I took a big bite of the brownie, making exaggerated *mmmm* sounds for Ty's benefit.

"Cathy," Ty said.

"We can stop talking about her if you—"

"Hi, Cathy," Ty said a little louder.

I looked up. Cathy was standing in front of us. She was crying.

I shot to my feet and grabbed her hands. "I'll kill him."

Cathy's shoulders shook. "I—I—"

"I'm taking the un out of undead. I swear," I said, pulling up a chair for her. "Cathy, what did he do? What's the matter?"

"N-n-nothing!" Cathy said sinking into the chair. Despite the gush of tears down her face, Cathy's eyes were shining.

"I'm so happy," Cathy wept. "I had to come tell you guys right away!"

"Tell us what happened?"

Cathy glowed through her tears. It was like seeing the sun rise behind a waterfall.

"Francis asked me to be with him forever," she said. "He asked if I would—if I would consider becoming a vampire."

My hands went numb. Cathy's hands would have slipped out of them, except she gripped mine tight, as if she could pass her sheer delight to me through her finger-tips.

This was it, then. This was the real reason I'd hated the thought of Cathy with Francis so much. I'd been afraid, without ever being able to even think that it might come to this.

Cathy smiled. "I said yes."

CHAPTER EIGHTEEN

Francis Says . . .

I'm not stupid. I knew telling Cathy she was about to make the biggest mistake of her life, reciting all the statistics about her odds of becoming a zombie instead of a vampire, or of flat-out dying, were not going to be heard with receptive ears. I knew that at this heady moment, with Cathy floating in bubbles of joy, my puncturing them with capital-R Reality would not go well.

And yet what were the first words out of my mouth?

"Are you INSANE?" I screamed. "HAVE YOU COMPLETELY LOST YOUR MIND?"

The busy coffee shop was suddenly a lot less busy. Everyone turned to stare. Literally everyone. Even the fat baby in the stroller stopped sucking on its own fists and stared.

I hadn't meant to scream.

Cathy was also staring. Her big eyes had gotten even bigger. She looked stunned, as if she couldn't believe I wasn't overcome with delirious happiness for her. But when had I ever given Cathy any indication that I thought her ending her life at the age of seventeen was a super-fantastic idea?

"You could die," I said as calmly as I could manage. Which was not very. Everyone was still staring. "If you don't die, you'll wind up a drooling zombie. If you don't become a drooling zombie—"

"It's illegal," Anna said, cutting through me. "You're underage."

Cathy looked as if she was relieved to have someone making a reasonable point. I didn't feel like it was very reasonable to be reasonable right now.

"I'll get my mother's permission," Cathy answered quietly. "We're going to do the whole thing legally. Of course."

"I think it's romantic," Ty said.

I punched him hard in the shoulder. So hard I saw him draw back automatically to return the blow.

The look on my face must have stopped him. He rubbed his shoulder instead.

"What?"

I glared at him. Looking at Cathy hurt too much.

"It's not romantic. It's the end of her life! She's giving up everything and she'll probably die. This is the worst mistake of your entire life, Cathy. This is the end of everything. You can't do this! You can't!"

Another voice broke in at the end of my tirade. A stranger's voice.

"Excuse me," a good-looking guy in black with too much eyeliner on said, coming up to Cathy. "You have a sponsor? You're going to cross over? I wanted to wish you good luck. I know not everyone understands."

He shot me a look. I opened my mouth to set the rude vamposeur straight, tell him that I understood perfectly well what Cathy was doing.

Anna grabbed my arm. I hadn't even realized I'd clenched my fists again. Or maybe I hadn't unclenched them. Anna was right; there was no point arguing with a vamposeur.

"Wow. You're so lucky. So blessed. I can't tell you how jealous I am. Can I hug you? Maybe the luck will rub off on me."

He hugged her. Cathy let him, still looking stunned.

"That's insane," said an older man at the next table over, lowering his newspaper. He was at least forty. Probably the oldest guy in the room. "Vampires are death. You should listen to your friend. A friend of mine did what you want to do. My best friend. Know where Leif is now? Dead. Leif didn't make it, did he? Dead at nineteen. Very glamorous. Do you think his vampire lover gave it a second's thought? Nope. But here's me twenty years later still thinking about my best friend, who died way too young, because he fell for a lie!"

"It's not a lie," the vamposeur said, releasing Cathy and wheeling on the man. "It's a risk. And the reward is worth it. It's an unbelievable opportunity, the kind most people can only dream of, to live forever, to see everything the world is going to become."

"To become a monster?" the man asked quietly.

"Hey!" snapped Ty. "My aunt's a vampire."

"Yeah, cut it out, you bigot," called a woman from another table, looking up from her laptop.

"How old are you?" asked the mother with the baby in her stroller. She stared at Cathy, then at her baby, and back again.

Before too long the entire coffee shop was giving us their nickel's worth of advice.

Anna, who hated scenes even more than Cathy did, started packing up. She nodded at me and Ty to do likewise and then grabbed Cathy, who was crying again, and hauled her out of there.

"We'll walk you home," Anna said as she steered Cathy past various people who wanted to touch her for luck or warn her that her very soul was in peril.

Outside Ty rubbed his shoulder again, looking at me pointedly. I was shaking, I was so angry and upset. How could she even be contemplating turning into a vampire? Let alone already have said yes.

"Thank you, Ty," Cathy said, as her tears continued to flow. "It means a lot to have your support."

"No problem," Ty said.

I was about to point out that it was, in fact, a huge problem, when Anna grabbed my hand and squeezed warningly.

"None of us wants to say anything we'll regret." Anna glanced back at the coffee shop, where dozens of people were staring out the windows at us. "Let's keep walking."

We headed north in the general direction of home. I couldn't help thinking of how close to the Shade we were. Cathy was probably thinking about that too.

"Cathy," Anna said. "All three of us love you and care about you. Do you think you could at least listen to our calm and rational comments about this?"

"Mel's not being calm or rational."

Anna squeezed my hand even harder. I remained silent even though I was on the verge of an explosion. "She will be. You get that she cares and worries about you?"

Cathy nodded.

"We want you to consider this decision. It seems like you're rushing things."

"I agree," Ty said. "I do think it's romantic. Honestly, Cathy," he added when she shot him an *Et tu, Brute?* look. "I think you two are great together. But it's a big deal."

"Very big," Anna said. "And it seems like you haven't considered how huge a decision this. It's not like picking which college to go to. It's not even like deciding to get married or having a baby. This is the biggest decision you'll ever make. And the most dangerous."

"I love him."

Anna's voice remained level. I didn't know how she was doing it. "We know you do. Can you tell us what you discussed once you said yes? Did Francis make it clear that he would turn you legally? That you'd apply for a license?"

"Of course! I already said we're doing it legally. Francis is even willing to wait until I turn eighteen."

"Big of him," I muttered, so low none of them heard.

Or at least, they all pretended not to hear. Anna continued with her quiet, reasonable line of questioning as I stood there watching them all and wanting to punch something.

"You discussed licenses?"

"Yes. I said I'd ask Mom for permission to change before my eighteenth birthday. Francis might be happy to wait, but I've decided. I'm going to have a new life. I don't want to waste any more time on the one I'm leaving. I want to go ahead as soon as we get a license."

Cathy's voice was very earnest. As if I believed for a second that any of this was her idea.

"Your mom will never agree."

Anna gave me a quelling glance. "You do know they give out very few licenses," she said. "And that applying when you're underage, even with parental permission, is not going to help your chances."

"Francis told me. But if Mom says no, or if the council

149•••

turns us down, I can always try again after I'm eighteen. I think it's worth trying now. It can take a long time to get approval. I'd like to be the same age as he is, and once they see our application and how much in love we are—"

Anna nodded thoughtfully, as if Cathy was doing well in a debate. I couldn't believe how cool she was being—she who'd been terrorized by a vampire, she who'd told me our whole city was a mistake. It was like she'd already given up on Cathy.

"Did you talk about the possibility of the process not working?"

Cathy nodded. "Francis says that the percentage of unsuccessful transformations is very low when it's legal and properly supervised. He says the majority of deaths and zombies happen when it's unauthorized and the vampire in question doesn't know what they're doing."

If Anna hadn't been clamping down on my hand, I would have expressed myself on the subject of what total crap that was. Sometimes it didn't work. Everybody knew that.

"I have a friend I want you to meet, Cathy. A friend of my"—Anna hesitated—"of my dad's, who knows a lot more about this than any of us. She's seen lots of trans-formations. She works in zombie control. Would you talk to her?"

Cathy nodded. "Francis said I should make myself prepared. It's a condition of getting a license."

"I have to go," I said. It was that or start screaming

and punching Ty again. I couldn't stand hearing Cathy say the words *Francis says* one more time. Because what Francis had said was "End your life."

That's what she was listening to.

CHAPTER NINETEEN

My Enemy's Enemy Is My Date

I didn't sleep that night. I couldn't sleep. I couldn't eat dinner. I couldn't talk to anyone, not Mom or Dad or even Kristin, because what if I tried and they talked like Ty had, or like that vamposeur at Kafeen Krank? What if they said it was an honor, a privilege, and a blessing for Cathy to get all her blood sucked out and to never laugh again?

She'd never laugh again if she became a vampire. And she'd never laugh, or smile, or speak if the transition didn't work.

If she died.

I didn't know why Ty and Cathy weren't thinking of that. I couldn't think about anything else.

I had to fix this. I had to change her mind, but I was so far from understanding what she wanted that I had no idea how to build an argument. It was as if she were saying: "Apples are blue!"

No, they're not. Sky is blue. Apples are red. (Or green, but *not* blue!)

Instead she was saying: "Risking my life to become a vampire is a cool idea!"

No, it's not, and what kind of person would agree with you that it was?

Apparently, Ty did. And lots of random people in coffee shops.

Cathy's mom would never, ever give her permission. No parent could do such a thing, could sign off on something that might kill her kid. Cathy would be eighteen in eight months. I had eight months to change her mind.

It didn't seem like a lot of time.

Failing wasn't an option. I had to convince Cathy not to throw her life away. I had to find some way. And I had to find some allies.

✦

The next day at school there was that feeling you get after a fight: a sort of tentative hush in the air in the aftermath of a lot of noise, like the world feels after a thunderstorm.

Ty and Anna both said an awkward "hey" out of the corners of their mouths when they saw me. I looked at the floor and muttered "hey" back.

When Cathy approached me, her shoes squeaking on the green linoleum, I couldn't even manage a "hey." I was just glad to see that she wasn't accompanied by Francis. I wasn't ready to look at the guy who wanted to murder my best friend.

"Hi," Cathy said, in a low voice.

"Hmm," I said, and the bell rang.

I escaped to class without another word. I'm not proud.

Of course I was merely putting off the inevitable, which on this occasion was lunch and the lunchroom and Cathy sidling over to me.

"Could we try that one again?" she asked. "Hi. And I'm sorry."

Sorry she'd made such an insane decision, and ready to take it back? Sorry that Francis had drugged her food last night and persuaded her to agree to the craziness? Sorry I'd had to see her like that, and could I repeat all of last night's crazy talk, because she remembered nothing?

"Sorry?" I repeated.

"It's not exactly a secret you're not Francis's biggest fan," Cathy said. "I know how you feel about vampires, too. And how Anna feels."

"That's not fair. I—"

Cathy plunged ahead before I could finish. "I can't believe I told you like that. I should have known you'd be shocked. I was just so happy, and I guess it rendered me entirely incapable of thought."

"When will you be capable of thought again?" I asked.

Cathy chose to ignore this perfectly reasonable question. "I know this is an important decision, and I know it came as a shock to you. I know you're scared for me. I know this seems sudden. I never dreamed this would happen to me, but as soon as Francis said it . . . it was a revelation. I want it more than anything. You're my best friend in the entire world, so I want you to understand."

I clenched my fists instead of grabbing Cathy and shaking her the way I wanted to.

"You're my best friend too," I said. "That's why I can't let you commit suicide."

"That's not what becoming a vampire is!" Cathy said. "Look, Mel. Can you admit that you might be a tiny bit biased against vampires? Don't you feel that you might have judged them a little quickly? What if I asked you to learn more about them?"

"We could read a book about them together if you wanted," I said, with visions of highlighting all the bits that said POTENTIALLY FATAL.

Cathy smiled. "You know how I love books. But I was thinking about a more hands-on experience."

"You want me to put my hands on Francis?" I made a face. "Isn't that kind of a best friend no-no, Cath?"

"No, not Francis," Cathy said patiently. "I was thinking we could go on a double date."

This was such a new side of Cathy. A side full of total craziness.

"Errr," I said. "I don't want to go on a date with a vampire!"

It's not about being prejudiced. Loads of girls won't

date a guy shorter than they are. Or won't date a guy with red hair.

I won't date a guy with no pulse.

Anyway, guys who don't laugh at my jokes are out. So guys who *can't* laugh at my jokes might as well be in outer space.

"You don't have to," said Cathy. "Not a vampire." She hesitated. "I thought you and Francis's ward seemed to get on rather well."

"Francis's what now? You mean Kit?" I almost yelped.

Cathy didn't even know Kit's real name or how he'd gotten it. She didn't know that if things went the way she wanted them to, people would leave unwanted babies on her doorstep so she could *eat* them.

"You laughed at each other's jokes," Cathy said delicately.

"He was funny," I admitted grudgingly. "He was just . . ."

"Weird," I almost said, which Kit definitely was. He was part of the strange world of the Shade. The world that Cathy wanted in on. He was someone I didn't understand and I wasn't sure I wanted to.

He had been funny, though, and there were a few things we agreed on.

He'd said something about not wanting to *encourage this madness* to Camille.

He'd made fun of Francis's stupid ballad. He'd mentioned Cathy's age.

He'd made it pretty clear that he wouldn't want the immortal love tale of Francis and Cathy going on in his house.

I needed an ally.

"Hot," I said. "He was hot! Definitely not weird."

"Oh," said Cathy, looking startled but pleased.

"And," I continued—it was evil, but I could not resist—"I was thinking of going to the beach this Saturday, anyway. It's been so warm and it won't be for much longer."

"Oh," said Cathy.

She looked a lot less pleased.

CHAPTER TWENTY

Double Date of the Damned

The weather report had said it was going to be sunny, and for once the meteorologists had not lied. It was bright and the air was crisp: a nice day to be at the beach.

White Sands was by far the more popular beach, and this was the perfect time of year to visit: fall, when it was not so crowded. But for some reason Kit had insisted on Honeycomb Beach.

That was not helping my mood. Anna's parents had met on Honeycomb Beach, and so she'd always wanted to go here before this summer: I think she was hoping to meet a guy.

The beach didn't just suck because of Anna. It wasn't as pretty as White Sands, and the currents weren't as good for swimming, though at this time of year it wasn't a lot of fun going in the water.

There was one old man bravely swimming. He looked like an asphyxiating prune in a Speedo. The few people on the beach weren't looking at him. I doubted if they would look at him if he drowned.

Everyone on the beach was looking at us.

Cathy had brought a picnic blanket and a bottle of lemonade she'd made herself. Francis had brought his suit. He sat stiffly on the picnic blanket, the sun shining brightly on his helmet.

You might think I'd suggested the idea of a beach date with a vampire in the spirit of terrible, unholy mockery.

But no: That was just a bonus.

I wanted Cathy to see what she would be missing out on: a day in the sun, blue ocean, and silver sand. I wasn't letting the fact that it was fall get in the way. I may have also been hoping that a date with a sulky undead astronaut outside during the day would take some of the shine off her romance. But Cathy's attention was fixed with dreamy happiness on Francis's helmet, so I had obviously—once again—underestimated the strength of her delusions.

Speaking of romance, of course, there was my own date.

Kit wasn't really my date. I didn't want to date him, and I highly doubted he wanted to date me. I knew why he was here. His mom wanted him to spend time with humans. Possibly because she thought bringing up Kit was like bringing up a baby lion or something: Eventually, it had to be reintroduced to the wild and its own kind. You couldn't keep it forever. You didn't want to.

They'd called him Kitten. They didn't think of him as a person.

But Cathy had called it a date, which was making me feel a little awkward. I found myself glancing at him.

"Uncle Francis," Kit said over Francis's muffled protest. He leaned forward and rapped on the side of Francis's helmet. "Uncle Francis."

"What, Christopher?" Francis demanded, his helmet swinging away from his contemplation of Cathy.

"Knock knock."

Francis turned back to Cathy. Kit grinned. He was able to look pleased with himself without also looking smug. It was kind of adorable. I'd steal a look and catch the grin or the cheekbones or the brown burst of curls.

Okay, so I hadn't been lying to Cathy. He was hot.

This mainly annoyed me. I was on a mission to save my best friend; I had no time for some weird guy to be hot.

My thoughts came to a sudden halt when a volleyball hit me in the back of the head.

I twisted on the picnic blanket, grabbed the ball, and stood up, coming face-to-face with the guy who had presumably thrown it. He saw my look and edged back toward the volleyball net. It was possible he could intuit from my eyes that I was not in the best of moods.

And I was armed.

"Heh, heh," he said, putting his arms up defensively. "Do you wanna play?"

I threw the ball at him pretty hard; he caught it more with his stomach than with his hands, and made a sort of grunting sound.

I had to do something that would help me work off this prickly, furious feeling. I had no chance of convincing Cathy of anything unless I could be calm, and calmly refrain from doing things like punching her boyfriend in the helmet. Also I needed a chance to discuss this whole situation with Kit.

"Yeah, I wanna play," I said, glancing over my shoulder at Kit. "Coming?"

Kit blinked, then grinned again. "Sure."

"How about you, Francis?" I inquired, so Cathy could see I was including him.

Kit was getting up as I spoke, and our eyes met in a moment of perfect accord, sharing a mutual shining vision of Francis getting a volleyball to the helmet.

"I thank you, no," Francis responded. "But Catherine, if you would like to play, please do. I would not want to mar your enjoyment of the day for an instant."

"I'm very well content where I am," Cathy said shyly.

Francis took her hand in his clumsy glove and lifted it to within an inch of the dark visor of his helmet. Kit, with his back to them, did a short silent impression of someone getting sick. It was my turn to grin.

CHAPTER TWENTY-ONE

Volleyball and Sex

I was sort of riled up, and anyone in the fencing club will tell you I'm pretty competitive at the best of times. The sun was beating down on my head and my bare arms, I was kicking up clouds of sand every time I spiked the ball, and we were killing the team on the other side of the net.

I'd only had to yell, "Get back, I'll hit everything that comes close to the net!" once at Kit, which was pretty awesome. A lot of guys pull the "I've got that, little lady" routine. Though I'd taught Ty better, after a game of mixed doubles and a racket to the head.

I jumped up to slam the ball into the sand on the other side of the net. The guy who'd initially thrown the ball at me didn't even try to lob it back. He just gave a sort of damp squeak of sadness and defeat.

I stood, hands on hips, and laughed. "You guys want a break?"

"Oh, yes, please yes," yelled a girl in a green bikini, and they began to trail toward their collection of folding chairs.

Covered in sweat and sand and feeling pretty great, I turned to Kit and grinned. "You're good at taking orders."

"You're not bad at giving them," said Kit easily, and gave me an extremely sandy high five. He grinned again, looking at his hand. "My first high five. I'm savoring the moment. Also my first volleyball game."

"Beach volleyball."

"I stand corrected. First beach volleyball game. A day of excellent firsts."

I couldn't help smiling back at him. Then I looked across the stretch of sand and saw Cathy's blue picnic blanket, deserted, anchored only by a lemonade bottle. The edges of the blanket were flipping back and forth in the breeze, in a tiny distress call.

"Where are they?" I demanded.

My eyes tracked along the curve of the bay, back to the cliffs. None of the people walking by the sea were an astronaut vampire and his lady fair.

I headed for the cliff.

We followed the rough rock wall, the cliff walls curved by the wind into almost the same shape as the bay. I stumbled over loose rocks in the shadow of the cliffs and for a moment thought the opening of the cave was another shadow. Only it wasn't: the darkness had a blue tinge that suggested coolness and depth rather than the flat black of a shadow. I walked forward into the mouth of the cave and saw them.

Francis had taken his helmet off, his fair hair glowing in the dim light. His head was bent to Cathy's. They were a tableau in the shadows, storybook lovers with their mouths about to meet.

Obviously, I'd wildly underestimated the romantic potential of this date.

I turned and stamped away across rocks and sand back to the sunlight.

Kit followed me. I sent him a furious look over my shoulder. He was part of it, part of the world that wanted to swallow Cathy. I kicked my way down to the waves and stood there looking out to sea, not caring if the ice-cold water turned my feet blue. Kit stayed near, a mere step behind.

"Enjoying yourself?" I snapped, and then regretted it. This wasn't Kit's fault.

"Yeah," Kit said eventually. "It's cool to see Honeycomb Beach. My mom talked about it."

The bay's name did not match its history. Centuries ago it was the center of smuggling in this part of Maine. Boats used to come in from all over the country, and the rest of the world, full of slaves for vampires to feed on. Even when slavery was legal it was never legal, to sell to vampires. And yet it happened; hence the smuggling.

Hard to know who was worse—the vampires or the humans who sold to them.

I stared at Kit. I hadn't thought Camille was that old.

He raised his eyebrows. "When the English soldiers landed here during the War of Independence, and the people of the city, humans and vampires, were waiting for them? My mom was there."

Did he hear himself? His mom was biting soldiers during the Revolutionary War. I wondered if Camille had eaten slaves too. Did she think of that time as the good old days? When vampires were a huge part of keeping the slave trade alive? Yet now she was a vampire cop arresting vampires who so much as nibbled on humans who weren't donors. Times change, huh?

I wondered how many vampires wished they didn't.

"It's great to finally see it," Kit said.

"It's only a few miles from the city," I said. "You could have come anytime."

"Yeah," said Kit. "But a day at the beach with my shade would be the least fun outing ever." He looked around, and I saw with his eyes for a second, and then just saw his eyes, the color somewhere between sky and sea, taking it all in. "It's nice," Kit told me. He sounded slightly wistful.

The knot of anger eased in my chest a little. "It's okay."

"Spoiled is what you are," Kit teased, and poked me in the ribs with sandy fingers. "Minty always said lavishing buckets of sunshine on children makes them uncontrollable."

"Raised a lot of children, has she?"

Kit laughed. "No, just me, and not really. She says pretty much everything makes me uncontrollable."

"Great choice of words. *Uncontrollable*? She sounds lovely."

Kit poked me again. "She's not exactly my favorite. But no shade is perfect."

"Is that one of your mom's sayings?"

He went to poke me again and I grabbed his hand. Fearing some sort of poking retaliation, he grabbed my other hand. And then we were standing there, the surf almost reaching our feet, with our hands linked.

"So, thanks for inviting me," said Kit. I could feel his pulse racing, and I realized he might not know this wasn't actually a date after all.

Perhaps this was not a good time to tell him that I hadn't invited him.

Instead, I drew one hand free of his grasp, stood on my tiptoes, and pulled his head toward mine. The sun beat warm on my hair, and his mouth was warm against mine. All the energy from the game, all my misery and confusion over Cathy, poured out into the kiss and changed to something new and fierce.

Kit's lips pressed against mine as the kiss turned more certain, and my sandy palm reached for the back of his neck. His hand went to the small of my back and I stepped in, my body curving along the lines of his, our mouths locked, standing together hot and close and human.

Kit pulled back and murmured, "I don't want to have sex, okay?"

"What?"

"I know how humans are always up for it," Kit said. "Which is totally fine! I'm not judging. It's just, you know, I'm not ready and my mom would have a fit and—"

I shoved him so hard he stumbled into the surf.

I will now use a seaside metaphor. It was the emotional equivalent of being stung in the pride by a jellyfish.

"You know how humans are always up for it?" I repeated, my voice rising. (It was a bit like a seagull's cry, if we want to continue with the seaside theme.)

Kit rubbed the back of his neck and looked at me warily. "Well," he began. "There are these guys and girls who hang around the Shade and—"

"They are groupies, Kit!" I snarled. "They are vampire groupies. They are there because they want to have sex with vampires! They are not how all humans behave."

"Oh," Kit said. "Oh, right."

He was beginning to go a bit red.

"Here is a lesson about how humans behave," I said. "When a guy assumes a girl wants to have sex with him on the second occasion they meet, we humans generally regard him as an enormous jerk! In fact, that goes for any guy assuming a girl wants to have sex with him anytime before she says, 'Yes, sex sounds terrific!'"

My fists were clenched again. My mood was not improved by the realization that I'd just yelled "Sex sounds terrific" at a guy loud enough for everyone within shouting range to hear.

"Okay," Kit said, sounding very serious. Which I already knew was rare for him. "Wow, I'm really sorry. I didn't know. I didn't mean to offend you or insult you or anything. I'm sorry."

It served me right, didn't it, going on some kind of weird fake-maybe-real date with a guy who didn't even know how to be human and then stupidly kissing him.

Vampires were ruining my life!

"It was my first kiss with a human. Told you this was a day of firsts."

I did not want to know about those other kisses. He meant vampires, didn't he? I suppressed a shudder. How could he live the way he lived? How was Cathy going to live like that?

Which reminded me that I needed an ally.

"Okay," I said, mimicking the way Kit had said it. A brief grin flashed across Kit's face, not quite comfortable enough to stay. "You have, however, ruined the moment." I paused. "Speaking of the moment—what do you think of this new Cathy-and-Francis development?"

"Those two crazy kids," said Kit, still looking a little wary. "It does seem like they should wait to celebrate a month's anniversary at the very least before thinking about eternal life together. I've made this point, but Francis told me I was to go to my room for having no poetry in my soul. Camille told me to ignore him, which I did."

"See," I said, vindicated. I'd been right: He was on my side. "It's weird for him to be dating Cathy. They can't make it permanent."

We both stepped farther up the beach as the tide moved in. "It seems like a bad idea to me, too," Kit said. "But it's not really our business."

"It's my business if Cathy's making a decision that will make her unhappy forever. Or kill her!"

"It's not like Francis is going to chain her down," he said. "He's a good person, and he really cares about her. If the relationship doesn't work out, they can always break up."

"She can't break up from being a vampire," I snapped. "And she'll never be happy being one of those things!"

Kit went very still.

"Those things?" he repeated.

"No," I said, scrambling. "Look, I'm sure Camille— uh, your mom—is really nice, but—"

"Yes, my mom," said Kit. "She is my mom, and you can stop saying it as if you're putting quotation marks around it."

"I wasn't!" I protested.

"Yes, you were," said Kit. "Let me tell you something about *those things*. Humans left me on a doorstep. Vampires took me in. If there's a choice to be made, I'd go with the vampires every time."

"That would be a pretty dumb decision, as you don't know anything about humans!" I yelled.

"What more do I need to know?" Kit yelled back. "It doesn't matter. I'll know all I need to know in a couple of months, when I can forget all about humans and turn into one of *those things*!"

It was my turn to go still. I felt cold—as if the shadow of the cliffs had fallen on me, or a different shadow.

"What did you say?" I whispered.

"I'm going to become a vampire as soon as I turn eighteen," Kit said, very coolly. "Of course."

CHAPTER TWENTY-TWO

Fun with Zombies

The waiting room was pretty much like every waiting room in the history of the world. Really, it could have been a dentist's, or a doctor's, or even a beauty salon. Magazines everywhere. Posters on the walls. Even a penned-off area for small kids to play in.

The only tip that this was not your regular waiting room was that the posters were all about zombies and vampires and the dangers of transitioning. Oh, and the doors leading in and out were made of lead and had more locks and security than Fort Knox.

I smiled awkwardly at the receptionists yet again. Though were they still just receptionists when they were armed and trained in zombie neutralizing?

Other than the receptionists/zombie neutralizers, I was alone. That made the waiting even worse. I couldn't help thinking about what would happen if one of the zombies got loose and attacked Cathy. Supposedly that was impossible. This was a secure facility, blah blah blah.

But it was a facility with *zombies* in it, and my best friend was currently being shown those zombies as part of her preparation for deciding whether to become a vampire or not. Along with Kit of the Unfortunate Kissing Incident, who I hadn't talked to since. Neither Francis nor Camille was with them. Something about bias and undue influence.

Kit had not smiled when he'd seen me this morning (the first time since the Unfortunate Kissing Incident). All I got was a brief stiff nod, which could mean "Oh, that girl who kissed me who I presumed was going to demand sex, how incredibly awkward this is" or "Oh, that girl who hates all vampires, including my mom, how incredibly awful she is."

Not that it bothered me, not really. I was much more concerned about Cathy, who—though she wasn't admitting it—was very nervous about the whole morning. She'd never seen a zombie before. Neither had I. Or even Kit. Or anyone we knew, except for the vampires.

When a transition goes wrong and a zombie is created instead of a vampire, the Zombie Disposal Unit (ZDU) is called in immediately and all traces of the zombie are erased. They have to be. The minds of zombies might be gone and they may be slow moving, but they're highly contagious. If you get bitten, you have about a day to have the affected area cut out or off, or else you turn into one. Nasty stuff. These days, even the smallest cities have their own ZDUs. There hasn't been a serious outbreak in decades.

But still. Zombies.

Somewhere on the other side of those incredibly secure-looking lead doors, Cathy was within spitting distance of a zombie. Maybe more than one. I knew they kept several in some institutes, and replaced them when they fell to pieces.

I went to a protest once with my mom, for people advocating the erasure of all zombies. The other side says people need to see zombies to be fully prepared for all the potential consequences of transition.

Personally I think that the other side will reconsider their position if there's ever another zombie outbreak. But it'll be a little too late, won't it?

I went over to the water cooler and poured myself a cup.

"How long does it usually take?" I asked one of the ZDU receptionists/elite zombie disposers.

He looked up from his work and gave me a small smile. "Depends. Sometimes they're out within a few minutes." He screwed up his face. "They tend to not look so good. You know what I mean? If you're hoping your friends will change their minds, you're in luck. Of those who do this tour, more than half change their mind."

"Really?"

He nodded. "It's not pretty back there. For most people the risks don't seem real. They think to themselves, A ten-percent risk of zombification doesn't seem so bad. Forgetting that the chance is as good that they won't even be a zombie—they'll go straight to the being-dead part. Seeing an actual zombie and how we deal with zombies? That makes the two chances out of ten failure rate absolutely real to them."

I shivered. "No need to convince me. I'm totally Team Human."

He laughed, then said, "Uh-oh," before coming to my side of the counter with a bucket in his hand.

The door that Cathy had disappeared through banged open. My heart did a metaphorical high jump into my throat.

Kit took a few unsteady steps forward with the woman beside him lending a hand. "If you need a bucket," she began.

Kit bent over. The receptionist got the bucket to him just in time.

CHAPTER TWENTY-THREE

Of Vomit and Kisses

"I'm glad that Mom wasn't here," Kit said. "Human illness kind of grosses her out."

We were in the recovery room, which looked remarkably like a hospital ward, complete with curtains surrounding each of the six beds. Only one of the beds was currently occupied. Kit lay with an ice pack on his head. The doctor had checked him over, given him a clean bill of health, and decreed that he hydrate and rest for a minimum of half an hour before leaving. I sat beside him and tried to be supportive.

I was practicing for when Cathy re-emerged.

"Well, vomiting is not high on the list of activities I like to witness either. Or partake in. Vampires are not alone in their vomit distaste." I did not point out that my parents had never been grossed out by me when I was sick. Or if they had been, they hadn't told me about it.

"Right," Kit said, looking dismayed. "I hadn't thought of that."

"No problem," I said, patting him below the knee. He shot me a strange look. "Um, no," I told him. "My touching your knee does not mean I want to have sex with you."

Kit blushed. "I didn't—"

"You know, when you're a vampire, you won't be able to blush anymore."

He went even redder. "I may not miss blushing. Sorry again."

"It's fine," I lied. I hadn't told Cathy what had happened between me and Kit. Accused of nymphomania by a weirdo raised by vampires? I wasn't going to tell anyone *ever*. "I'm teasing you, Kit, which is probably not that nice of me, given that you just vomited your guts up multiple times after seeing a zombie."

Kit grimaced. "Many zombies."

"Many?"

"Okay, three. But one was more than enough. Way more than enough."

"I'm sorry. It sounds awful." Though this was the most he'd said about it. I was dying to ask for more details. What did they look like? Up close, I meant. Was it true they could remember what it was like to be human, at least for a little while? Did they talk? Or just groan? Did they smell as bad as everyone said?

"I can't imagine turning into something like that," Kit said, reaching for his glass of water. "It's too . . ." He shuddered. "And there's two chances in ten."

"Actually," I said, repeating the receptionist's words, "I think it's one chance in ten of becoming a zombie. The two chances in ten are of winding up dead, either by just dying instantly or by becoming a zombie. 'Cause, you know, zombification leads to immediate eradication."

"Right. Well, that's *much* better," Kit said. He took a sip of water and sat up a bit more. He glanced at me and his mouth twitched. He seemed to be attempting a grin, even though he still looked shaken and pale.

He was always smiling and trying to get everyone else to smile. I guess you learn to be persistent about that around vampires, or you give up. Clearly Kit wasn't the giving-up type.

"Why do you want to be a vampire?" I asked suddenly. "I mean, you said yourself you don't even know what it's like to be a human."

"I didn't say that. I said I didn't know much about humans. Why do you think vampires are things and not people?"

I bristled and then bit my lip. He looked kind of pitiful lying there, which wasn't surprising considering he'd vomited four times in quick succession.

"I shouldn't have said that," I admitted.

"But you did mean it. Why?" Kit asked. "No vampire's ever hurt you."

I felt my lip curl. "Well, I'm not sure about that. Vampires have hurt friends of mine," I said, and hurried on because Anna's situation was none of his business. "Francis is trying to take away my best friend. Plus the way he talks harms me. And his poetry!"

Kit laughed. I smiled seeing him laugh.

"You haven't even heard any of his poetry!"

I punched his shoulder. "That doesn't mean I want sex either. By the way."

"Oh, hush," Kit said. "Answer the question. Vampires. Why are you against them?"

"Kit, I'm honestly not. I mean, I do think the vampire groupies are ridiculous."

Kit looked away and coughed.

"But it's just that the vampires are over there." I pointed in the direction I figured the Shade was. "We humans are in the rest of town. And that's the way I prefer it. Francis is the first vampire I ever really talked to. They're easier to deal with as an abstract concept, but I guess even the idea of them grosses me out. Alive, but not really. Dead, but not really. And they're like leeches or mosquitoes or those bats: They drink our blood. It's hard not to have a reaction to that, you know?"

Kit frowned. "Obviously I'm no expert—you're the only human I've ever had a real conversation with. I mean, beyond, 'I'll have the thin crust with extra pepperoni.' Or, 'Stop bothering my mom—she doesn't want to make you her sex slave.' But vampires are as varied as humans.

They're people. Some are mean and selfish—Minty, for example. Some are caring and responsible—my mom. Some are annoying but mean well—Francis. They're all sorts. Some are good, some aren't. Some really would eat you if they could. Some want to study you. Some don't care about you at all. You can't tell me there aren't humans like that."

"That want to eat me?"

"The Donner party?" Kit pointed out. "Jeffrey Dahmer?"

"Okay, but humans eating humans happens in extreme circumstances involving a very few individuals, unlike with vampires, where it happens on days ending in *y*!"

Kit stopped looking smug about his brilliant historical point. "I'm only saying that they're people," he mumbled. "They're just different."

"They're very different," I told him. "It's hard not to be scared of that. It's harder to understand that my best friend wants to be one of them."

"Well," Kit said, "maybe the zombies will make her a bit less keen?"

"I don't know," I said. "Did they make you less keen?"

Kit looked away, lashes lowered, at the suddenly fascinating hospital curtains. "It's different for me," he said. "They're my shade. They've always expected that I'd become one of them. I don't know how to be anything else—I don't want to be anything else," he added defiantly.

"Okay," I said.

"Okay," said Kit, his hackles going down. "I can see how you might want something different for your friend," he admitted, almost reluctantly. "She's got a lot of options. It's a big decision to make. Also, and I say this with, like, affection and everything, but risking being a zombie for Francis's sweet sweet love does seem a bit crazy."

"A bit?" I said. "You think?"

I grinned, and, still pale and a little shell-shocked, Kit grinned back. Just like that, I had an ally.

"Do you think you could talk to her? Tell her what you told me?" I asked.

If someone besides me said it to her, maybe it would sink in.

"Sure." Kit smiled at me. Not a pay-attention-to-my-wit smile. This smile was slow and warm, and made me want to kiss him again. Not that I would. I coughed and changed the subject. "How was Cathy doing back there with the zombies?"

"Not getting sick," Kit said, his smile turning wry. "Which makes her tougher than me, at least."

"Oh," I said.

"Don't worry. I'll talk to her. She's not going to transition without hearing all the pros and cons."

I sighed and bowed my head. "She's so in love."

"Mel," Kit said suddenly. "I know this might not be the perfect moment to mention this, since you just saw me get sick four times and all, but I liked that kiss."

My head jerked up so fast, I almost bit my tongue. (It occurred to me that biting your tongue was probably very painful for vampires. Another thing to point out to Cathy.)

Kit was blushing again. "When you and I kissed the other day at the beach, I mean."

"I know which kiss."

"Right, of course. I'm trying to say it was nice and, um, I don't think I told you that. I wanted you to know that I liked it. It was warm. And, um, oh, Cathy!" He turned. "How are you doing, Cathy?"

I turned too. Cathy was possibly a bit paler than usual. The overly bright lighting made it hard to tell. She did not look anything close to as shaken as Kit had.

"Are you okay, Kit?" she asked.

"I'm fine. I'll be up and ready to go in a few seconds. The doctor said quite a few people respond to the smell like that."

"It was bad," Cathy agreed sympathetically. "Nobody could blame you for losing it. That was quite possibly the worst thing I've ever smelled."

"Or looked at."

"Oh, yes." Cathy shook her head. "The poor things are all old and withered. They can barely move. It seems cruel to keep them alive just to look at."

That was so Cathy. Not overcome with horror, not swearing she would never risk becoming such a thing.

No, she'd decided that she felt bad for the zombies.

"The pamphlets say that zombies don't feel anything—that part of their cortex is the first thing destroyed by zombification," I pointed out to her.

There had been a lot of pamphlets in the waiting room.

"But their eyes, Mel, their eyes! They were so full of pain." Cathy shuddered, more upset by the horror she could imagine than the horror she had seen. "Francis has promised me that if that happens, he will end my suffering himself."

My hands clenched. Kit caught my eye, his own eyes steady. "No second thoughts, then?" he asked, very lightly. Much more lightly than I would've been able to.

"Of course not," Cathy said, sounding surprised. "It was terrible, of course, but we haven't learned anything we didn't know already."

So the zombies' eyes were full of suffering? There was a lot of suffering going around.

CHAPTER TWENTY-FOUR

Clues over Cantonese

"**I** can't believe you didn't even get to see the zombies," my little brother, Lancelot, said scornfully at dinner that night. "That's such crap."

"Lance," Mom said, her voice stern.

We were all sitting down to a proper Cantonese meal. My dad's only third-generation American, and occasionally he has fits of guilt about us kids being raised not knowing about our heritage. My mom's family has been here since the Gold Rush and she's a lot more easygoing, but if Dad wants to cook us a ton of Cantonese dishes, she's not going to turn that down.

Mom is always very keen on someone else doing the cooking.

Normally, I wouldn't turn it down either. But today my gai lan—Chinese broccoli, so much better than normal broccoli—in oyster sauce didn't look as good as usual. I might've read too many zombie pamphlets.

Or it might have been the memory of Cathy's face, distressed but still totally determined to do something that would destroy her.

Or maybe Kit's face, pale and sick, talking like he had no other choice.

"I can't believe Cathy didn't take one stupid picture," Lance continued. "She's always said I was like her own little brother. What good is that, if it doesn't score me one lousy picture of a zombie with its eyeball on its cheek?"

"Lancelot!" Dad exclaimed. "We're trying to have a nice meal and celebrate our heritage. Celebrate it now, or celebrate it at Cantonese classes over the summer. It's your decision."

Lance planted his face in the honey-garlic spareribs.

"You'll be doing the dishes for that," put in Mom, looking pleased. Any excuse to not do them herself.

"But, seriously, how was the whole business down at the ZDU?" Mom asked, deploying her chopsticks to steal a massive wedge of the flowering chives stir-fry. "I hear it's pretty rough on the younger ones who go down for the first time."

"Yeah. A boy I know got sick," I said without thinking. "But Cathy was fine."

Mom clicked her tongue against her teeth. "I don't know what Valerie is thinking."

I raised an eyebrow. My mom and Cathy's mom

weren't exactly friends: They're not each other's kind of people.

My parents used to have dinner with Anna's, though.

"Valerie was down by the courts investigating the laws related to vampire transitioning," Mom said. "She told me Cathy had asked her to sign the permission forms for transition. The idea is crazy. Cathy's got her whole life ahead of her. There's no need to let her rush into a decision. I don't think anyone should be allowed to transition before eighteen. Except the underage terminal patients, of course."

"In some states, you can't transition until you're twenty-one," Dad said. "I think that's fair, myself. Why should you be able to drink blood before you can drink alcohol?"

"They'd never pass something like that in Maine," Mom said, rolling her eyes. "Not in the vampire state."

Mom and Dad swung into a debate about the laws controlling vampirism. I passed the time by grabbing a hank of Lance's hair and lifting him off the spareribs. He had honey-garlic sauce on his forehead.

"Sōng, the fact of the matter is that vampires signed the Declaration of Independence as well—"

"Megan, I'm not disputing that—though I also don't believe the rumor that Thomas Jefferson was a vampire—"

Lance leaned toward me, one elbow on the table, and whispered: "Want to play soccer later?"

"I have homework," I whispered back.

"Just for a little while," he said, giving me a sweet, winning smile. The effect was spoiled by the honey-garlic sauce. "Besides, you've already gotten perfect SATs. Any college you want to go to will take you. Why do your homework?"

"Almost perfect is not perfect. Plus there's the little matter of my GPA, Lottie. Like you'd ever skip your homework."

He rolled his eyes at me yearningly. "Soccer's good for your brain."

Because I am weak, I said, "Maybe," which any little brat of a brother knows how to parlay into a "yes."

The whole Cathy situation had obviously totally demoralized me.

"I still can't believe Valerie," Mom said, veering back to the original topic. "I know Cathy's very romantic but I still can't believe she's considering it! She knows what a vampire did to the Saunderses."

That was a cue if I ever heard one.

"Have you—talked much to Principal Saunders since Dr. Saunders, you know—" I said, laying down my chopsticks.

"Leila won't even return my calls," Mom said. "I wanted to tell her how sorry I was. I couldn't believe it of Chris Saunders. He was such a good doctor: Everyone said so, and you could tell, the way he talked about his patients. So much sympathy, but at the same time, the right distance. I would never in a million years have thought he'd do something like that."

I thought about Anna saying she didn't think her dad could fall in love with someone like that. I thought about Francis asking me not to tell Principal Saunders what he was doing at school.

"I'd have expected a vampire to attack him first," Dad said, nodding in perfect agreement with Mom for a change. "Not that Chris ever spilled anything he shouldn't have, but that secretary of his—Adam Wasserman—he used to tell stories that would scare you away from the Shade for life."

"Really?" I asked, and made an encouraging *hmmm* sound as Mom and Dad told a couple of stories about vampires who took breakups very badly—household pets were mentioned—and this one vampire who was sure she was Lord Byron, and not in a past life, either. "So the secretary still works at the Center for Extended Life Counseling, right?" I asked at last, as innocently as I could.

"That's right," Mom said. "Honey, do you remember the one about the vampire with the drinking problem? He'd hang around bars and pay people to get drunk and then let him feed off them. . . ."

When they had exhausted all the stories either of them could remember, Dad looked at me, frowning in that particular parental way, half worry and half love.

"This whole Cathy business got you down, my

melodious one?" he asked. "Don't worry about it. She's a smart girl. I'm sure she'll think better of it."

I looked at the table so he wouldn't see me planning.

"I'm sure she will."

I'd make sure she would.

◆

Later, after I'd played penalty shootout with Lance until it was dark out and he'd scored four goals on me—little weasel!—I left the scene of my horrible defeat and bounded up the steps to the porch swing.

"Oh, c'mon, Mel, just a bit longer."

"Don't push your luck, Lottie!" I yelled.

My T-shirt was stuck to me with sweat. I pulled the material free so I could feel the night air on my skin, plucked my phone out of my pocket with my other hand, and called Kit.

He'd agreed with me about Cathy. He was an ally in the enemy camp. So I'd asked him for his number. It had nothing to do with any kissing incidents or the liking of them. Well, almost nothing.

Kit answered on the third ring.

"Hi!" he said. "Hey! Don't go away, okay? I have to run outside with the phone because my shade have super hearing and they're all incredibly nosy."

There was a sound I couldn't quite hear on Kit's end of the line.

"Sorry," said Kit, already sounding out of breath as he ran. "Except for my Uncle Francis, who wishes to inform us both that he would never dream of displaying unseemly curiosity or eavesdrop on any conversation, personal or otherwise."

"Oh, Francis," I said, sighing dramatically. "What a man. If only Cathy hadn't got there first."

Kit yelped with laughter, and then there was a series of bumps and rustling noises.

"Hi, Kit?" I called out. "Kit?"

"Sorry about that!" said Kit. "Jumped over a fence, dropped the phone. Don't go away."

I smiled. "Okay."

Kit's breathing came faster, and it sounded like he'd dropped the phone again. Finally, he said: "That should be far enough."

"I imagine so," I said. "Since I imagine you're now on Mars. You need to get your breath back?"

"I'm good," Kit gasped. "You sound a bit short of breath too."

"Mmm," I said, and was tempted for an instant to tell him I'd been kissing some extremely handsome guy who hadn't been raised by vampires and thus hadn't presumed it was a prelude to monkey sex. "I was playing soccer with my baby brother."

"I'm not a baby!" screamed Lancelot, bouncing the soccer ball from his head to his foot and back again.

"Isn't it past your bedtime, Lottie?" I yelled back.

"Don't call me Lottie!"

"You have a brother?" Kit asked.

"Yes," I said, sitting the other way on the swing to get away from Lancelot's shrieks.

"And you play soccer together?" Kit asked, as if I'd mentioned deep-sea diving instead of soccer. "That sounds nice."

"Your family's not that into soccer?"

"Well, no," Kit said. "Not that we don't do activities together. Francis taught me how to waltz."

I burst out laughing. "I'm sorry—what?"

His voice warmed. I could imagine him being delighted he'd made someone laugh, even over the phone.

Maybe not just someone. Maybe delighted he'd made *me* laugh.

"Yes, well. At first he tried to instruct me and Mom together, but Mom said she'd never liked waltzing much herself, and Minty thought it was hilarious to go too fast deliberately so I felt sick, and in the end Francis said that we were all impossible and nobody was properly dedicated to the child's education or ever thought about how I would conduct myself in society and how it would reflect on them all. So Francis ended up waltzing with me himself."

"Are you a credit to Francis?" I asked, solemnly.

"Oh, I'm an excellent waltzer. Sadly, I don't actually know how to lead . . ."

I thought of several excellent jokes about Kit's first ball gown and also his dance card, but I pulled myself back. This was not flirting time, especially not flirting time with someone who was determined to become a vampire. This was for Anna and Cathy: This was saving-friends time.

"What are you doing tomorrow?"

"Uh," Kit said. "Nothing! Nothing, I am free. What do you—do you want to do something? With me?"

"I thought we could go down to the Center for Extended Life Counseling."

Maybe Dr. Saunders's secretary, Adam Wasserman, would have something to say that would cast light on what was going on with Principal Saunders. It was worth a shot.

And from what my parents had said, he'd have stories to tell about what went wrong with vampires even when the transition went right. I'd have Kit with me, someone Cathy couldn't possibly think was biased against vampires. Someone who could tell Cathy exactly what he'd heard, and be believed.

"Um, dunno," Kit mumbled.

"Kit—" I started, not actually above begging.

"Sorry, Mel!" Kit said quickly. "I wasn't talking to you. Yes, I'll go with you to—uh, that sounds like an extremely strange date."

"Well, it's not a date," I said. "I just thought—that you'd maybe find it interesting. Er. We could get coffee afterward."

It was only polite! I didn't want to seem like I was using him as nothing but an anti-vampirism mouthpiece.

"Great," said Kit.

"So who were you talking to?"

"Huh? Oh, Mrs. Appleby. You remember her?" Kit asked, and I did: the fourteen-year-old married vampire. "She, uh. She asked if I was talking to my sweetheart."

I had nothing to say to that. So I went with: "See you tomorrow, Kit, bye!" and hung up extremely fast.

These saving-your-friends missions were turning out to be very complicated.

CHAPTER TWENTY-FIVE

The Center for Extended Life Counseling

"Hi," I said. "I don't have an appointment. I mean obviously I don't, on account of I'm not a vampire." Beside me, Kit squirmed. "Not that there's anything wrong with that," I amended.

Adam Wasserman, former secretary of Dr. Saunders, had kind eyes and looked as if he enjoyed a bit of a laugh. Unfortunately, right now I suspected he was quietly laughing at me.

"Actually, the doctors here see many humans. Ones who are dating vampires, ones who are considering transitioning. Some who work with vampires and are struggling with it."

He nodded at the patients, and Kit and I turned slightly to look. Even though we'd arrived at the center not long after dusk, almost half were human.

"Right," I said.

Now that I came to think of it, Anna had mentioned that Dr. Saunders had human patients, too. It was just that the vampire stories were the dramatic ones, and I'd assumed that human patients were pretty rare. I supposed it shouldn't be a surprise that so many humans had vampire problems. Wasn't I dealing with them myself?

I decided the subtle approach was getting me nowhere, laid my hands flat on the desk, and leaned in.

"Look," I said quietly. "I'm friends with Anna Saunders, Dr. Saunders's daughter, and—"

"Excuse me," Adam said, answering the phone. "Center for Extended Life Counseling."

I drew back from my conspiratorial lean-in. "No, absolutely, that's fine, I don't mind waiting at all," I whispered to Kit.

He was eyeing the blank walls and the people sitting in rows.

"Is it just me," Kit whispered, "or does this place look a lot like the ZDU waiting room? More potted plants and a little bit ritzier, but there's magazines and posters and an area for small kids to play in. Why do all waiting rooms look basically the same?"

"I know," I said. "I thought the exact same thing when I was waiting for you and Cathy at the ZDU."

We shared a smile. Then I glanced away.

Adam finished his call and looked up. "You said

you're friends with Anna?"

I nodded.

It had been the right thing to say. Adam's already kind brown eyes basically turned into little melty chocolate pools of sympathy.

"That was so awful. How's she doing? She used to come in occasionally on Saturdays and have lunch with Dr. Saunders. Sweet girl."

"It's been hard," I said, feeling wretched about using Anna's pain as my ticket in with this guy. But she wanted to find out more about what was going on with her mother. She'd want me to. She'd thank me if she knew.

I was almost sure.

"I can imagine. No one here can believe what happened. Dr. Saunders was the last man in the world who would have run off with a patient."

Just when things were getting interesting, the phone rang again and another patient came in. A human one. He was as tall as Kit but much thinner, and around my parents' age. He ignored me and Kit and said loudly, "I have an appointment."

Adam signaled to the man that he was on the phone.

"My appointment is right now. It's very important," the man said even louder. Both Kit and I edged away. "I must see Dr. Yu RIGHT NOW!" he shouted.

Adam put down the phone. "Dr. Yu is with another patient right now," Adam said calmly. "I have let her know you are here."

"How?!" demanded the man. "You were on the phone!"

"See these buttons here?" Adam said. The man leaned forward. "When a new patient arrives, I press the button next to that doctor's name. See where it says 'Dr. Yu'? She knows you're here. Right now she is dealing with another patient. There was an emergency visit earlier, which means that she is running late. You will have to wait."

The man opened his mouth and then shut it and then did the same thing again. He looked like a fish. He went and sat next to an older woman, who gave him a look that would have been uncharitable to a cockroach. She was also human. Five humans were sitting on one side of the room and seven vampires on the other. The separation was as marked as that between boys and girls at freshman prom.

Adam turned his attention back to me. "Did you want to make an appointment to see a counselor?"

"No," I said. "Actually I wanted to talk to you. I thought you might know a bit more about what happened. With Dr. Saunders."

"I really don't—"

"Anna's so miserable," I said shamelessly. "I really want to help her."

The phone rang again.

"Well," Adam said, "we can't talk here. I've got a break in about ten minutes. I'll go down to the courtyard in front of the building. Why don't you join me?"

CHAPTER TWENTY-SIX

Hard Out There for a Vamp

The courtyard had dozens of trees in it, possibly in an attempt to make the center look like a friendly and welcoming place. Sadly, only two had any leaves left on them, and those leaves were shaking violently in the brisk wind. A few dead leaves lay on the top of our picnic table. The spell of lovely fall weather had obviously ended, though at least it wasn't raining. I was glad of my coat.

Kit shivered in his. "Tell you what," he said. "When I'm a vampire, I will not miss being cold."

I didn't answer. It would only lead to another fight as I listed all the wonderful things he would miss when he was a vampire. Such as those warm kisses he'd mentioned.

Kit leaned toward me. "I hope you don't think I'm

being overly curious, but I was wondering—why are we here?"

"Anna's worried about her mom."

"Right," Kit said slowly. "Who's Anna?"

Yes, I could see how the whole situation might be incomprehensible from Kit's point of view.

"My other best friend," I explained. "The one who's not in love with a vampire. Her father—"

"Ran away with a patient from the clinic. I got that."

"Her mom's been kind of out of it ever since. She's also the principal of our school, and she and Francis seem to be afraid of each other. Or something. It's weird."

I kept handing the boy who'd been raised by vampires more opportunities to think I was strange. I was pretty surprised when the smile spread across his face. Not the "Come on, smile too, you know you want to" smile, but the slow "Isn't that amazing" smile.

Actually, since he was looking at me, I guessed it was the "Aren't *you* amazing" smile.

It was a good smile.

It made me want to kiss him again.

"So you're investigating," Kit said with glee. "You're an amateur detective! I love it!"

I grinned and wished I'd detected the weather well enough to bring a hat and scarf. My ears were getting cold. "Something like that. I've kind of always been the person who solves problems. Believe it or not."

"Oh, I believe it," Kit said. "From what little I've seen

of you—you're very capable."

"Thank you."

Adam emerged from the center in a big coat and a wonderfully warm-looking woolen hat. He looked completely cozy, and yet so rumpled and nice, I didn't even want to steal his gloves.

Much.

"Hi there," he said, sitting down and pulling out his sandwich and taking a bite.

We returned his hi. "I'm Mel," I told him. "And this is Kit."

"I'm her trusty sidekick," Kit said, grinning.

"That must be fun," Adam observed. "I'm Adam. You have questions? Fire away. I'm afraid I can only take twenty minutes. We're short staffed right now. Usually there's two of us at the desk."

"Is it usual for the patients to be so shouty?" I asked.

Adam gave a rueful smile. "It's usual for all the patients to be agitated, human or vampire. But, hey, they pay me really well. I'm one of the few receptionists to last longer than a week."

"How long have you been there?" Kit asked.

"Ten years," Adam answered in a matter-of-fact way.

"Wow," I said, trying to imagine dealing with shouty people for ten years. Yet another job to cross off my list.

"I like it. The doctors are mostly great. Like I said, they pay me well to be their receptionist-slash-secretary-slash-troubleshooter. And the patients are fascinating.

I've started writing a novel, but I worry no one will believe it."

"Is the novel about human doctors running away with their sexy vampire patients?"

"Oh, no, everyone would believe that," Adam said, smiling again. His eyes crinkled up behind his glasses. "Though it's actually fairly rare. It's happened twice in my time here. Though, frankly, I still find it very hard to believe Dr. Saunders ran off with Rebecca Jones."

I hadn't heard her name before. She'd just been the man-stealing vampire, Anna's horror in the night. Now she had a name: She was a person.

They're people, Kit's voice said in my head, and I cast a guilty look over at him. He looked back at me wide-eyed, obviously expecting me to carry on with my fine detecting self.

"Was she very beautiful?" I asked, thinking of Principal Saunders's thin, haunted face.

"I suppose she was," Adam answered slowly, as if he wasn't convinced. "She was very sick. She'd been in and out of psychiatric treatment for twenty-three years, ever since she transitioned. It seems so unlikely to think of Dr. Saunders being attracted to her, or acting on that attraction if he was. She was clearly obsessed with him, yes. Transference is very common, and—well, everyone wants to believe being loved will change their lives."

I thought of Cathy and Francis.

"Rebecca wanted to change her life more than most,"

Adam said, sounding tired and sorry for her, for Rebecca in particular, even after ten years of patients. "So she would come by when she didn't have an appointment, try to meet him as he left work. But Dr. Saunders was one of the best at handling that kind of thing. He was a total professional. He never gave the slightest hint of returning her feelings. I'd never have believed he would leave his wife and little Anna. I can still hardly believe it—I mean, he emailed his letter of resignation—but Principal Saunders called up and told us herself." Adam sighed. "I shouldn't be telling you any of this, but—I miss him."

I stared at the white plastic tabletop, pitted with the weather. "So does Anna."

"Poor girl. It's an awful way to lose your father. He hasn't been in touch at all?"

"He texts."

"Harsh," Kit muttered.

Kit's voice reminded me that I was supposed to have my detective hat on.

"Have you seen Rebecca Jones since?" I asked. Tracing Rebecca would lead to Dr. Saunders, and that might give Anna some answers, at least.

Adam shook his head. "She never returned to the clinic either. Not that she would, what with having her own therapist on tap now. So to speak."

I shuddered at the image.

There was a brief, uneasy silence.

"So—what are the events you've borrowed for your

book that we wouldn't believe?" Kit asked. I could tell that he was quite sure *he* would believe it, having grown up with vampires.

"You know that some vampires can't adjust to being vampires? They cling to human things. Try to carry on as if their life is exactly the same?"

We both nodded. I thought of the jogger in the Shade.

"One of the things that those patients find hardest to deal with is that they can't laugh."

I looked at Kit out of the corner of my eye. He was actually wearing an expression of studied indifference, with an edge of boredom, as if to say that anyone who knew anything about vampires knew that.

"I've lost count of how many patients we've had who perform surgeries on their throats trying to make themselves able to laugh again. Some of them get backyard operations from disbarred surgeons. Respectable surgeons won't do it because it can't be done."

"Oh," I said.

I felt sick. Kit looked it.

"They heal, of course. Being vampires. But they keep on trying. A lot of those cases end in suicide."

Vampire suicide is very easy. All they have to do is walk out into the sun.

"Do you lose many patients?" I asked reluctantly.

I didn't want to look at Kit, and yet I couldn't help it. I didn't want to think of Cathy, but I couldn't stop.

Adam nodded. "There are some humans who should

never become vampires," he said, and I could have kissed him. Kit was listening and looking grave. "They can't live without the sun, without laughter, without pain. I know that sounds odd. A life without pain sounds great, doesn't it? But too many of our patients say it leaves them empty, feeling nothing at all."

"But you only see the worst cases, right?" Kit asked. "Lots of new vampires adjust fine."

"Sure," Adam said. "It's a skewed sample. There are some who thrive as vampires so well, they never come to us. But the human-to-vampire adjustment is difficult even when it goes perfectly. Not enough people who want to transition realize that. They romanticize it. They tell themselves it's a gift, that it will solve all their problems. That attitude's a large part of why this clinic and clinics like it exist."

"I have a friend who wants to transition," I said. "I think she needs to talk to you."

Adam looked mildly surprised.

"Well, it's a condition of getting the license that she have a minimum of three sessions with doctors like ours. Trust me, they'll tell her all about it."

"I hope she listens."

I didn't care who made her see reason, as long as she saw it.

"Is there a particular type who adjusts better to becoming a vampire than others?" Kit asked.

"Some think so. Dr. Saunders used to say that not

having much of a sense of humor was a big plus for a successful transition. Having a strong enough reason to become a vampire is also key. But, mostly, being more in love with death than life is the biggest help. You know the type."

I wasn't sure I did.

"That's my twenty minutes," Adam said. "Back to work. I—it would be great if you didn't mention this conversation to anyone like Leila Saunders. It's not exactly professional of me to tell you all this, and she and I had a few words over what I told the cop: that I couldn't believe Dr. Saunders would run away with a patient."

"Told . . . the cop?" I repeated.

"Officer de Chartres," Adam said. "Now that's a vampire lady who seems well adjusted. But she was bothered by the case, just like I was. She came back and talked to me a few times. I think her superiors had to pretty much slam the case closed on her. Well. Me being shocked isn't going to help Anna, is it? And that's what I'd really like to do. Call me if you have any more questions. It's been nice to meet you, Mel. Give Anna my love."

"I will."

He nodded at Kit and disappeared into the building.

"Officer de Chartres," I said, and looked at Kit. His mouth was a thin, flat line.

"That's my mom," Kit told me.

I wasn't all that surprised—there had to be a connection between Francis and Principal Saunders somewhere,

although I didn't have the faintest idea what it meant—
but I was startled to see how upset Kit looked.

"And . . . ?" I asked delicately, trying to look as if I
could be trusted with any clues he might possess.

Kit had his hands shoved deep in the pockets of his
coat.

"That guy doesn't know what he's talking about,"
Kit said. "Mom has a sense of humor. So does Francis.
Even Minty does, though it's definitely of the drowning-
puppies-how-hilarious kind."

Oh. So this wasn't about Anna at all.

"Uh-huh. Minty begins to grow on me," I lied.

I hadn't noticed much of a sense of humor in Francis,
but I wasn't going to argue with him. Kit looked bleak.

"That was not fun," he said. "Did it help you with
your investigation?"

I thought of Mom, Dad, and Adam Wasserman, and
how surprised they had all been about Dr. Saunders,
about how even Kit's mom didn't believe it.

But that was how Principal Saunders said it had happened.

Maybe she was lying.

Maybe she had a good reason to lie? If that vampire
had kidnapped her husband, and said she'd kill him if
Principal Saunders didn't lie, that would explain everything.

But if it was true, how could I fix it? It would be a
problem for the cops.

I didn't have any evidence to show them. The police were unlikely to launch a rescue mission based on a teenage girl's wild guesses.

"Hard to tell," I said carefully.

Kit continued to look bleak. "Huh."

"How do you feel about some hot chocolate?" I asked, trying to sound cheerful and afraid I was failing miserably.

Kit smiled, though it was unconvincing. "Sounds great," he said.

One more thing to cross off the careers list. I didn't think either of us had a future on the stage.

CHAPTER TWENTY-SEVEN

Kit at Kafeen Krank

Kit was as much out of place at Kafeen Krank as I'd been at Francis's fancy coffee shop. Times about a million. He looked at people talking to each other, tearing apart muffins and cupcakes as they spoke. I wondered if he'd ever seen this many people eating at once.

A baby cried. Kit flinched and looked around as if it had been a gunshot, which made me wonder how many babies he'd heard crying in his life.

"Kit," I said. "Maybe this wasn't such a—"

"Mel!" Ty shouted.

I looked in the direction of the shout and saw Ty sitting at a table with Anna and a guy I thought was from the soccer team. Anna, who despite being superhot is mysteriously shy around guys, looked very pleased to see me. They both waved.

"I'm going to do some detective work of my own and intuit that those are your friends," Kit said. He took a deep breath and lifted his chin. "Well. Why don't we go see them?" He hesitated. "Unless you're embarrassed to be seen with me, that is."

I think he meant it to come out as a joke, but it didn't quite.

Was it reasonable for me to be embarrassed? He didn't know how humans worked. He was from bizarro world, vampire world, a world I had no interest in being near.

But he was funny, and he was nice. We might come from different worlds, but we laughed at the same jokes.

"No," I decided. "I'm not. Let's go over."

I meant to touch his hand as reassurance, but he misunderstood and slid his hand into mine, which felt remarkably good. I blushed a little. We went to the table holding hands.

Our accidental hand-holding count was up to two. Doing it once might be carelessness, but doing it twice made the claim it was accidental seem less likely. So did my extreme consciousness of his hand right there in mine. I wasn't going to let go anytime soon.

Ty and Anna both noted the hand-holding, of course. My friends, the gossip fiends.

Ty didn't look entirely pleased. Of course, he hadn't been thrilled when I was dating Ryan. It's not that he's pining for me. (Ha! Far from it.) But you know that feeling when you see an ex with someone new. It feels like they're winning the breakup.

Anna raised her eyebrows, and while Kit was nodding at the boys, she mouthed, "He's hot."

It's especially like winning the breakup when your someone new is hot.

I grinned and mouthed, "I know" and then when Ty glanced at me, I said, "Hey, guys! This is Kit."

Anna obviously recognized the name. Her face wiped itself of expression. It was like seeing a computer crash, the screen going abruptly blank.

"Hi, Kit," Ty said. "I'm Ty, this is Jonathan."

"Just call me Jon. 'Sup?" said Jon. He was sandy blond, cute in that scruffy soccer-boy way. I wondered if Ty was trying to fix up him and Anna. Everyone was looking a bit self-conscious.

"Kit?" asked Jon. "Weird name."

"Uh," said Kit. "My mom says I was named after Christopher Marlowe."

"Huh," said Jon.

I shared a grin with him over his sneaky phrasing. Then I realized everybody was looking blank about the Christopher Marlowe thing.

Maybe if he'd been a famous Elizabethan soccer player . . .

"Old dead playwright," I explained.

We grabbed two hot chocolates and pulled up chairs. Ty asked Kit if he played soccer.

"No," said Kit. "I did play volleyball once, though. Beach volleyball."

"Right . . . ," said Ty.

At which point, Anna broke in: "Kit was raised by vampires."

She looked at him as if he'd committed a crime. I'd reached for Kit's hand again without thinking about it. He grabbed hold, and I squeezed.

"Whoa," Ty said. "Seriously?"

"Uh, yeah," Kit said. "My mom's a vampire."

Jon frowned. "So you don't, like . . . take after her, or something? My mom says I'm all my dad's side of the family."

"I'm adopted," Kit told him.

"Oh," said Ty. "Well. Cool. We have a vampire friend, don't we, guys? His name's—"

"Francis," said Kit. "He's part of my shade. He helped bring me up."

"Dude, that is weird," Ty observed in a pained voice, and for a wild minute I thought Ty was talking about a human guy referring to "his shade." "No offense," Ty said hastily. "I've got a vampire aunt. It's a bit strange, though, thinking of the fact that our Cathy is dating someone who used to change the diapers of someone her own age."

"I am certain Francis would never dream of performing such a menial task," Kit said, tilting his chin and speaking in a beautifully modulated English accent.

"There is the additional fact that it would be exceedingly aesthetically unappealing, and Francis is a great lover of beauty."

It was exactly like Francis. The boys burst out laughing, and Kit started and then beamed, his hand relaxing in mine. Even Anna smiled.

"So," Kit said. "The television is my window into all things human. There's loads of sports on it, and I decided not to take on too many. Soccer was one of the ones I skipped. How do you play?"

The boys plunged into action. Ty said, "Okay. Okay, so if this marshmallow is the ball, and this saltshaker is the goalkeeper, and this packet of ketchup is—"

Normally, I would've been happy to join in the soccer conversation. But soccer isn't really Anna's thing, and I wanted to talk to her.

I leaned back in my chair, regretfully pulling my hand from Kit's.

"Hey," I said in a low voice. "I went and talked to Adam Wasserman today."

"My dad's secretary?" Anna bit her lip. "Why?"

"I wanted to follow up every lead," I said quietly. "I didn't want you to think I'd forgotten about you, with the whole Cathy thing."

Anna smiled faintly. "I knew you hadn't." She leaned in closer, over the yells of "Offside! That ketchup is totally offside!" and said, "I'm sorry I burst out with— that about Kit."

"It's okay," I said.

"He seems nice," Anna offered.

She was looking at me, waiting for an explanation or just wanting to talk about boys, and I was trying to think of a way to ask her something awful.

"At least he's not a vampire," she said.

"Not yet," I muttered.

"What?" Anna asked.

"Oh, nothing. Adam's a really nice guy."

"Did he tell you anything useful?"

"He was very surprised by the way your dad left. By how sudden it was. That he didn't even come in to say good-bye or stay to help his patients adjust to a new doctor. Adam said everyone was surprised."

"Yes." Anna's mouth twisted. "My parents were so in love. No one could believe it."

"When's the last time you heard from your dad?" I asked, wishing there was a more delicate way to phrase it.

"When school started, he texted to wish me luck with my senior year. I was too upset to reply. I know I should have. But he hasn't texted since. Some father, huh?"

"Yeah," I said. Now that I was questioning Principal Saunders's versions of events, I was finding it very hard to imagine Anna's dad being so neglectful and, well, cruel. "Do you think, maybe . . ." I trailed off. "Never mind."

I couldn't help thinking about Rebecca Jones howling at Anna's house, scratching up the door. The chill from earlier was back, even in this hot, crowded coffee shop full of yelling and laughter. I shivered, and Anna saw it.

"What?"

"Your dad was always so nice," I said. "Remember when he made us the cabbage costumes?"

Anna smiled sadly.

When Anna and I were thirteen, we were cabbages in the school play (don't ask), and my parents both had big cases on, so Dr. Saunders made my cabbage costume. He said it was no trouble. Made us laugh at our cabbage humiliation. It had been a lot of trouble. Those cabbage leaves had been gigantic.

I'd always liked him.

"I don't get him running away like this. Being so cruel to you. It's not like him."

"It's okay, Mel," Anna whispered. "I guess he was too much of a coward to tell me, to explain things. Some midlife crisis, huh? We all know boys, I mean men, can be selfish and awful."

"Is that what your mom says?"

"No. Mom doesn't talk about it. Not since she brought me back from camp."

I frowned.

"I'll be okay, Mel. It's my mom I'm worried about. She loved him so much, you know? I don't think she'll ever get over it."

I wished I knew exactly what "it" was. Some of the

"its" I was thinking of were so terrible, and I didn't know how to suggest to Anna that her father might not have hurt her deliberately.

That someone might have hurt him instead.

CHAPTER TWENTY-EIGHT

Jumping to Conclusions?

I wasn't sure Kit had heard any of what Anna and I had been talking about until we told the others good-bye and Kit insisted that he had to walk me home or Francis would make him memorize more books of etiquette.

I might have dangled my hand sort of invitingly in the space between us, but he didn't take it. He was staring straight ahead, as if he found the sidewalk really interesting and possibly a little bit upsetting.

"Your friends seem cool," he said. "Ty mentioned you guys often have a pickup soccer game in the park on Sundays."

"Come along," I said, and when Kit smiled faintly, I winked. "I'll kick your butt as well as Ty's. Be a pleasure."

"It's a date," said Kit. I thought about objecting, but

who was I kidding? It was a date. "Your friend Anna," Kit continued after a pause. "She has it pretty rough. I didn't know—I didn't know your detective work was about something so serious."

"How do you mean?" I asked warily.

"Well," Kit said, "her dad's gone, after doing something massively uncharacteristic, and he's just been texting since he left."

He glanced at me, as if for confirmation. Of course he would have the same suspicions I had. It was obvious, wasn't it?

"What if Dr. Saunders has amnesia?" Kit asked.

I stared at him. Okay, we didn't have the same suspicions.

"No, I'm serious," he continued. "What if Dr. Saunders had head trauma and when he came to he didn't know who he was, but Rebecca Jones was there to tell him who he was and how he hated his family and loved her—pretty convenient, huh? And that's why he's abandoned his family even though it's totally out of character. Dr. Saunders doesn't know who he is!"

I didn't say anything.

"Makes sense, doesn't it?" Kit said, waiting for me to be impressed by his crazy theory.

"Um. Amnesia?" Not rolling my eyes took all my concentration. "What made you think of that?"

"I saw this excellent show all about it. There was this one guy who stood up too fast in the kitchen, whacked his head into a cupboard door, and didn't know who he was for six months! And then there was this woman who was hit by a car on the way to her own wedding, and when she got her memory back it was three years later and she was living in a hut in Alaska. Apparently it happens all the time."

"I guess we can't discount it," I said to be kind. I wondered what show Kit had been watching. *Days of Our Lives?* "But, um, I don't think he's in a hut in Alaska. Besides," I said quickly when Kit started to protest, "how does that explain how strangely Principal Saunders has been behaving?" I took a breath. "I think Anna's dad may have been kidnapped—"

"Kidnapped? By Rebecca Jones?"

"Yes. And that's why Anna's mom is behaving so weirdly. She's being threatened."

"By Rebecca Jones?"

"That's my theory, anyway. It seems more likely than amnesia."

"Amnesia is way more common than you'd think," Kit said. "It happens all the time on TV shows. But either way, don't you think we should we go to the police? I could ask my mom to look into it? She would, you know. We know she's interested in the case."

"But what if it's exactly what it looks like?" I asked, suddenly unsure. Was what I was thinking any more likely than amnesia? "Dr. Saunders had a midlife crisis and ran away with a beautiful vampire, and his wife is miserable. She really loved him. *Loves* him. Could be that both our theories are nuts."

"Beautiful crazy vampire," Kit said. "You heard what Mr. Wasserman said."

"If he has amnesia, why is he texting his wife and daughter at all? If he's been kidnapped, why hasn't Principal Saunders gone to the police?" I asked.

"Because she doesn't want her husband killed?"

"Thin. Very thin. Principal Saunders can't believe that Rebecca would ever give him back," I said. "The vampire is nuts. Principal Saunders would go to the police. Besides which, Rebecca Jones didn't sound like a criminal mastermind."

"I guess not," Kit said. "It's horrible to think that a vampire would do something like that."

"Vampires do all sorts of horrible things," I said.

"As do humans," Kit replied.

"Right. Sorry. Dr. Saunders running away without saying good-bye, without letting his daughter know how much he loves her—texts don't count—that's really horrible."

If he'd done it.

Someone else could have used his phone. Someone else could have sent those texts.

But if he hadn't, if my theory was true, then Principal Saunders was being stupid. She'd always been so sensible: She'd know the only thing to do was go to the police.

Love made you do dumb things, though, I mused, thinking of Cathy. Maybe we were letting our imaginations run away with us. Especially Kit. Amnesia? Seriously?

"Yeah. And depressing."

"It's hard to accept it's true. But Occam's Razor says—" I began.

"The simplest explanation is usually the right one," Kit completed. "But crazy Rebecca Jones turning kidnapper is an explanation too. So is amnesia." He saw the look on my face. "Okay, possibly not *as* likely. But if my mom thought there was something fishy going on . . ."

"I hope I'm not right," I said. "With or without his memory, I hate the idea of Dr. Saunders being held prisoner by a crazy vampire."

"Me, too," Kit said. There was a long pause. "I hated hearing all those things Mr. Wasserman said, about vampires getting botched surgeries to let them laugh and committing suicide."

He shuddered and hugged himself reflexively, as if he was cold. The boy who lived in a chilly vampire house.

It occurred to me that like Adam's patients, Kit's samples were skewed. Vampires who lived in the Shade tended to be older and more traditional. They were successful, established vampires who had adjusted well. Kit didn't know any badly adjusted vampires. This must've been the first time he'd faced the downsides of becoming a vampire.

I wanted to hug him.

Kit shoved his hands in his pockets. "I should get going. But I had fun."

"Uh-huh," I said, looking at his pale, strained face. "Loads of fun."

Kit made a crooked attempt at a smile. "Well, some of it was fun. And—I'm sure you're going to find out what happened with Dr. Saunders. So," he said.

"So," I said.

He looked at me, and for a moment I thought he was going to kiss me.

I suppose technically he did. He leaned forward and gave me a quick peck on the cheek.

Yes indeed. The I-think-of-you-more-as-a-maiden-aunt kiss.

"I'll call you," Kit told me. "I've got a lot to think about."

A peck on the cheek? I nodded and turned away. My throat felt tight. "I'll call you"? I knew what it meant when a guy said that.

Ryan had said that he needed time to think about how things were going, and that he'd call me, the day before he hit on Cathy at a party I hadn't been invited to.

I felt a bit disgusted with myself feeling blue about the fact that Kit wasn't going to call, when something else Kit had said was much more important.

His mom thought something fishy was going on. She'd interviewed Adam Wasserman too, after all.

Francis had chosen our school, out of all the schools in New Whitby, to attend. Principal Saunders was terrified of Francis. Francis had asked me not to discuss him with Principal Saunders.

Francis was on record as having written several volumes of his magnum opus already. Francis had a plausible cover story to be in school.

Francis lived in a shade with a vampire cop. Was Camille secretly investigating what had happened to Dr. Saunders? Was Francis her man on the inside?

CHAPTER TWENTY-NINE

Desperately Scandalizing Francis

At school the next day I was in the worst mood in the history of bad moods. I went to my locker, not because I needed a book but because I wanted to stand in the hall, stare into my locker, and brood.

I'd realized that our conversation with Adam Wasserman hadn't gotten me any closer to knowing what had happened with Dr. Saunders. Had he just left Anna and his wife? Or had Rebecca Jones kidnapped him and was she now terrifying Principal Saunders while Camille investigated the whole thing by placing Francis at Craunston High as her spy?

Francis would be the worst spy ever.

It was entirely possible I was crazy. Or at least the worst amateur detective ever. Was Kit's theory really that much worse than mine? Maybe amnesiac Dr. Saunders was now living off kelp and whale meat in Alaska.

On top of that, Kit had broken up with me. Not that we had been together or could ever have been together, what with his desperate need to become an eternal member of his shade.

I'll call you. Yeah, right.

He hadn't even said why. Was I too human for him? Too bossy? Had he lied about liking our kiss? He'd pecked my cheek last night. A mere peck!

Ugh.

"Are you all right, Mel?" Principal Saunders asked.

I started. "Just lost in thought!" I said, extremely relieved she couldn't read them.

"And late for class, it would appear."

"On my way, sorry!"

I so wished that I hadn't told Kit my Dr.-Saunders-kidnapped theory. It had been bad enough thinking it myself. Now, thanks to Kit, I couldn't *stop* thinking it. But every time my brain went there, I started to imagine all the awful things that crazy vampire Rebecca could be doing to him, and my thoughts recoiled, going into painful spirals and heading toward a headache.

Stop it, Mel, I told myself. There was another explanation that made perfect sense: Dr. Saunders ran off with Rebecca Jones. Love makes people crazy. Look at Cathy and Francis. She was going to change species for a guy she'd known for less than a month! Love made people deranged.

I was so relieved I wasn't in love with Kit. That jerk.

I confess I did not take in much in trig or bio. Cathy was, of course, in all those classes. We always took the same classes. She wasn't paying much attention either, which was very unusual for her. She seemed to be reading a book under the desk. I'd never seen her do that before.

We exchanged "hi"s and "how are you"s but that was it. It felt like I was already losing her.

At lunch instead of joining us or going off with Francis, Cathy squeezed his hand, smiled meltingly at him, and then headed for the library. Francis, shockingly, did not join us either. Anna, Ty, and I were getting used to each other's company without Cathy. They were good friends to have, and it was especially lovely having Anna back, but I was starting to really miss Cathy. Since we were little we'd practically lived in each other's back pockets.

"So," Ty said, as soon as we had all gotten our lunches and acquired a table. "This Kit guy. Kind of cool. I suppose." He paused so I could contemplate how he, Ty, was much cooler.

"You broke up with me, Ty," I said.

Ty coughed. "That's got nothing to do with anything. I was saying I like your new boyfriend."

"He's not—" I began. I wasn't going to tell them the barely begun friendship had come to an end. "We only just met."

"Do you like him?" Ty asked. "Not that I care."

"I do," I said, because it was true. Even though it didn't matter anymore. "Not that I care that you don't care. Though you clearly do care, and I don't care about that, either."

"Well, I don't care that you don't care that I don't care. In fact I'm glad. Because, um, if I was seeing someone that I liked, I'd want you to be happy for me."

"Are you seeing someone?" I asked, pretty sure he wasn't. "Not that I care."

"You two are making my head hurt," Anna observed. "I like Kit. He's cute and he's funny. We can't all have living families." She smiled to show she was joking.

"Aunt. Vampire," Ty said, but he was smiling and clearly not offended. "I'm sure she'd love to meet Kit."

"Cathy's been a bit odd today," I said to change the subject.

If Kit had been my boyfriend, or even potential boyfriend, which he'd made clear last night he wasn't, it was a pretty short relationship. Not my shortest—at four days, Ryan was the winner and still champion on that front—but still pretty short.

"She's reading every book in the library about vampires, zombies, and transitioning," Anna said. "Preparing herself. She's turned it into her Local History major assignment. A history of the transitioning process in New Whitby."

I admit I was a little jealous. How did Anna know that

and not me? It must have shown, because Anna shrugged and said, "I've been in the library a lot. So has Cathy."

"Of course. Typical of her to turn the whole thing into an assignment. I bet Kaplan was thrilled."

Anna smiled.

"I can't believe she's really going to do it," I said. "Do you think they'll give her a license?"

"Don't know," Anna said. "I've never known anyone who transitioned before. Who's even tried to."

"My aunt transitioned so long ago, it's probably not how they do it anymore." Technically Ty's aunt was his great-great-aunt. "But I could ask her about it if you like."

"Thanks. Can you imagine Cathy not laughing?" I asked.

"I kind of can, actually," Ty said. "She's not that much of a laugher. Not like you or me or—"

"Cathy laughs!" I protested, trying—and failing—not to think of Adam Wasserman's words about the kind of person who made a good vampire. "She has a sense of humor!"

"She does," Anna agreed. "But I don't think of her as a laughing person. Not like you, Mel. She's more of a wry smiler. With a very low-key sense of humor."

"Right," Ty said. "That's exactly it. Kind of like Francis."

I bit my tongue to prevent myself from saying that she was *nothing* like Francis. But was that true? They did seem to be sharing several private jokes already.

I had a sinking feeling that Cathy could tick the three boxes Adam Wasserman said were essential for successful vampire transitioning: not much of a sense of humor—it was true that she wasn't a big laugher; strong reason to become a vampire—true love (I didn't think it was enough of a reason, but Cathy certainly did); being more in love with death than life—I wondered if thinking an early death was romantic counted as being more in love with death than life. Cathy had long been obsessed with Thomas Chatterton, John Keats, Wilfred Owen, Sylvia Plath, and Anne Sexton. All of them died young and wrote loads of death-obsessed poetry. But Cathy had never said that *she* wanted to die young. Was being obsessed with death the same thing as wanting to die young?

Not that I wanted to calculate Cathy's chances of a successful transition.

I didn't want her to attempt transition at all.

◆

The bell for the end of lunch sounded, and I grabbed my bag, got up, and trailed off to class. I walked so slowly that by the time I got to within sight of the classroom, the corridors were deserted. At least they were until Francis turned the corner.

"Francis!" I called out, not as quietly as I should have.

He strode toward me, his ever-so-perfect and ever-so-expressionless face not displaying annoyance, even though I knew he must be annoyed. I'm sure real ladies didn't raise their voices.

"Miss Duan?"

He *was* annoyed. Normally he called me Melanie.

"I need to talk to you," I said, grabbing his arm and pulling him into the girls' room. Now, no way was I stronger than Francis, but he was a gentleman who would never throw off a lady's guiding hand, even a lady he didn't entirely consider to be one.

When I let go of his arm, he smoothed out his sleeve as if attempting to erase all Mel contamination.

"This is the ladies' powder room," he said, eyebrows rising in the vampire equivalent of total horror.

"The girls' bathroom, yes, where we go to—"

"I am quite aware of the personal business which ladies conduct here," Francis said. "The question is, Why am I here?"

"Because what I want to ask you is, um, confidential and everyone's in class." I waved at the row of empty stalls. Francis did not follow the direction of my arm. Apparently gentlemen did not look at the empty stalls in the girls' bathroom. "No one will hear us in here."

Francis's posture was even more ramrod stiff than normal. He was clearly torn between being scandalized and being forced to accept a sort-of lady's confidence.

"Please proceed with haste," he said, and forgot himself to such an extent that he added another "Please."

"Are you here to investigate Principal Saunders?"

For a moment Francis looked almost uncertain. "But you know I am," he said at last.

"No, I don't."

"Then pray tell, Miss Duan, why you claimed you had such knowledge? You threatened to reveal the undercover nature of my endeavors here!"

"I didn't!" What was Francis talking about?

"You informed me that you were aware of the true reason for my sojourn at this fine establishment."

Fine establishment? Did he mean this school? Apparently he did. "Yes," I said. "To write your book. You thought that I . . . Oh." But of course his secret hadn't been the book. Cathy knew about it. The school knew about it.

"This is most perplexing," Francis said at length, which I thought was Francis-speak for "What the hell is going on?" Typical Francis, not even making it a question.

Since it wasn't a question, I didn't have to answer.

"Isn't it?" I said sweetly, and cut to the chase. "What's going on with Principal Saunders? Her husband didn't really run away, did he?"

Francis was still for a moment, sky-blue eyes scanning my face. I tried to keep my face as expressionless as his.

Stupid vampires. There's a reason it's illegal for them to play poker.

"Miss Duan," Francis said carefully, "I am not about to reveal the true nature of my investigation here."

"Are you working for Camille?"

"I can only repeat: I am not about to reveal the true nature of my investigation here," Francis said firmly. "It is unfortunate that you're aware that there is such an investigation. I shall ask you—and this is for your own good—to put it from your mind and cease to interfere."

For my own good, like Francis's leaving had been for Cathy's own good. Look how that had turned out!

I resisted the impulse to kick Francis in the shin and instead tried for an ingratiating smile.

"C'mon, Francis. You can tell me."

Francis looked—well, to use his own words, I believe he looked most perplexed. (It was possible that I had never smiled at Francis before.) Then he looked cold and decided.

"I most assuredly cannot. And now, if you don't mind, I am late for my class. As I believe you are also. Good-bye."

Francis left so quickly, there was no time to beg him again to change his mind. A breeze in my face was all that remained of Francis's unspeakable presence in the ladies' powder room.

I'd been all set to tell him of Anna's suffering and how he could help her.

I leaned back against the sink. At least now I knew for certain that there was an investigation.

Oh, poor Dr. Saunders and Principal Saunders. Could my kidnapping theory really be true? How was I going to tell Anna?

Francis's being involved in the investigation meant Camille must have been the one who sent Francis.

Camille must know, or at least suspect, something. I had to find out what. Anna had a right to know. Which meant I had to talk to Camille. She was a mother. She would understand that Anna needed help.

She was also the mother of the boy who'd just dumped me. And a scary vampire cop who moved so fast she became a blur.

Piece of cake.

CHAPTER THIRTY

Interrogation with the Vampire

Obviously it would have been bad manners to visit Camille when she was still asleep. So I waited until it was almost dark before heading to the Shade on my bike. The sun set as I rode through the empty streets; it colored the ornate buildings orange, red, and purple before fading to a dull pink and then darkness. As I got closer to Camille's house, one or two vampires began to appear. It was almost more eerie than when the vampires were all out promenading. Almost.

When I reached the house, I carefully left my bike against the low fence. (I did not want to destroy any more flower beds.) I took a breath, reminded myself that Camille was a tea-making mom, and knocked on the door.

Strangely, I'd decided to go with the front door rather

than continuing the tradition of breaking in through the wine cellar.

It was immediately flung wide open.

"Darling Raoul!" exclaimed a vampire with a cloud of scarlet hair and an even bigger cloud of perfume.

"Uh," I said. "No?"

"He can always be relied on," the redhead continued mysteriously. "Well, come in, child, come in! We're starving."

As invitations went, it was up there with "I hope you can attend the party at our place! Much love, the Manson family" or "Drop in anytime, our chainsaws are always buzzing." I almost fell backward off the porch.

"I think you've made a mistake," I said.

"I don't have all night, gel," said the lady vampire.

I didn't think she was actually English, like Francis. I'd heard a lot of vamposeurs pretending to be foreign, as if it made them more vampiric. I hadn't expected an actual vampire to do the same.

Great. Pretentious vampires: That was all I needed tonight.

"No, really, you've got it wrong."

"Children today are so indecisive," the woman said. "'Oh, bite me, oh no, wait, do, oh no, no, I've changed my mind, don't take so much, I feel all faint, call my mommy.' Every human who wants to experience the dark delirium of a vampire's bite is so whiny! I wish we attracted the taciturn, I truly do."

Something about the way she said "children today" made me pause and take a gamble.

"Minty?" I asked cautiously.

"Oh," Minty said. "Oh, just fine. 'Minty,' indeed. My name is Araminta. I presume you're Kitten's little girlfriend, then, and I expect you don't want to be bitten at all."

She gave me an accusing look. I shook my head apologetically but firmly.

"Splendid!" Minty exclaimed. "We'll all starve to death while entertaining a constant parade of humans, and the neighbors will think that we have set up a little human zoo. Absolutely splendid! I suppose you had better come in."

I edged in past her, my neck feeling horribly exposed. I was afraid she'd snap at it.

She didn't. Of course she didn't: She might be having donors make house calls, but no vampire that hadn't gone completely rogue would dream of biting someone without permission.

"Is breakfast here?" asked a vampire guy in a waistcoat.

If you ever wondered how fangs and a droopy mustache look on someone, I am here to tell you the answer: Very weird.

"No," Minty said, throwing me a bitter look. "This is Kitten's girlfriend."

"Kit. Honestly, Araminta, you must try to remember,"

said the man, and offered me his hand. I took it and he shook, hurting my fingers a little bit. A vampire's firm handshake is very firm. "My name's Albert."

"Mel," I said.

"You'll be wanting the lad, I expect. Let me see if I can fetch him for you."

"Uh—no, no, that's okay," I told him quickly. The last thing I needed was for Kit to think I was stalking him. "I was wondering if I could possibly speak to Camille?"

Minty and Albert both paused. They had poker faces as good as Francis's, but I'd had experience of the vampire version of "very perplexed" today already.

We all stood staring at each other in extreme perplexitude, and who knew how long that would have continued if not for the interruption of yet another strange vampire.

"Hi," I said, before someone else could introduce me as Kit's girlfriend. "I'm— friends with Cathy?" At the last moment, I couldn't bring myself to utter such a total lie as saying I was friends with Francis.

Minty sniffed. "We are positively besieged by humans."

The new vampire, a small woman with a sweet heart-shaped face, zoomed over with vampire speed that made me jump, and before I knew it, she had her finger on the pulse in my neck.

Calm down! I ordered myself. Calm down, it's probably a vampire thing, it's like the vampire version of Eskimo kisses, it's probably totally normal.

"You're so unkind, Araminta," she murmured. "I think she seems very nice."

"Ulp," I said. "Thank you?"

"My name's Marie-Therese," she continued dreamily. "I am so fond of Kit. I hope we can be friends."

"Friends, awesome, yes," I said. "Do . . . friends always stroke other friends' veins?"

"Sorry about her," Albert told me. "Spanish, you see. Very volatile people. Best to indulge her."

I stayed very still as Marie-Therese's cold fingers traced up and down my neck. I'd never been outnumbered by vampires before. I felt fragile, crushable in a way I'd never felt before. I wondered if this was how Kit felt all the time.

Then, unexpectedly, Marie-Therese stepped back and called out "Camille!" in a piercing tone. She stopped and gave me a sweet smile. "Camille is lucky to have such a charming visitor," she said. "Come back and have tea with me anytime."

Marie-Therese drifted out of the room. There was a glimpse of a chandelier in the next room before the door swung shut.

"She gives herself all these unearthly vampire airs around humans," Minty said in her fake English accent.

"The Spanish are a dramatic people," Albert said stoutly.

"If she's Spanish," I asked, "how come she's got a French name?"

"Nobody knows," Albert said.

"Nobody cares, more like," Minty said with a sneer.

I was grateful to see Camille coming down the stairs, hardly what I'd felt the last time I saw Camille coming down some stairs.

It was still eerie. I'd been thinking of her as more human than she was, more Kit's mom. I'd aged her, softened the cold lines of her face and the icy glitter of her eyes. But here she was, all vampire, in her uniform with her black hair hanging in a braid down her back.

"Mel?" she inquired. "Shall I fetch Kit for you?"

Did all these vampires have to keep harping on Kit?

"I was wondering if I could have a word with you, actually."

Camille nodded, with not even the faintest sign of confusion. She led me silently into the kitchen.

Behind us, I heard Minty and Albert conferring on whether I might have come to ask Camille for Kit's hand in marriage.

✦

"What can I do for you?" Camille asked in her remote voice, sitting with perfect posture in the chair across from me.

She'd already insisted on making me a cup of tea. I sloshed the cup around in my hands as I tried to think of a way to put this.

"The thing is," I said, "I have this friend called Anna Saunders."

Camille folded her hands on the table. "You seem blessed with many friends."

"And—I may have sort of guessed that you sent Francis to our school so he could keep his eye on Anna's mom. Our principal. Principal Saunders."

Because I was so sure that if Camille suspected Principal Saunders of lying to the police, she'd forgotten her name.

Camille actually made a slight expression. Sadly, it was not an expression that said, "Mel, you clever girl, you've guessed so much, you might as well know it all."

It looked more like frustration.

"Francis," she muttered, in a tone that let me know I'd gotten Francis in trouble.

Which was excellent, but not really the point.

"Anna's really worried about her mom and her dad," I said in a rush. "I mean, she has no idea that something might have happened to her dad. That he might not have run away." I studied Camille for a reaction. "But Principal Saunders has been acting strange for a while. I saw, the day of the Ratastrophe—uh, the day all the rats got loose at school—that she was terrified of Francis."

Camille's whole posture changed so swiftly that I spilled tea on my jeans.

She was hunched over slightly. The way she sat made me think a word I didn't want to be thinking—predatory.

"You observed Principal Saunders's behavior on that day?" Camille asked, and fished out a notepad with a pen clipped to it. "Can you describe it to me?"

I immediately felt like a complete fool. Of course Camille looked intent. She was a cop. She wanted me to give an eyewitness account.

But an eyewitness account of the Ratastrophe? She wasn't a vampire health inspector.

"Why do you want to know about the rats? What could that possibly have to do with anything?"

"Mel," Camille said, "can I make myself perfectly clear? I am a police officer. You are a seventeen-year-old girl. That means I ask you questions, and if you respect the law, you answer them. It does not mean that I tell you confidential information about any of my cases."

"Of course," I said. I glared into my half-full cup of tea.

"Can you tell me about the rat incident?" Camille said.

I told her.

"Thank you for your help," Camille said when I was done, serene as if we'd both gotten what we wanted when all I'd gotten was a lapful of tea. "Shall I call Kit down?" she asked. "I am certain he would be pleased to see you."

She was a lot more certain than I was.

"No, thanks," I said. "I have to get going."

Camille hesitated. "I do hope you two haven't had a falling-out."

"We kind of did," I said, getting up from my chair. "But it's okay. I don't see us as having much of a future."

Camille looked at my face for a moment, as if she

wanted to say something.

"Perhaps you're mistaken about that?"

I shrugged. "Can I ask you one thing? Do you know where Rebecca Jones is?"

"You needn't worry about her," Camille told me crisply. "Rebecca Jones is dead. She killed herself."

"What?" Rebecca Jones dead? Then she couldn't be a kidnapper. She couldn't be *anything*.

"But—"

"That's all I can say," Camille said, making it plain that our conversation was over.

I left the kitchen and stumbled into the hall with my head spinning. I didn't notice Kit on the stairs, not until he spoke.

"Mel?" he asked.

I felt too shaken up to even pretend I didn't care about being blown off. I did care, and I didn't know how to stop.

"Don't worry," I snapped. "I'm not here to see you."

I slammed the front door, ran down the steps, threw myself onto my bike, and took off pedaling as fast as I could down the middle of the street. Any vampire that had a yen to try my blood was going to have to run for it.

I hadn't realized how much I wanted everything to be as it seemed: Principal Saunders was understandably upset about her husband living in Rebecca Jones's vampire love nest. Which made perfect sense and did not send the world spinning off its axis. Even the wild story

I'd come up with wasn't true.

Rebecca Jones couldn't be threatening Principal Saunders. So what did Principal Saunders have to hide?

And if Rebecca was dead, where was Anna's dad? I was pretty sure he didn't have amnesia.

I could think of only one reason for Principal Saunders to lie: if she was covering up something she had done.

CHAPTER THIRTY-ONE

Friends Don't Let Friends Become Undead

Rebecca Jones could not be holding Dr. Saunders hostage. Dr. Saunders could not be living in her vampire love nest.

Rebecca Jones was dead.

I tried to digest this world-exploding information as I pedaled. I needed to talk to someone. I couldn't talk to Kit, on account of the blowing off. I couldn't exactly call Anna, either.

Ordinarily when I needed someone to talk to, I turned to Cathy, but, well, I wasn't sure I could do that now. She was so caught up with Francis and the whole wanting-to-become-a-vampire thing. We hadn't had a real conversation since the disastrous double date.

Yet somehow I found myself pedaling all the

way to Cathy's house.

I dismounted and looked up at her room. The light was on. Feeling almost as nervous as I had when I'd knocked on the door to speak to Camille, I hauled my bike up the steps, hid it on the porch (vampires might suck your blood, but at least they wouldn't steal your bike), and rang the bell.

Then waited and waited and thought maybe she wasn't home after all? Maybe I should call Kristin instead?

The door opened.

"Hi, Mel," Cathy said, looking genuinely pleased to see me.

"Hi. I was in the neighborhood."

"You live in the neighborhood." She smiled and beckoned me in.

"True," I said, following her up the stairs. "Your mom's not home?"

"No. She's working late."

Cathy ushered me into her room, which was not as tidy as usual. By Cathy standards, I mean. There were piles of books on the floor and bed and desk and every other flat surface, most of them festooned with forests of Post-its. A glance at a couple of the titles—*Cell Transition in Vampirism, Encyclopedia of the Undead*—told me more than I wanted to know.

"Hard at work, huh?" I said.

She nodded and cleared off a chair so I could sit down. She sat on an uncluttered corner of her bed. "Are you okay?" she asked as I sat.

"Fine," I said. "No, not fine. It's Anna."

"Yes?"

"She, well, really it's her dad. If he did run away with Rebecca Jones, he's not with her now."

"Rebecca Jones?"

"The vampire he supposedly ran off with. She's dead. Killed herself. But he hasn't come home. So where is he?"

Cathy was pale and horrified. I could barely look at her: I didn't want to see how serious this was.

"How do you know all this?"

"Camille told me," I said, apparently unable to stop talking now I'd started. "Anna said her mom was acting strangely. More than just being hurt and mourning because her husband left her. So I've been looking into it. I think I know why, and it's not good."

Cathy waited for me to continue.

"*Really* not good."

She nodded to encourage me to finish. She looked totally understanding, like nothing I could say would shock her.

"Anna's mom? Principal Saunders?" I said, lowering my voice although no one could possibly hear me. "I think she might have—done something to her husband."

I said "something" because I couldn't say "hurt."

I didn't know how to even think the word *killed*. I'd known Principal Saunders all my life.

But Dr. Saunders had vanished, and his wife was lying about where he was.

"No!" Cathy gasped. "She didn't. You're not serious."

It was my turn to nod. "Yeah, I am. Completely serious." I filled Cathy in on everything I'd learned, skipping bits that involved me being rude to Francis or too cozy with Kit. "I don't know how to tell Anna."

"You're not going to." Cathy took my hands in hers and squeezed them. "You don't know what happened. All you know for sure is that if Dr. Saunders did run away with Rebecca Jones, he's not with her now."

"But—" I began.

"What about the texts?" Cathy asked. "Anna showed me some of the texts her dad sent her after he left them."

"If you have the person's phone," I pointed out, "anyone can send a text. Same with email."

"If Principal Saunders killed her husband, why isn't she in custody?"

Cathy said it so coolly that for a moment all I could do was stare. She stared back, as if she didn't realize I was freaked out she'd said the unsayable. "She *is* being investigated."

"Did Francis or Camille tell you that?"

"Not explicitly."

"Of course not. Camille can't let you in on the true nature of her investigation. And Francis is working for her, so he has to operate under those same rules. He's so honorable," she added.

I tried to not feel queasy at Cathy's obvious pride in Francis.

"You need to separate out what you do know from what you suspect. You can't go to Anna with any of this until what you have to tell her is fact, not conjecture. Have you thought of simply asking Principal Saunders?"

"Cathy, something is up. She's acting weird. She's scared of Francis. She's hiding *something*. She obviously isn't in a mood to confess, or the police wouldn't have to investigate her."

"You don't know that they are investigating her."

"Francis is at the school because Camille asked him to keep an eye on her."

"Francis *isn't* a police officer. So whatever he's doing for Camille must be informal, right?"

I hadn't thought of that.

"Has Anna mentioned the police?" Cathy asked. "She asked for your help. Surely she would have mentioned if she'd been interrogated. Surely we would have heard if there was a police investigation. You know how fast gossip spreads."

"Good point."

"Maybe Dr. Saunders ran away with the vampire, then changed his mind and wanted to return to his family. Maybe that's why she killed herself."

That did sound more reasonable than what I had been imagining. I began to feel foolish.

I bit my lip. "Then why hasn't he come home?"

"Maybe he's afraid to. Maybe he's gearing himself up to beg their forgiveness. Maybe he's still shocked at his lover's suicide. There are lots of explanations for the few facts you have."

"Maybe he has amnesia?"

"Mel," Cathy said, "stick to the facts. Why not simply ask Principal Saunders?"

"I can't ask her without letting her know what I know, and if she did do something to Dr. Saunders—even though I agree there's no proof of that—how's she going to respond to me asking about it? Even if she didn't do anything and she just got dumped, she's not going to take it well."

It felt good to be talking to her about this. Almost like we were back to being best friends.

"I'm still me," Cathy said.

"What?" I asked when I meant, "How did you know what I was thinking?"

"I know you think I'm all about Francis all the time now. But I'm still me. We're still friends."

"Of course," I said.

She did seem like the old Cathy. I could almost forget about Francis and her insane desire to become a vampire. All I had to do was ignore the fact that she was completely surrounded by books about becoming a vampire.

"You don't have to do it, you know," I said quietly.

"Do what?" Cathy said, though I knew she knew.

"Change. You can still be with Francis as a human.

Why do you have to change?"

"It's something I really want," Cathy said. "I wish I could make you understand. I think I've always wanted this."

"To be dead?"

Cathy started to say something and then stopped. She took a deep breath. "Being a vampire is not being dead. You know that. You've talked to Francis and to Camille. You've talked to Kit. He's spent his whole life with vampires. It's a different way of living. Francis says—"

"Francis says!" I shouted, losing my temper. "When did you become so brainwashed? Ever since you met him, it's been 'Francis says this! Francis says that! Francis says I should die now!' When did you stop thinking for yourself?" I stood up. "I can't believe you're going to give up on humanity. And I'm sorry, but that's what you're doing. That's what becoming a vampire means. At least it does if your transition *actually* works. If you don't wind up dead or zombified and *then* dead. Plus there's the little matter of whether or not you'll adjust to being a vampire. Do you have any idea how high the vampire suicide rate is? Or how hard most of them find being a vampire? And you're going to go through all of that BECAUSE FRANCIS TOLD YOU TO!"

Cathy stood up too. She looked even paler than usual, her lips were thin, and her eyes narrowed. I'd seen that face before. That's how she'd looked when Tommy Lewis had lied about kissing her behind the girls' room in the third grade. How she'd looked when her fifth-grade teacher, Ms. Hildergardt, had accused her of plagiarizing her first-prize-winning, end-of-year, best-of-Maine competition essay. She had never turned that face on me before.

"How long have you known me?" she asked.

"Since we were born, I guess."

"Have I ever made any major decisions in my life simply because someone told me to? Have I ever shown myself to be a sheep? Have I ever made any major decision without weighing every pro and every con? Do you think I have been researching every single aspect of what I'll be undertaking *because Francis told me to?*"

"But you—"

"If anyone here rushes into things, it's you, Mellifluous Li Duan. You're always rushing into situations thinking you know best, when you haven't got the faintest idea. Like deciding Anna's mom has murdered her husband!"

"What!" I shouted at her. "I'm the one who always knows what to do!"

I thought Cathy understood me. She'd known me for years. She was the only person besides my family who knew my real name. If Cathy didn't know who I was, who did?

Cathy kept talking in that cool, precise voice. "For other people, perhaps. For yourself? You went out with Ryan after you had known him for precisely three seconds. Dozens of his previous girlfriends could have told you what a jerk he is. You didn't even have to ask his girlfriends—casual acquaintances could have told you the same thing! You started fencing because you had a crush on Raj Singh. You didn't know a single thing about fencing except that some cute guy did it. You don't even choose your own classes! Every year you pick the same classes as me. What are you going to do when we're at different colleges? How dare you tell me I can't think for myself!"

I had the strangest feeling in my chest. I was going to yell back at her, tell her she was wrong, scream at her about her being Francis's puppet, but I found myself on the brink of tears, a knot in my chest. Sometimes, yes, I did stuff because Cathy or Anna or Ty or Kristin or whoever was doing them. I mean the classes thing was because I didn't care that much about school. It was easier to do what Cathy did. I wasn't a sheep. It was just that I didn't have as many passions as Cathy. I wasn't like her. I'd never known what I wanted to be when I grew up.

It wasn't the way she was making it sound. I could make decisions.

I couldn't let her make me cry.

"I think you should go now," Cathy said.

"Right," I said, moving toward the door.

"One last thing," she said. "You're the first to know: Mom gave me permission. I can apply for a license whenever I want."

CHAPTER THIRTY-TWO

The Craziness of Humans

I stumbled out of Cathy's house, trying to pretend my eyes weren't swimming with tears—trying to pretend so hard that I tripped on the porch steps and hit the ground on my hands and knees.

Beauty and grace in distress, that was me.

The knees of my jeans were dirty. I tried to brush them off, but the stain seemed to be sticking, and I didn't care. My palms stung, and so did my eyes. I blinked fiercely, then realized I had to climb back up the porch steps to retrieve my bike.

Obviously, I thought as I pedaled furiously, heading for home, obviously Cathy figured she didn't want or need friends as long as she had Francis for all eternity. She'd decided to make it clear that she didn't want me tagging around after her anymore, taking classes because she took them, studying hard because she did.

Not that I tagged around after her! She was being like Francis, contemptuous of all humans. She might talk about caring for Anna, but I was the one Anna had come to for help. I was the one who had found out everything we knew so far, and I was the one who would get to the bottom of it.

Cathy could study her vampire books and dream of endless bliss with Francis—oh, it rhymed, I should tell Francis so he could put it in another ballad!—I was going to help Anna.

The blood was pounding in my ears so hard, I thought that it was the thudding I heard. Everything was a blur of refusing to cry and wanting to show Cathy. Then someone tapped me between the shoulder blades.

I swerved on the sidewalk, wheeling my bike savagely to a stop that nearly sent me careening into the road, and found myself staring at Kit.

He was looking sweaty and disheveled, curls springing every which way.

"I have been . . . running after you . . . yelling your name. . . for three blocks!" he panted.

Now that I thought about it, the thudding had been a bit like running footsteps.

"I was thinking," I said, summoning up all the dignity I had left. "Thinking deep thoughts."

"I went to your house and you weren't there," Kit went on, regaining his breath. "Where were you? Why were you cycling as if the hounds of hell were coming after you in a Mack truck?"

"Never mind that," I snapped. "Why were you chasing after me?"

Kit looked at me as if I was dimwitted in some way. "You came to my house and talked to my mom instead of talking to me. In fact, when I saw you, you said you weren't there to see me, and you ran out of the house and banged the door."

"Well, I'm terribly sorry if I'm not as courteous as all your undead acquaintances."

"Courteous?" Kit asked. "What?"

He ran a hand through his hair. I could've told him that was a bad idea. It already looked like there was some sort of localized tornado going on directly above his head.

"I've obviously upset you in some way," he said carefully. "Tell me how."

"All human girls are upset when they're broken up with!" I yelled at him.

Did vampires take it easily? I guess they had a lot of experience. Centuries of experience getting rejected. After a while you wouldn't even raise an eyebrow in response to the latest dumping.

Oh yes, Cathy was so right, vampirism was a dream come true.

Kit stared at me. "Broken up with? I didn't break up with you!"

Technically, that was true. Because technically we

hadn't been going out. But I didn't think it was very gentlemanly of him to point that out. Had Francis taught him nothing?

"You said you'd call!"

"Yes," Kit said. "Because I was going to call you. Did I not call soon enough? I was about to call you when you showed up at my shade."

It was my turn to stare at him. "You were about to call me? But you said 'I'll call you.'"

"Yes," Kit said. "You haven't gone deaf, have you? Or stopped understanding English? Because you're not making any sense."

"When a guy says 'I'll call you,' it means they're not going to call you. It means they're dumping you."

"What?" Kit said. "I said I was going to call *because* I was going to call. Why would anyone say that if they weren't going to? That's completely insane! How do humans even function as a society? That's like me going to the cheese store and saying 'Oh, hello, I'd like to buy some cheese with this money of mine,' and getting arrested for shoplifting brie! Actually, I don't think my cheese metaphor makes sense, though compared to 'I'll call you' meaning 'get out of my life,' it's crystal clear. But that's because humans don't make any sense! None!"

He stopped, out of breath.

"Oh," I said in a small voice.

The knot in my chest eased a little. The fact I hadn't been dumped was the only good news I'd had all day.

"It's a whole thing," I continued, in the same small voice. "When a guy says, 'I'll call you,' and he doesn't say when—that means he won't call you."

Kit pulled his phone out of his pocket and pressed a couple of buttons. My phone vibrated in my pocket. I fished it out, smiling.

"Madness," Kit whispered softly into his phone. "I meant I'd call you. This is me calling you."

We stood staring at each other over the handlebars of my bike on the phone to each other.

"Cathy and I just had an enormous fight," I said. "And Rebecca Jones is dead. So she can't have kidnapped Dr. Saunders. So where is he? Is he even alive? Don't even think about mentioning amnesia. And I can't tell Anna any of this. And Cathy's going to become a vampire, like, tomorrow. And I still don't know what college to go to, or what I'm going to be when I grow up. And I thought you'd dumped me."

Kit pushed the handlebars aside and wrapped his arms around me. It felt warm and wonderful and uncomfortable because my bike was between us. I placed it gently on the sidewalk. Then we held each other even tighter. Kit stood in the gutter and leaned down and our mouths were touching. The intensity of the kiss pushed the cold and sadness away.

"I didn't dump you," Kit whispered, pulling me closer. "I didn't even realize we were going out. But if we are, I'm glad."

"I see that," I said, kissing him again.

"We'll fix this," he said. "You'll fix it."

The next kiss was deeper and warmer than the last.

"I should get home," I said, not wanting to in the least. "My parents will be worried." I pulled my phone out to check the time. "Possibly also mad."

"I'll walk you," Kit said.

It was only two blocks away, but our progress was slow. Slow and glorious. It took us another twenty minutes to say good-bye outside my house.

"Good-bye," I said yet again.

"Bye," Kit said.

We were still holding hands. I moved a step up; Kit moved one down.

"Do you want to go somewhere with me early tomorrow morning?" I asked, taking one more step. We were holding on with the tips of our fingers. "Very early?"

"Will it be as exciting as our visit to the Center for Extended Life Counseling?"

"I hope not," I said.

Our fingers slipped apart, and Kit ran halfway down the street, where he stopped, fished keys out of his pocket, and opened the door to a battered-looking car.

Kit had a car?

That might come in handy.

◆

Kristin called me that night to talk about her latest breakup, which was with a girl called Elspeth Moonfeather (not her real name) who had six gargoyle tattoos.

"No more crazy wenches!" Kristin said, as she always did. Yet somehow the next girl was usually even more insane. "So," she added. "How's your love life? I have heard reports from a very reliable source that you now have one."

"You mean Lottie," I said.

Our brother is not a reliable source of anything except amazingly terrible farts. And ridiculous gossip, apparently.

"I may mean Lottie," Kristin said airily. "He may have also mentioned this boy is called Kit, and you looooove him. That'd be a direct quote."

"Augh," I said.

"Oh wow," said Kristin, sounding all of a sudden incredibly overexcited. "You didn't deny it."

"I deny it!" I told her instantly. "I am not, and hope I never will be, in looooove with anyone. I deny it absolutely. I am in utter and complete denial." I paused. "Uh. Scratch that. Don't snicker at me!"

Kristin snickered. I was lying on my bed, staring at the ceiling. I pounded my head against the pillow a few times.

"I may be kind of seeing someone," I said. "Sort of. His name may, in fact, be Kit. But it's not serious. I mean, it can't possibly go anywhere. He was raised by vampires. He doesn't even know anything about humans. He was under the impression that human girls want to have sex all the time and he had to tell me he wanted to wait."

"There are human girls who *don't* want to have sex all the time?" Kristin asked. "They do with me. Huh. I guess I should just put that down to my irresistible charm and good looks."

"He's going to become a vampire himself in a couple months."

"Ah," Kristin said. "Well. That is a problem. I know how you feel about vampires."

"What?" I asked. "Why does everyone keep acting as if I have a problem with vampires? I don't have a problem with vampires. You said Cathy shouldn't be dating a vampire. You agreed with me!"

"Well, sure," said Kristin. "I think vampire groupies are dumb. And I know Cathy gets way too intense and serious about things, and getting intense and serious about a vampire seems like a terrible idea. But I'm not saying I'd never date a vampire. You, though, Mel. You love to laugh. Not to mention you're always fierce about your friends, and the way you saw it, a vampire hurt Anna. None of those things are bad! It just means you are less likely than anyone I know to be Team Vampire."

It didn't sound as bad when Kristin said it. Not like it had when Cathy had been yelling at me.

But then, Kristin couldn't stop being my sister. While apparently Cathy could decide to stop being my friend.

"This is why I'm delighted about Kit!"

"Uh," I said. "Sorry, I can't make any sense of what

you just said. Possibly because it makes no sense!"

"Well, you know," Kristin said, "you tried dating Ty because you were such good friends, even though it was pretty clear neither of you were that into each other. Then you got burned by that jerk Ryan, may he be afflicted with pustules. You've not had much luck in love, which has made you cautious, which is reasonable. Totally reasonable. But now Cathy is not being cautious. She's never been serious about a guy before, right? It's scaring you. Do you think that's part of why Francis freaked you out so much?"

"No. You haven't met Francis. He's freaky."

"What I'm trying to say is that you concentrate on your friends," Kristin said. "And that's awesome. But I also think it's awesome that you've met a guy and you're seeing him in spite of the fact that it's totally not sensible. Raised by vampires, Mel! That is nuts!"

"Well, yes, but—he makes me laugh. Like, a lot."

"Oh, Lancelot was so right," Kristin said. "Listen to you, this is precious."

"Shut up."

"You really like him, don't you?"

I thought about Kit, about everything he'd told me about his shade, about his life. About how whenever I smiled, he smiled back at me, brilliant and amazed.

"On the understanding that there will be no follow-up questions," I said, "yes. I like him. A lot. But I'll tell you something. He gets any gargoyle tattoos or changes his name to Moonfeather, he's so dumped. And since it can't go anywhere, can we talk about something else?"

"How's Cathy?" Kristin asked.

My throat had gone tight at the thought of Kit's smile, how that smile would vanish off the face of this world when he became a vampire.

It closed up almost entirely at the thought of Cathy.

"Can we talk about something even more else?" The tone of my voice sounded odd even to me.

Kristin must have agreed, because for once she didn't push.

"How are things on the Anna front?"

"Not good," I replied, thinking of all that I suspected and everything I feared. "But someone gave me a clue today. I know what I'm going to do next. And you know I always feel better when I'm doing something."

CHAPTER THIRTY-THREE

What We Found in the Basement

Kit had a car, but he was not a very good driver. On the short drive from my place to the school, he barely took his foot off the brake, causing the car to shudder in a way that could not have been good for it.

"Who taught you to drive?" I asked, trying not to clutch the seat. I had been imagining a much more romantic trip. "Francis?"

Kit laughed. "No, Francis hates cars. June taught me."

"June?"

"Also in our shade. She's the youngest. Other than me, I mean. She turned in the 1950s."

"Which is when this car is from, right?"

"Seventies, I think. It's a Ford Country Sedan. That's why it's so roomy. Though it breaks down a lot. Just got it out of the shop the other day. Exhaust pipe fell off."

I believed it.

"June's the only one who likes cars. Not that she drives much anymore. No point really. In the city, vampires can move about as fast as a car."

They can certainly go faster than this one, I couldn't help thinking.

Kit slammed on the brakes because a traffic light had turned red half a mile ahead.

"Um," I said. "I don't think you need to stop quite this soon."

"Oh, right," Kit said, cheerfully, easing his foot off the brake a little and causing the car to make its shuddering way to the traffic light, which was now green.

Fortunately, Craunston High was just around the corner. Kit did his version of parking and we both got out of the car. Me more shakily than him. We walked the block to the school in silence.

Kit was staring at my high school as if it was something awe-inspiring and strange. The pale morning sunlight made the chunky redbrick building sitting squatly in front of us look slightly less hideous than usual.

"So hundreds of you go here all at once?" he asked, his voice wondering. Because going to Craunston was so mysterious and exotic, as opposed to being homeschooled by vampires.

"Thousands," I told him. "Well, two thousand, but that still earns the plural."

"Wow," Kit breathed. "That's a lot of high school students. How do you remember everyone's name?"

"You don't," I said. "Just the ones in the same classes as you."

"Huh," he said, looking overwhelmed.

"Yeah," I said. "It's handy to have people around for gym."

"Yeah," Kit said, and as well as looking weirded out, he looked a little wistful. "That does sound like fun."

"But I bet you learn a lot more history than we do."

"Also waltzing," said Kit, grinning.

I raised my eyebrows. "How could I forget?"

Anna hadn't seemed at all sure about it, but she had given me the keys to the school when I'd promised her that I would return them as soon as I could. I'd also assured her that I was a mere step from finding out what was going on with her mother and that I would tell her everything as soon as I was sure.

She'd run out to give me the keys still wearing her pajamas, with her hair a red riot around her face. We'd hidden behind Principal Saunders's SUV to make the exchange, crouching down by her sandy tires as if we were spies.

I couldn't tell her what I suspected. I wasn't even sure I suspected it anymore. Cathy was right. The leap from what I knew to Principal Saunders being a murderer was a big one.

My hands shook a little as I fitted the key into the lock of the front door.

"So," Kit said, bouncing nervously behind me. "You want me to come look at this basement with you."

"Yes," I said. "Your mother interrogated me about the time a huge flood of rats came bursting out of there. She made it seem important."

"Rats?" Kit said. "That's not normal, is it?"

"No, it's really not."

Kit followed me closely as we went down the halls, eyeing the art projects lining the walls with fascination.

"Anna's mom is the principal. She should have been where the students were, trying to make us leave in an orderly fashion, getting us not to panic," I continued. "Or she should have been the one making announcements. She wasn't doing any of that. She was down in the basement, getting her tights all ripped up. Why? What was she doing down there? Why did your mom ask so many questions about that day?"

"Are you sure you want to be the one going down there? It could be dangerous. We could ask Mom—"

"No," I said.

I didn't think Camille would be pleased to hear from me again. Not to mention we probably wouldn't find anything. I had no idea what we were looking for.

There might also have been a tiny part of me that wanted to do this myself. If Cathy could see me now, breaking into a school on a Saturday morning intent on searching the basement, she wouldn't think I was such a sheep.

My thoughts of showing Cathy stuttered to a halt as I remembered everything she'd said. I stopped. Kit took my hand in his, pulled me to him, and held me tight. "It's just a basement, right?"

"Right."

It was extremely unlikely that if Dr. Saunders had murdered her husband, she would have buried him in the school basement. But it didn't hurt to have a look around, did it?

I went to the door at the bottom of the stairs where Cathy and Francis had once stood and sorted through the keys, trying first one and then another, the jangle very loud in the silence of the school.

When the right key turned in the lock, I heard Kit suck in his breath. I opened the door.

It looked very dark down there. I could barely make out the flight of steps.

I was glad I'd asked Kit along, because otherwise I might have chickened out. Instead I pulled my small-but-more-powerful-than-the-light-of-my-phone flashlight out of my pocket and turned it on.

See, Cathy? I told her in my head. I can think ahead. I can be prepared! Sheep don't use flashlights.

I took one step, then another, carefully walking down the stairs.

Halfway down, the entire room burst into brilliant light. I gasped.

"Er, sorry," Kit said from the top of the stairs. "But

there was a switch right here. It's easier to move around when you can see everything."

"Right, yes," I said. "Thank you."

The basement was not in the most pristine shape. It smelled dank and moldy, though the stairs and floor showed signs of recent cleaning. I guessed by the clean-up crew after the Ratocalypse. They hadn't done a great job. But at least there were no rat corpses.

"I have to say, the beach is winning as the best date location," said Kit from behind me, "by a lot."

We were in a giant gray room with bare brick walls. Why use up the budget on painting the basement? There were cobwebs everywhere, and naked old pipes crowded the low ceiling and tops of the walls. Most of the room was filled with old desks and chairs and piles and piles of boxes. All of it liberally covered in dust.

The janitor had his own office and staff and several ground-floor storage rooms for cleaning supplies and tools. I imagined he and his staff only ventured down here to dump stuff. It certainly looked like it.

The floor was concrete. I decided that was a good sign. It would be awfully hard to bury someone in a concrete floor without a jackhammer, and Principal Saunders could hardly show up at school with a jackhammer and a corpse. Wouldn't she also need a cement mixer to make the cement to fill in the hole? They weren't the most fashionable accessories. Somebody would have noticed. Not to mention the noise. No such thing as a stealthy jackhammer.

"Seriously," Kit said. "I loved the beach."

"I may take you someplace fancy next time," I told him. "But you'll have to dress all pretty for me."

I looked up and caught Kit's grin. It made me feel braver about moving on. I had to explore every inch of the basement. There was a large gap instead of a door at the far side of the room. "This looks like a corridor."

"And here," Kit said, "is another handy light switch." He flicked it and the corridor lit up, revealing more concrete floor and more old pipes along the ceiling. If anything, this one was even lower. Kit began to stoop. "So what exactly are we looking for?"

"I don't really know. Something unusual? Some signs that the floor has been disturbed?"

"How do you disturb concrete?" Kit kicked the ground with the heel of his shoe. "Feels pretty solid."

"It is. I'm probably barking up the wrong tree."

"But you have a theory, don't you?"

"Um," I said. I'd decided that the basement was starting to look a lot more cheerful. Nowhere to bury a body, and although some of the rooms we passed had junk in them, it was hardly enough junk to conceal a body.

"Come on, tell me."

"It's stupid and insane and probably wrong. I mean, hopefully wrong."

Kit adopted the traditional waiting position, crossing his arms across his chest and raising an eyebrow. His waiting stance was rendered somewhat awkward by his having to stoop his head.

"I think, no, I don't think, it's just a guess, a wrong guess, most likely."

"Go on."

If Cathy could talk calmly about a woman we'd known all our lives murdering her husband, so could I.

"What if Principal Saunders killed her husband and faked the whole running-away-with-Rebecca-Jones thing? And what if she buried the body down here? And what if when she was doing that, she disturbed the rats and that's why they invaded the school?"

All right. So not *that* calm.

"You're right," Kit said. "That's quite a leap. Why would that many rats freak out at someone burying a body? Wouldn't the rats happily eat the body?"

"Ugh. I don't know. Maybe. I'm not a rat expert. But trust me, I'm hoping my theory is totally wrong."

We hit the end of the corridor.

"I guess we have to start looking in these rooms," I said, flipping on the switch in the first one. Lots of junk. We walked in and started poking around. No bodies rolled out. Though a few dead moths did. Same in the next room and the next and the one after that. I was regretting not bringing a water bottle. It felt like my entire throat was coated with dust.

"Is that a piano?" Kit asked at the fifth room we investigated.

It was. Kit pulled off the cover and plunked at the

keys. We both grimaced.

"To call it out of tune is an understatement."

"Hey, is that a door behind it?" Kit asked.

It was. With surprisingly little effort—wheels on pianos, an excellent idea—we rolled the piano out of the way. The door opened easily, revealing a small room with an old boiler, and running from the boiler were more old dusty pipes.

In the shadow of the boiler, on the pipe, there was a flash of silver.

We walked into the room and flipped on the light switch, which did not work.

Time for the trusty flashlight. I'd been sure it would come in handy. I aimed the flashlight at the glint of silver as I knelt by the pipe, and realized I was looking at a few lengths of bike chain.

Except it was too long to be a bike chain. They were real chains.

In the shadowy corner of boiler and pipe, on the brick wall, there were crisscrossing lines. The bricks were scarred with long deep marks.

"Whoa, Mel," Kit said, in a low voice. I felt him lean against me, shoulder pressing solid and warm into mine. He took my hand, the one that was holding the flashlight, and held on tight.

There were four gouges in the wall like someone had made them with his hands.

In one of the deepest gouges, there was something

pale and irregularly shaped.

I pulled it out and shone the flashlight on my palm. It looked a lot like a fingernail.

Someone had clawed at this wall so desperately, he had left a fingernail behind, lodged in the brick.

If Dr. Saunders had told Principal Saunders he was leaving, and she'd decided she wasn't going to let him . . .

"She can't be keeping him prisoner. She can't be," I whispered. "She'd have to be totally crazy."

CHAPTER THIRTY-FOUR

Human Crazy, Vampire Crazy

"We have to tell Mom," Kit said.

I didn't argue with him. I was too busy trying to put a positive spin on what we'd seen. Maybe it had nothing to do with the Saunders family at all, but had been caused by someone else entirely. How long did it take for a fingernail to decompose?

"Mel? Mom really needs to know what we found down there."

"I know. But she's asleep, isn't she? We don't have to bug her right away. Also I have to return these keys to Anna."

"I can call and leave a message for Mom," Kit said.

He didn't ask me if I was okay. He didn't have to. My agitation was all too clear.

"Right, yes, do that."

Kit did that while I called Anna.

It wasn't a long drive. Ty was the only one of the four of us who didn't live in the neighborhood. In its own way, it was as cozy as the Shade was for vampires. Almost all my friends close together and close to school and . . . Principal Saunders couldn't really have been keeping her husband prisoner, could she?

The car shuddered along Anna's street. It felt like my brain was rattling in my skull. Why did Kit have to be such a bad driver?

When we reached the house, Anna was waiting outside, looking even more anxious than she had two hours earlier.

"I'm sorry, Anna," I told her, squeezing her hand. "We still don't know anything for sure."

"Except that the basement is very dirty." She gave me a small smile and pulled gray thread from my hair. Cobwebs, I realized.

Kit nodded, looking down at his dust-streaked jeans. "Very dirty."

"Lucky it's Saturday, and we don't have to rush off to school now," I said. "See you later, Anna?"

"Okay," Anna said. "You sure there's nothing you can tell me, Mel?"

Kit and I exchanged a look, neither of us meaning to.

"Mel? I know you've found something. Why can't you tell me?"

"Because I don't know what it means. Because I'm not sure. Because—"

"You don't think I'm strong enough?"

"No! No, not at all." I gave her an awkward hug, which she only half returned. "You're one of the strongest people I know. It's just that I'm—"

"She's an amateur," Kit said. "She doesn't know what she's doing and if she told you something that turned out to be wrong, or that she misinterpreted, she'd be causing you unnecessary pain."

Anna didn't say anything, but it was plain that Kit's words hadn't relieved her anxiety any. The opposite, more like.

She didn't ask me any more questions. "I'll see you later," she said, and walked back inside her house. I wondered if her mom was home. Or if she was off some-where— No, I had to stop thinking like that. Anyway, I knew Principal Saunders was in the house. Her new truck with the sandy tires was still in the driveway.

Poor Anna. I was starting to think that my investigating was a terrible idea and had only made everything worse for my friend.

"So," Kit said, breaking into my thoughts. "Where to now?"

I'd had something to do today, before I'd found out about chains and craziness. I'd had a plan.

For a moment my mind was terrifyingly blank, and then I remembered.

"I have to go talk to Cathy's mom."

I had to do something, or I'd go crazy.

"Are you cool with me tagging along?"

"Of course."

He started to walk to his car and I grabbed his arm. "Mind if we walk? It's such a lovely day."

"Okay. You don't think it's too cold?"

"It's nice and brisk. Thanks for sticking with me."

"Pleasure," Kit said. He leaned down and kissed my mouth lightly. I wished there was time for more. Instead I took a deep breath of the cold air.

"It'll be good for you to see more human stuff." I tried to keep my voice neutral.

I'm not very good at neutral.

"So my mom always says. But fingernails embedded in basement walls? It's true I haven't seen much of that in the Shade," Kit said. "But I really wasn't prepared for it to be a regular part of human life."

"Very funny," I said, even though it wasn't.

"Sorry," Kit said, looking down.

"It's not you. We will have a normal date very soon," I promised. "Things are not usually this . . ." I waved my arms around, trying to find the right word.

"Crazy?"

"It is crazy, isn't it? I suppose vampires are all so cool-headed and unemotional, they never get into crazy situations."

Kit started laughing. Then he kept laughing. Harder

and harder. He laughed so much, he had to sit down on the curb, two blocks from Cathy's house.

"What?"

Kit tried to answer, but he was laughing too hard.

His laughter was so contagious, I started to giggle even though I wasn't entirely sure what at. Kit slowly started to recover. He held out his hand, and I helped pull him up.

"I was thinking of the last fight Albert and Minty had. Over a teapot. It lasted months. Then there's all the bizarre love triangles Marie-Therese keeps getting mixed up in. The triangle is her favorite shape. Also instrument. Then there's Francis and his book. And lots more, of course."

"So there's crazy all over?" I said.

Not that I had ever doubted it. Personally, I would have said that vampires outcrazied humans, but at this point I was willing to admit that it might be a tie.

Kit nodded. "Vampire crazy, human crazy. I'm sure if we could talk to birds or snails, we'd discover their brands of crazy."

"No doubt."

"So Cathy's mom? You planning to get her to join your campaign to stop Cathy from transitioning?"

I raked a hand through my hair. More cobwebs came off on my fingers. "Cathy says her mom's given her permission to apply for a license while she's still underage."

"Ah," said Kit. "My mom wouldn't give me permission to do that, and my mom is a vampire. Cathy's mom must be an unusual lady."

"Oh," I replied, "she is."

CHAPTER THIRTY-FIVE

Eternal Youth and
Endless Nodding

We stood outside Cathy's house. During the day it looked even more run down.

"That's quite a pile," Kit observed.

I hadn't ever thought about it like that. I was too used to it. But the old Beauvier house had once been majestic. It was still one of the biggest houses in the neighborhood. More than three times the size of my house. It had been built with servants' quarters and stables.

Cathy's ancestors had had loads of money, but it had disappeared sometime around her grandfather's day. Now the stables and servants' quarters had been converted into residences and the lands were gone. All that remained was the old house, surrounded on all sides by smaller houses, looking shrunken and forlorn.

What had once been the most commanding balcony for miles now sagged in the middle. The imposing white columns had lost most of their paint and were more green mold than white paint. The steps leading up to the house were broken and uneven, with weeds growing in the cracks. If someone had told you the Beauvier house was haunted, you would not be surprised. Cathy's mom insisted her great-great-grandmother Isabelle liked to float around in the old ballroom. Though neither Cathy nor I had ever seen her.

"It's amazing," Kit said. "No wonder she's interested in Francis. He'd fit right in here. You'll be shocked to hear he doesn't hold with new architecture. By which he means anything built after he transitioned."

"Wouldn't he *tsk-tsk* the fact that it's about to collapse?"

"Oh, no," Kit observed cheerfully. "He's always bemoaning the lack of proper ruins in the New World. By which he means European ruins. Specifically Roman. Aztecs need not apply. So, are we going in? Or are we going to stand here and make bets on how long before the balcony collapses?"

It was possible that we had been standing there for a little while. Okay, maybe twenty minutes.

"I'm gearing up."

"You're worried about running into Cathy, aren't you?"

"No, no. She has an all-day Go tournament."

"Go? The Japanese game?"

I nodded.

"Figures. Francis loves it. It's about the only non-European thing he does love. He tried to teach it to me one time. I'm not really a games kind of person. But at least it wasn't as bad as chess."

"Nothing is," I said. "Cathy's been playing it for years. She's a junior champion."

"They really are made for each other, aren't they?"

I didn't say anything.

"Sorry," Kit said.

"No, it's okay. I can see that they have a lot in common. I just don't think that's enough of a reason for her to . . ."

"Become a vampire," Kit completed for me.

"Maybe you should wait outside? No, wait, you should come with me! Er . . . because I'm sure Cathy's mom would want to meet you. I've known her all my life. She's interested in my life, in who my friends are."

"You're nervous."

"No, I'm not," I said, marching up the stairs and losing my footing twice, narrowly avoiding a fall. Kit, being much taller, took them three steps at a time. "Show-off," I muttered.

The front door opened before we reached it.

"Hello, Mel," Cathy's mom said, in her usual vague, smiling way, as if she was pleased but puzzled by the whole world. "Cathy's not here."

"I know. I came to see you. This is Kit."

"Ah," she said, brightening slightly. "The boy who was raised by vampires. How fascinating. Do come in."

She ushered us into the parlor, muttered something about cookies, and then disappeared. Cathy's was the only house I'd ever been in that had a parlor.

The windows looked out on the street. The room was filled with furniture that smelled—and looked—as old as the house. When we sat down, puffs of dust went up in the air. Kit let out a sneeze, and I valiantly suppressed mine.

"Not big on cleaning, are they?"

"It's just the two of them and there are a lot of rooms. They don't normally use the parlor. I guess she thinks you're special."

"Awesome," Kit said, and he sneezed again.

Cathy's mom returned with a silver platter piled with a plate of cookies and two glasses of milk.

"Do you like living with vampires, young man?" she asked, sitting down.

"Kit," he said. "My name's Kit."

"Do call me Valerie," said Cathy's mom. She was that kind of mom: She wanted you to call her by her first name and act a little like a friend. Sometimes I suspected it was so she didn't have to be a responsible adult.

Kit coughed, instead of calling her anything at all. "I do like living with vampires. Not that I've ever lived with anyone else. But they've been very good to me."

She leaned forward, knees on her elbows. "Do you think my daughter will be happy as a vampire?"

"Er," Kit said. "It's hard to know. The vampires I live with are happy. Mostly. I mean no one's happy all the time."

"She's very happy right now. I've never seen her so happy. Her Francis seems like a good man."

"He is," Kit said, looking at me nervously.

"He's like a father to you, isn't he?"

Valerie said it as if that was a good thing, her eyes brightening, as if Cathy's boyfriend should be like a father to someone her own age, because that wasn't creepy at all.

Kit bit his lip. "Er, well," he said awkwardly. "He's taught me many things."

Like waltzing.

"Don't you think he's too old for Cathy?" I asked, staring at Valerie and willing her to be a real parent for a change.

Cathy's mom nodded. "I did worry about that. It's more than a century and a half since he changed. Though he was only seventeen when it happened. I think he has a young soul. And Cathy has such an old soul. They seem to have evened out."

I took a deep breath. "Why did you agree to let her apply for the license early? She could have waited a few months!"

I hadn't meant to yell.

Cathy's mom nodded again. She had the very annoying habit of saying yes or nodding even when she was disagreeing with you. "She could have waited," Valerie said. "But is it right, to ask love to wait?"

"Love should wait," I said between my teeth. "If it's the right thing to do. She would have to wait if you refused permission."

"Yes," Cathy's mother said, a little sadly, as if it was out of her hands.

It wasn't out of her hands. Cathy's life was in her hands. "You could still withdraw your permission. She hasn't applied yet."

Valerie leaned forward again, drawing close this time as if she was going to pat me.

"Mel," she said, "you've been Cathy's friend for so long. Can't you be happy for her? Becoming a vampire is a great honor, you know. Some would say she's been blessed: to stay young forever, perfect forever, to defy the passage of time."

Cathy's mother looked around the parlor, her eyes trailing over those dusty tables. I thought of the balcony on the front of their house, sagging like an old, disappointed mouth, and felt dread because I saw that Cathy's mom might believe she was doing the best for her daughter, making sure she never grew old.

"She's only seventeen," I whispered.

"I remember what it was like to be seventeen. I was so impatient. In a hurry for my life to begin, and it all went by so fast," Valerie said. "Sometimes I still can't quite believe it. Cathy is so much more mature than I was. She makes me proud."

"I bet," I said. I couldn't help thinking that Valerie's own immaturity was a big part of why Cathy was so grown up for her age. She'd been looking after her mother all her life. "She's sure to get into Oxford. She has a perfect GPA and SATs. She'll probably win the Go tournament today. She's the smartest person I know."

"Yes," Cathy's mom said. "She's brilliant."

I heard my voice get louder than I'd intended. "So don't you think it's, I don't know, a bit of a waste for her to throw her life away?"

"Oh, yes," Cathy's mom said. Her yes-means-what-ever-I-want-it-to-mean strategy had never been so annoying. "*If* she was throwing her life away. But Mel, Cathy is so brilliant. I try to let her go her own way. She's never let me down yet. Would you like another cookie?"

Given that I hadn't touched my first cookie, I declined. I had forgotten how impossible she was to talk to.

"What school do you attend, Kit?" she asked, as if this was a social call and Cathy's life or death a subject that could be changed, as if we were debating the weather.

"I'm homeschooled," Kit said carefully, eyeing me as if he was afraid I might explode.

He may have had some basis for that fear.

"If you refused your permission," I said, "then Cathy would have to wait. You'd be making sure she doesn't rush into this enormous decision."

"Rushing is never good," Valerie said pensively. "I don't believe my Cathy would rush into anything. You can't blame her for wanting this. We all want it: the promise of eternal love."

"I don't blame her," I told Valerie, and I was trying not to. "Please, will you'll talk to her? About rushing?"

"Cathy and I talk all the time," Cathy's mom said. She stood up. "I must buy groceries. You're welcome to stay until you finish your milk and cookies. Lovely to meet you, Kit," she said, shaking his hand.

She bent to kiss my cheek.

"Will you even consider withdrawing permission?" I asked desperately.

Cathy's mother's hands were light on my shoulders. "I simply do not feel as if it is my decision to make," she murmured. "Not truly. And Mel, if you don't mind my saying so? I don't think it's yours, either."

CHAPTER THIRTY-SIX

Whatever Happened to Lily Jane?

"Well, that was—"

"A total waste of time?" I said. "Yes, I noticed." We walked away from Cathy's house. I was trying not to stomp or kick the grass. I didn't think it was my decision. How could she say that? I just wanted Cathy not to make the biggest mistake of her life!

Kit patted me on the back. "Not a total waste of time," he said. "We both scored cookies."

It surprised a laugh out of me. "I didn't even eat mine."

"That's okay," Kit assured me. "I had three. One for you, one for me, and one for luck."

I laughed again. I was glad Kit was with me. If he hadn't been, I probably would have started stomping. I didn't know where we were heading. Away was enough for the moment. I lifted my face to the crisp blue sky and took a clean, cold breath of morning air.

"Cathy's mom has always been strange," I said. "But I never thought she'd agree to Cathy becoming a vampire. I thought she loved Cathy. What kind of a mother would do that?"

Kit said nothing.

"To let her take such a risk!" I said. "Cathy could *die*. How could she say her daughter would be better as a vampire? That it's okay for Cathy to give up everything! To give up laughing—to give up being herself! It's like she's saying Cathy's not okay the way she is now. What kind of a mother would say that?"

"Don't you think that's a bit simplistic?" Kit asked, and it dawned on me that his mother was also allowing him to become a vampire.

"Oh," I said. "Oh, Kit. Crap. I didn't mean that. I'm sure it's different for Camille. I mean she *is* a vampire. Cathy's mom is human, so—so crap."

"Ah, the compelling 'so crap' line of argument," Kit said. "A classic."

His smile was stretched up too tightly at the corners.

I congratulated myself on my famous tact. (People stop and stare and whisper, "There's Mel Duan. Born completely devoid of the tact gene. A miracle of science." See? Famous.)

"I'm so sorry, Kit," I said. "Don't listen to me. I'm not doing Cathy any good. I'm not doing Anna any good. I'm not doing myself any good. I don't even know what I want to study in college. I have no idea what I'm doing."

"Hey, you're seventeen," Kit said. "Some of the most interesting people I know are two hundred and seventeen and still don't know what they're doing with their lives. You care about Cathy. She knows that. See? You're doing fine."

"Really?" I said.

"Sure. I think you're wrong about vampires. But Cathy probably is rushing things." Kit coughed. "I've been thinking about transitioning my entire life, and yet since I met you and threw up due to zombies, I've discovered it's a bigger decision than I thought. There's more to being a vampire than I realized. More to being a human, too. How long has Cathy been thinking about it? A few weeks. You *should* be concerned. You're a good friend. As for Anna, sure, you're doing her good. We detected stuff today, didn't we? I mean, you detected chains and fingernails, and I sidekicked like a pro. Am I right?"

He kicked the side of my sneaker lightly with his own, and I looked up and saw a real smile.

"I thought your sidekicking needed maybe a bit more practice," I said, grinning slyly up at him. "But you do show some natural talent. We'll work on it together."

✦

We had to kill time until Camille woke up. We must have walked all over the city talking about almost everything.

Kit had a ton of questions about my life and my family, what I liked to do for fun.

But, unlike Francis's, his questions weren't about research. They were about me.

Also, Kit laughed at all my jokes.

I told him about fencing, and attempted a demonstration with an invisible saber that earned me some funny looks.

We blew our allowances on hamburgers and fries and way too much ice cream. As dusk fell, we were walking through Lily Jane Memorial Park on our way to the Shade. Lily Jane is my favorite park. A big stretch of real grass, excellent for playing Frisbee or soccer or anything else you wanted to play on a long summer's day.

Lily Jane Boothby was a little kid in the 1910s with spina bifida. The Boothbys were important people in New Whitby back then. She was dying, and she got turned. The Boothbys had enough money that all the people objecting to six-year-old vampires forgot their objections and wandered off to spend their new money.

It was a mess.

Lily Jane killed fifteen people, including her mother, before the vampires came out of the Shade and took her down.

That was when vampire law enforcement changed from being a motley volunteer bunch to becoming an official branch of the police force. It was also when all the age restrictions were laid down. No one under fourteen gets turned—even terminal patients. You know how most kids don't understand why they can't have another cookie? Well, superpowerful kids who never grow up tend to be really bad at understanding why they can't have another delicious, person-shaped cookie.

Also, I imagine babysitters are hard to find.

Mr. Boothby built the park as an apology to New Whitby, and maybe as an apology to his daughter, too.

There are flower beds in overlapping circles all around the circumference, and at the back of the park, near one of the benches, there's a statue of Lily Jane.

"She's cute," I said.

Kit nodded. "Sad story."

Birds started to sing. Kit fished his phone out of his pocket.

"Hi, Mom," he said.

I stood looking at the statue of the little girl, with her stone curls and her hands spreading her skirts in a minicurtsy, while Kit talked to Camille. I may have been slightly eavesdropping, more on his tone than what he was actually saying: His voice went from pleased to quiet and concerned to surprised and a bit annoyed, and then to subdued in the way everyone gets when their mom yells at them.

"What—what did she say?" I asked.

"She said they're totally aware of the situation. She knows what was in the basement," Kit said. "And we're to stop messing around with things that don't concern us."

He went over and kicked the base of Lily Jane's statue.

"I mean," he continued, "what the hell? Mom's a

policewoman. They're the police. Isn't the whole definition of the police 'People who deal with chains and fingernails and don't leave them lying around looking suspicious and terrifying'? How are they dealing with it by ignoring it? This makes no sense!"

I looked at Kit, and at the statue of Lily Jane, and thought about the police. It *was* weird. I mean, surely that was enough evidence to call Principal Saunders in for questioning. Dr. Saunders's supposed vampire lover was dead, he was missing, his wife was behaving suspiciously, but the authorities hadn't done anything about it. Why? Then I remembered what Cathy had said about the investigation, about how it might not be official.

"Did Camille say it was an official investigation?"

"What? Um, no, I guess not. Not in so many words."

"Maybe it isn't one. Maybe your mom's doing this on her own time. I mean, Francis is her undercover cop. He's not exactly undercover material, is he?"

Kit laughed.

"What if she hasn't been able to investigate the school herself? What if she doesn't have enough evidence?"

Kit considered. "Mom's pretty thorough. Even when she's not doing an official investigation. I mean, Mom's thorough about how she makes tea."

"What if your mother left the evidence there so—so Principal Saunders wouldn't know she was being watched?"

"Why?"

My brain was suddenly whirring, things falling into place at last.

"Because she doesn't want Principal Saunders to think they're on to her? What if they're lulling her into false confidence? What if they want her to lead them to something?"

"But you said she seems to know that Francis is spying on her—" Kit began.

"Maybe she doesn't actually *know* it. Maybe she's not sure, so she's just all jumpy because of her guilty conscience and because she really doesn't like vampires."

I stepped in closer, grabbing Kit's arm. "What if they want her to lead them to Dr. Saunders?" I whispered. "Wherever she has him hidden."

Or buried, said a tiny terrible voice in my mind, but I refused to listen to it.

Principal Saunders had been down there, the day the rats came. The chains being down there could not be a coincidence. She must be doing something wrong.

I wanted Dr. Saunders to not only be alive but to be okay. I wanted Anna to get her father back. I wanted Cathy to see them reunited and to see that I was right sometimes, that I could take care of my friends.

CHAPTER THIRTY-SEVEN

Taking a Running Leap
Down the Rabbit Hole

We hadn't even left the park when my phone let off its fire-alarm wail. Kit looked startled until I pulled the phone out and answered it.

"Hi, Anna," I said. "How are—"

"I found something," she replied. "Mel, you need to tell me what's going on. I think my dad's dead."

Anna sounded about as you might expect, having to say that. I gripped the phone hard. "Where are you?"

"At home," Anna said, her voice wavering. "Mom took off a few hours ago, and you'd left with the keys to the school, and when you came back and didn't tell me what happened, I got to thinking—"

"I'll be there as quick as I can. I'm still with Kit. Is it okay if I bring him?"

"Sure," Anna said, so fast I didn't even know if she'd taken in the information. "Whatever. Just get here."

"I'm running. Anna? It's going to be okay," I said, even though I wasn't sure of that at all.

"Anna's place again?" Kit said as I slipped the phone back into my pocket.

"Yeah. She thinks her dad is dead."

"Which he could be," he said, matching my pace.

"Maybe," I said. "Maybe not."

I felt so bad for Anna. Should I have told her my suspicions earlier? Now that Anna had said it aloud—*I think my dad's dead*—it seemed so much more real. At least I could truthfully tell her that the police, meaning Camille, were investigating. But would that be reassuring? Was anything reassuring when your dad might be dead? Murdered?

I didn't even want to think about how horrible it would be if Anna's mother was the one responsible. Anna would have nobody.

No, I told myself, and sped up. She'd still have me.

But I kept hearing Cathy's voice in my head, and I knew I wasn't enough. Nobody could be a good enough friend to make up for this discovery, and I was the one who'd helped her make it.

"Consider me faithfully sidekicking," Kit said when we had to stop to cross the road and he had breath to speak. "We'll figure this out." His smile flashed out at the same time as the walking-man light turned on. "You know, you're good at this."

"I'm a tireless crusader for truth and justice," I agreed. "Green means go. C'mon!"

We were running past the corner of Le Fanu Avenue and Third when Kit grabbed my elbow. I looked at him inquiringly. He'd been keeping up so far.

He didn't look out of breath, though. He looked serious.

"I was wondering," he said in a rush, as if he'd been holding the words back for a while. "After I become a vampire. I was wondering if you'd still want to see me."

"No," I said without pausing.

Kit stood stricken.

Not for the first time that day, I kind of wanted to punch myself in the face.

"I mean," I said, talking fast partly to get it all out and partly because I had to get to Anna, "I mean . . . I do mean no. I wish I'd put it in a nicer way. I get— I'm starting to get that vampires are people. I know Camille's your mom. She seems great. I don't want to say anything bad about them. But a vampire wouldn't be for me. Not growing up, not seeing the sun, not having every bit of life: laughter, food, the highs and the lows of being alive. That's something I don't understand and I never will. It's like choosing to watch a movie that's stuck on pause.

"I couldn't do it. And being *with* a vampire? You'd never laugh at any of my jokes. I'll turn eighteen, nineteen, twenty, thirty, forty, but Kit, you'll be a teenager forever."

Kit swallowed.

"So when Cathy becomes a vampire," he said, "she won't be your friend anymore?"

"Cathy's not going to become a vampire!" I yelled at him, as if by shouting loud enough I could make it true.

Kit stood there on the corner of two of the busiest streets in the city, people flowing past him, carrying shopping bags, hurrying off to a movie or dinner, living their human lives. He looked wretched.

"Cathy and I have been friends since we were tiny," I said after a moment. "We'll always be friends. Nothing can change that. But I've only just met you and—I couldn't stand it. I'm sorry."

"I've only just met you, too," Kit said. "I'm not going to change the whole course of my life—what I was always meant to be—for you. I can't. I'm sorry as well."

I guess there should have been a pause filled with regret then. But we didn't have time.

"C'mon," I said. "I mean, if you still want to?"

Kit nodded. "Anna's waiting. She needs us."

Cathy was willing to change her whole life for Francis. She would've said that if we weren't ready to change our lives for each other, then Kit and I weren't meant for each other. I guess that also meant it was best this way and there was no need to be upset.

My throat was tight. I was upset. Even if Kit wasn't the One.

"Let's get to Anna's," I said, and started running again. Kit ran beside me.

"Can I ask one more question?"

"Sure," I said, my voice less than steady. I hoped he'd think it was because I was out of breath from running.

"Why is your ring tone a fire alarm?"

✦

Kit had barely closed the door behind us when Anna started talking, her face red and crumpled from crying.

"As soon as Mom left," she said, "I just, I had to do something. I started looking for something, I don't know what, and I found . . . I found . . ."

She held out a phone. "My dad's."

"Oh," I said.

"It was in the garage. You know what a mess it is. In this box."

The box was at the foot of the stairs. On top was an old and battered copy of *Alice's Adventures in Wonderland*.

"The book was my dad's too. He would never run away without it. It was his mom's before, and her mom's before that. He takes it with us on every holiday. He's taken it on conference trips. He wouldn't leave it behind."

I looked down at the book. It was really old. I didn't know what to say.

"He wouldn't have left any of this stuff behind."

Least of all his phone. I'd been right: Someone else had sent those texts to Anna.

I wished I hadn't been right.

"None of this makes any sense," Anna said, and her voice wobbled all over the place. "He wouldn't not call me. He would tell me he was going. He would tell me face-to-face. My dad wouldn't disappear and then text me about it. He's not like that. But that means my mom is lying. Why would she lie to me? Why would she hide his stuff?"

I handed the phone to Kit and grabbed Anna in a big hug.

Her shoulder blades felt fragile under my hands. I held her as tight as I could. After a few moments, Anna hugged me back. She started to shake a little. She was crying, her tears making a warm, wet patch on my shirt.

I led her into the living room, still holding her, and we sat on the couch. Anna kept her head buried in my shoulder.

"Should I make some tea?" Kit asked, showing that he was indeed Camille's son.

Anna sat up and wiped at her face. Kit handed her a tissue from the box on the coffee table.

"It's okay," she said, blowing into the tissue. "I don't want tea. I want to know what's going on."

I told her what I knew and what I suspected from start to finish, including Francis and Camille's involvement, including Rebecca Jones's suicide, including the fingernail in the wall.

"Thank you," she said when I was finished. She was still crying. And really, who wouldn't be? I tried to imagine how I'd feel if it was my dad. My mind wouldn't go there.

"I can't believe I ever thought he ran away with that— that *monster*!"

Kit winced.

"What was I thinking? How could I doubt my own dad?"

I hugged her again. "Why would you doubt your own mom?" I asked, and then wished I hadn't.

Anna looked as if she might be sick. "What do you think is going on?"

"I don't know," I said.

"But you have a theory?"

I swallowed and then spoke. "Maybe your mom's keeping your dad somewhere. Hiding him?"

"Why would Mom do that?"

"I don't know," I said helplessly.

"Why would she lie to me about Dad running away with that thing?" Anna asked.

"I don't know," I repeated, realizing how much I didn't know. I'd been feeling so detectivey. I'd been proud of myself. I'd basked in Kit's praise. One look at Anna's face wiped all those feelings away. Nothing I'd done had helped Anna.

"What if they're holding him?" Anna demanded.

"The monsters. The other vampires. What if they've got him and they're holding him hostage, and my mom, she has to do what they say or they'll kill him?"

"What would they want her to do?" Kit asked. "Vampires aren't monsters. It's much more likely that she—"

"Stop it! Shut up!" I shouted. Kit's face was red, but he shut up. "We don't know what's going on," I told Anna, focusing all my attention on her, "but maybe if we could find your mom? Do you know where she went?"

Anna shook her head. "She just went. She goes off like this a lot. I mean ever since Daddy ran away— *disappeared*. She bought that new car and drives in it for hours."

"The SUV?" I asked.

"She said she bought it to cheer herself up. It didn't work."

"Have you noticed anything unusual in it? Well, not unusual, necessarily, but, um, I don't know, something else that would give us a hint of where she takes it? Like camping gear? Or—"

"Does she come back with mud on the wheels?" Kit asked.

"No," Anna said. "I don't think she takes it off-road. Or if she does, she cleans it before she comes home. But I did notice in the last few weeks there's been sand in it. Especially in front of the driver's seat."

I'd noticed sand on the tires as well.

"What kind of sand?"

"Like beach sand," Anna said. "Honeycomb Beach. Dad and Mom used to go there all the time before I was born. It was their place. The least popular beach. Always so cold and windy."

"With lots of caves," Kit said, looking at me.

"Right," I said. "Caves."

Kit pulled out his phone. "I'm calling Mom."

"Wait," I said. "Wait just a minute."

Anna looked at me with alarm. Kit looked at me as if he thought I was crazy.

None of us knew exactly what had happened. But we knew we were talking about a crime of some sort. I knew that I couldn't handle this. I knew we were going to have to call Camille, and that there was a real possibility I'd uncovered a secret that would ruin Anna's life.

I could hear Cathy's voice in my head, telling me what a terrible friend I was.

It might still be possible for something good to come from this hideous situation. We didn't know what had happened, but we knew that this Rebecca Jones had been involved with Dr. Saunders somehow, and lives had been ruined. I wanted Cathy to see where involvement with vampires could lead.

If nothing else could be saved from this wreck, I wanted to try to save Cathy. I wanted to have done some good.

"I'm going to call Cathy," I said slowly, "and ask her to meet us at Honeycomb Beach."

Kit continued to look at me as if I was crazy. "I think we need slightly more impressive backup than Cathy at this point."

"Kit, we're going to call Camille," I said. "Right after we call Cathy, and then a taxi."

"I can drive us. My car's still where we left it this morning. Outside."

"That's great," Anna said, because she had not experienced Kit's driving.

"Why are we calling Cathy?" Kit asked.

"I'd like us all to be there for Anna," I said, which was true but not the whole truth. "And Anna—Anna has a right to see what's happening."

"Mel's right," Anna said, straightening up and looking at Kit with a martial light in her eyes. He was outnumbered. "I am going to see. I'm not leaving this up to vampires. I'm not leaving this up to anybody. Let's go now."

CHAPTER THIRTY-EIGHT

Principal Saunders's Crime

Cathy came running when I told her that Anna was in trouble. By the looks of her dress and makeup, she'd been interrupted mid-date, but she hadn't said a word about that. I was relieved to see that she hadn't brought Francis with her—even as I wondered how she'd managed to keep his chivalrousness at bay.

We crammed into Kit's crumbling car—me and Kit in front and Anna and Cathy in the back—and snapped on seatbelts, and Kit stuttered the car slowly out of its ample parking spot and onto the road.

"Can you go a little faster?" Anna asked.

"Sure," Kit said, easing his foot off the brake a tiny bit. The car continued to jerk.

"Maybe," I said as patiently as I could, "if you drive

without your foot on the brake the whole time."

"You can do that?" Kit asked.

"Yes!" Cathy and Anna yelled in unison.

"Seriously, Kit," I said, trying not to sound like I was begging, "you'll be able to go a lot faster if you only put your foot on the brake when, you know, you want to stop."

"Really? 'Cause that's not how June taught me."

"June hasn't driven since the 1950s!"

Kit gingerly removed his foot from the brake. The jerkiness stopped at once. The car started moving faster and smoother.

"So," Cathy said tentatively. "Why are we heading out to Honeycomb Beach?"

Explaining what was going on was not fun. Anna kept bursting into recriminations against vampires. Kit bit his lip to keep from leaping to their defense. Anna's tears probably played a big part in keeping his mouth shut. She was barely holding it together. Then every so often Kit would forget about the new no-foot-on-brake-while-driving rule and we'd all yell at him. Somehow we arrived in one piece.

When we pulled into the parking lot, Principal Saunders's SUV was the lone car there. We'd been right. It didn't make me feel very good.

Night was closing in. The moon was a sharp silver curve in the sky, the bay and sea forming the same sharp silver curves around each other.

"We could wait for Mom here," Kit suggested.

Anna said nothing, heading toward the path to the beach. I was pretty sure she'd heard Kit.

"I can't believe this," Cathy breathed in my ear as we walked down the path. She was trying not to shiver in her short black lace dress as the full force of the ocean wind hit us.

"We shouldn't do anything until Mom gets here," Kit said.

Cathy looked uncertain and distressed, her long dark hair tumbled and streaming in the wind, like the heroine in one of those old gothic novels facing unknown dangers.

"I don't know," she said. "Maybe—maybe we should wait."

We all looked at Anna. She was standing a little apart with tears dripping off her nose and her face turned toward the sea.

"I want to talk to Mom," Anna whispered, her voice almost lost to the wind blowing from the sea. "I should call her so we can find out where she is—if she's hiding in one of those caves."

I cleared my throat. "Maybe it would be safer if we waited for Camille."

"Safer?" Anna echoed. "My mom's not going to hurt me! I want to talk to her. I don't want to do it in front of vampire police!"

"No," Cathy said soothingly. "No, Anna, of course—"

"I'm calling her now," Anna said, more definitely.

She took out her phone. It fell. Anna dropped to her

knees in the wet sand and seized it.

I went down on my knees beside her and grabbed her free hand, her fingers sandy and shaking in my palm.

"Anna," I said.

Anna hit her mom's number. She pressed the phone to her ear, but we could still hear the other end ringing clearly above the waves shushing each other on the shore.

It went on ringing for so long, I thought nobody was going to pick up. We'd be left here on the beach with no answers.

That might be all right, I thought, my heart thumping as loud in my ears as the ringing.

The phone clicked and Principal Saunders answered, her voice breathless and upset.

That wasn't what made me freeze, seawater seeping through the knees of my jeans. It was the sound of the sea, magnified by an echo coming through the line.

She really was here. We'd been right.

I'd never been so sorry to be right.

"Baby, this isn't a good—"

"Mom," said Anna, and began to cry like a storm breaking, in a desperate rush. "Mom, I need you. I don't understand anything, I can't— You have to come right now!"

"Anna!" Principal Saunders said. "Anna, what's wrong? I'll come right away. Tell me what—what's happening, has something happened?"

Anna was sobbing too hard to talk. I held on to her

hand as hard as I could. "Mom—Mom—"

"I'm coming!" Principal Saunders gasped, love and fear in her voice.

"She's coming," I said, low, but loud enough for the others to hear.

Kit and Cathy looked at me, and then all of us looked at the cliffs, searching along the wide gray curve of stone for movement.

I heard Principal Saunders's breath through the line, coming fast. I heard the sound of her pounding footsteps in the sand. It mingled with the sound of Anna's sobs.

I heard her scream.

Anna dropped the phone again. I stood up.

Principal Saunders came racing out of the caves, no more than fifty yards away. I saw the look of terror on her face. She ran so fast that she was kicking up a cloud of sand as she went.

"Anna!" she screamed, as if she didn't see the rest of us. "Anna, oh my God! Run!"

None of us ran. We all stood absolutely still: Cathy with her wide, sad eyes, Kit with every muscle tense as if he wanted to run but could not, Anna crouched there on the beach as the surf came in. And me, responsible for them all being here, frozen.

The only person moving on that beach was Principal Saunders, running as fast as she could toward her daughter.

Then there was something else moving on that beach.

He came stumbling out of the cave, staggering through the sand as if it was deep water. My brain didn't process it properly for a moment because it was a human shape, but the way he moved was all wrong. Arms swinging heavily from the sides, feet not placed so much as thrown, one ahead of the other.

Principal Saunders glanced over her shoulder and then back, even more terrified than before. But she didn't look scared for herself, though he was gaining on her.

"Anna!" she screamed. "Oh, Anna, don't look!"

Principal Saunders ran toward us.

What was left of Dr. Saunders ran too. I'd known him for years. He was a big guy, but he always looked apologetic about it, shoulders stooping a little beneath his checked shirts. He was one of the parents you could always sucker into money for ice cream, and he used to spend ages searching for his glasses while Cathy, Anna, and I doubled over in silent laughter because we could see them in his shirt pocket.

Now he was big like a lumbering beast, casting a dark shadow on the silver sand as he came after his running wife, toward his sobbing child.

His skin was mottled like a bruise, made up of dull shades of gray and purple and green. There was a dark, spreading stain of rot across that familiar shirt. His right hand shone in the moonlight where the gleam of bone stuck out from his fingertips.

I'd been right. Principal Saunders was keeping him

imprisoned. With Anna's call, she'd gotten scared and distracted, and now he was free.

He kept moving toward us.

"Cathy! Kit!" I yelled. "Go!"

I stood and tried to pull Anna to her feet. She didn't move, didn't seem to feel my grip on her wrist. So I put myself in front of her.

What had been Dr. Saunders was making a low, moaning sound. It seemed like the only sound on the beach. He went "Ah—ah—ah—ah!"

The sound of his voice was curdled. Everything was broken inside him.

Sometimes the process of turning into a vampire went wrong.

The moonlight fell on his empty eyes. They glowed like car headlights in his ruined face.

Principal Saunders reached us first and shoved past me, falling to her knees beside Anna.

There was nobody between me and the zombie. I heard Kit and Cathy both scream my name. Why hadn't they run?

I seized a piece of driftwood and held it in a fencing stance.

Don't ask me. I know it was stupid, but they were my friends, and I'd led them here.

Dr. Saunders's headlong stumbling run checked for a moment, as if he registered a weapon.

A moment was enough.

A dark shape hit him from behind, moving at vampire speed, faster than the wind. Camille tackled him into the sand.

She looked at me through her black hair, fangs glittering in the moonlight, the perfect picture of a vampire in a movie, and said in the most exasperated mom voice imaginable: "Mel, please step back."

I exhaled a ragged, disbelieving breath and did as she asked.

The rest of the Zombie Disposal Unit, all vampires, appeared as quickly as Camille. So did Francis, who must have zipped back to his house after his date had been broken up, found Camille leaving, and realized what his lady love and her friends were up to.

Francis went right for Cathy, taking her into his arms, murmuring into her hair.

Principal Saunders held Anna, both of them kneeling in water with the cold tide coming in, clinging tight as they sobbed.

In the moonlight the blood running down Principal Saunders's arm looked black.

She'd been feeding him, as well as keeping him in our school until his restless presence made the rats, who like all animals hated the undead, flee the building. She'd moved him to the caves and kept feeding him her blood, kept him chained so he could not hurt anybody.

I could put the pieces together now, now that it was no longer any use, now that the Zombie Disposal Unit was restraining him, covering him with a net that held him trapped and shuddering on the sand.

Rebecca Jones had meant to make him a vampire so he would be like her, maybe hoping he would stay with her.

It had gone wrong.

Principal Saunders had hidden her zombie husband, hidden him knowing the risk, lying through her teeth to everyone she knew.

When Kit touched my hand, the piece of driftwood fell out of my numb fingers. He looked the way I felt, tears falling down his face. I didn't think he was aware of them.

I squeezed his hand tight. He squeezed back, so hard I could feel my fingers again.

Then I heard Cathy saying, "Let go, darling. Francis, I need to be with Anna . . ." and I let go myself.

Cathy and I walked, splashing through the icy seawater, to where Anna was crouching with Principal Saunders.

Anna got up slowly. Her face under her crown of wet curls looked bewildered, like she'd woken to find the nightmare was real.

Cathy and I walked on either side of her, Principal Saunders behind her, guarding her back. All three of us together, we got her to the edge of the net. She stood shaking, looking down at the body still moving under the net.

The Zombie Disposal Unit, including Camille, fanned out in a circle at a respectful distance, with their heads bowed but their weapons ready. Francis and Kit were standing by the shoreline, Kit's head dropped onto Francis's shoulder.

It was just us near the zombie, listening to his moans.

And I understood why Anna had to go to him, and why Principal Saunders had done what she had done. At this moment, more like a nightmare than any other moment I'd ever lived through, I thought about love as something that endured through nightmares.

It took a while for a zombie's mind to go completely.

"Ah—ah," Dr. Saunders said thickly. "Ah—nah."

He was trying to say his daughter's name.

Anna said: "Yes, Dad. I'm here. Don't . . . don't be scared. I love you and . . ." Her voice wavered, almost broke. "Everything's going to be all right."

Camille killed him then. He was quiet. Everything was quiet for a little while on that silver shore, in the shadow of those cliffs.

CHAPTER THIRTY-NINE

The Temperature of Rooms

Cathy came back to my house. Neither one of us wanted to be alone, and since we weren't allowed to go with Anna and her mom, we turned to each other. We said little as Kit drove us home, not even when he reverted to his brake driving. We were too shocked. Besides, what was there to say?

I'd called and let my parents know what had happened. Dad wanted to drive out and pick us up. It took Camille telling him that Kit would get us home faster to stop him. Cathy's mom agreed to let Cathy stay over at my place on the promise that she come home first thing in the morning.

Mom greeted both of us with a huge hug. Dad too. Even my pesky brother hugged me. Though at that hour in the morning he should have been asleep. We all should have been.

The trundle bed in my room was already made up for Cathy. Dad's doing, I knew. It wasn't something Mom would have thought of. She's a big-picture person, Dad says. Not great at details. It made me feel sad for Anna all over again. Her dad was gone forever.

I lent Cathy a pair of pajamas. My treasured green polka-dotted flannel ones. Treasured because she'd given them to me.

We slid into bed and I shut off the light.

"Do you think she's going to be okay?" I asked.

"Yes," Cathy said. "I do." She yawned. We were both exhausted.

"Good night, Cathy," I said, wanting to believe her. "Thank you for coming tonight. I'm glad I'm not alone."

"Me, too. Good night, Mel."

I thought I would never sleep. I felt as if I had run a marathon after I'd been hit by a train. My eyes stung, they were so sore. But I couldn't stop thinking about Dr. Saunders.

What if I saw him in my dreams?

The skin sloughing from his decomposing flesh, the glint of white bone, the dull gray of his eyes.

Wonderful. I hadn't closed my eyes and I was already seeing him. How was I ever going to sleep again? How was Anna? How was she going to deal with what had happened to her father? With what her mother had done? At least she knew Principal Saunders had done it out of love. But still, she had seen her father as a zombie. Then she had seen him killed. How did you recover from that?

I lay there with my eyes open and stinging, trying to process everything that had happened, but it was too much. I shut my eyes and was asleep at once.

◆

I woke to dawn light coming through the window. Great, I thought, that must have been two or three hours, tops. But at least no nightmares had interrupted my sleep. I hoped Anna was as lucky.

I doubted she was.

"You awake?" Cathy asked.

"Barely," I said, but as soon as I said it, I was fully awake, the look on Anna's face as her zombie father tried to say her name clear in my mind.

"Poor Anna," Cathy said.

"And Principal Saunders. Imagine keeping that secret for so long. Imagine watching someone you love change like that."

We both shuddered.

"Do you think Anna will ever forgive me?" I asked, though I was also thinking about what Cathy must think of me now.

"Forgive you? For what?"

Cathy sounded honestly baffled.

"Showing her what happened to her dad. Meddling—"

"Principal Saunders's keeping her husband alive was hardly your fault, Mel."

"I know, but if I hadn't interfered—"

"Anna asked you to interfere. Besides, if you hadn't, he might not have been found in time. Principal Saunders might have wound up as another zombie." Cathy's voice sank even lower. "There could have been a zombie outbreak."

"But—"

"You did right, Mel," Cathy said firmly, sitting up and looking directly at me. "You were brave and smart, and you helped Anna when she needed you most. You're a good friend. Anna was able to say good-bye. You gave that to her."

"It was so awful," I said, "seeing Dr. Saunders like that. His skin . . . seeing the bones underneath . . . and the smell."

"I keep thinking about him recognizing his daughter even after so much deterioration of his brain," Cathy said softly.

"I wish we could stop thinking about it," I said. Cathy was not going to think I was brave and smart if I vomited on my pillow.

"I've been thinking about it," Cathy said. "A lot. About zombies, about what can happen if a transition goes wrong. It's different when it's someone you know."

I was silent. Was Cathy about to say what I thought she was? What I hoped she would? Had she changed her mind?

"It's so real. I knew Anna's dad. We all did. Remember

how clever and funny he was? Then last night he could barely say his daughter's name."

"I can't imagine anyone I loved being like that," I said, looking away from Cathy. "It's too horrible."

"You mean me?"

"No. I mean, yes. You're my best friend. I love you. I couldn't stand to see you like that. But I won't, will I? I mean, not after what you just saw."

There was a long pause. I stared at the morning light on my bedroom ceiling.

"You think I've changed my mind?" Cathy asked at last.

"Well, yes," I said, sitting up. "You have, haven't you?"

"You know I've been doing a lot of research, right?"

I nodded.

"One of the things I've discovered is that it's true: There *is* a correlation between how someone is turned and how successful their transition is. Dr. Saunders was changed against his will. He would have fought his assailant—his murderer. You saw the result.

"The odds of my success are high. Not only am I willing, but we're doing the transition in a secure facility, with trained experts. We're not leaving anything to chance."

Cathy's face, lying on her pillow, was sad but serene. I couldn't imagine being that calm, talking about the odds. The odds of her not becoming what we'd seen last night.

"There's still a risk."

"Yes, but I'm willing to take it. I want this. And if—if it does go wrong, the ZDU will be right there. I won't end like Dr. Saunders."

I did not want to imagine Cathy as a zombie, not for a fraction of a second.

"You're still going to do it?" I said. I couldn't keep the misery out of my voice.

Cathy sat up now, hugging her knees and speaking in a level voice.

"Yes, Mel, I am. I love you. You're my best friend and I'm really sorry you don't want me to do this. But I am going to do it. I'm glad you're worried about me. I'm glad you care so much. But you have to trust me to make my own decisions."

She wasn't angry this time. She truly wanted me to understand.

"Even after what you saw? Dr. Saunders?"

She nodded. "Like I said, I've always known there were risks. But I'm going into this with my eyes open, knowing everything there is to know. We've minimized the risks as much as they can be. This is what I want. I know you don't want it for me. I respect that. But it's my life, Mel. I'm the one who decides.

"I don't want to lose you. I don't want our friendship to end. Will you—can you be my friend after my transition?"

She was asking me what Kit had asked. I thought of everything I'd told Kit about why I couldn't be with him if he changed. I'd told him Cathy wasn't going to change. But she was.

Cathy was going to change. There was nothing I could do to stop her.

She was going to become a vampire.

Cathy was watching me with her big eyes. She'd always looked a little wistful, even when she was a kid. As if there would always be something important to her that she could never have.

"I want you to stay in my life," Cathy whispered.

"I want you to stay in mine," I whispered back.

I was thinking about Camille. She wasn't so bad. She loved her son. She had a wry sense of humor even if she didn't laugh. And Anna and Ty were right: Cathy had never been much of a laugher. Even as a kid you could tickle her as much as you liked and barely get a smile out of her. Sure, she wasn't ticklish, but it was more than that. She was so serious. Cathy had been born serious. She would make a serious vampire. A little like Francis. A Francis who wasn't obnoxious and who could handle being teased.

"When I transition," Cathy said, then paused, waiting for me.

So I said, "Yes."

I admitted reality, at last. I admitted I could not stop it. Cathy was going to become a vampire.

"I want you to be there. I want my best friend to be there to see me leave my old life and welcome me to my new one."

"If that's what you want," I said, concentrating hard on not letting the tight awful feeling in my chest transition into tears.

Cathy held out a hand. I took it between mine. It was warm, human. I held on as hard as I could. "You'll be cold," I whispered. "Room temperature."

"You get used to it," she promised.

CHAPTER FORTY

Team Human

School on Monday was weird. Anna wasn't there, obviously. But news of what had happened had somehow spread. It hadn't come from me or Cathy. Yet everyone seemed to know. I didn't answer any of their questions. I really didn't want to talk about it.

Kaplan was acting principal in Principal Saunders's absence. Who knew when or if she'd be coming back? He called Cathy and me into his office first thing to see if we were okay and to assure us that we could take a few days off if we needed to. We both said we were all right.

I wasn't sure if that was true. We were both quieter than usual. I couldn't stop thinking about Anna and her zombie dad, and Cathy determined to become a vampire, and what a horrible mess everything was. I was relieved Francis wasn't at school. I didn't think I could stand to

see him on the day after I had finally accepted I was losing my best friend.

I was already calculating how long Cathy had left
before she stopped being Cathy and became . . . whatever
it was she wound up being. At best it would be Vampire Cathy. I could not imagine being BFFs with Vampire
Cathy. Though I would try, because I had promised.
Because she was Cathy, and I couldn't stand the thought
of losing her.

All day I was on the verge of tears. I am not much of a
crier, but there they were, like pins behind my eyes.

I found myself thinking several times during the day
that maybe I should have stayed home. My concentration
was not fabulous. But none of my teachers said anything
about it. I guess Kaplan had spoken to them.

Even Ty could see that Cathy and I were not our
usual selves. He gave us very fast hugs, mumbled that
he was sorry and did we think Anna would like him to
visit? Sure, we said. Though neither of us had any idea
what Anna wanted right then. Other than to have her
father back and to never have anything to do with vampires again.

During study period, unable to concentrate on a
single chapter of anything, I checked my phone. There
was a text from Kit.

Can you come over this evening? Having meeting
with my shade. Need you.

I texted back **Yes** even though I'd been thinking about whether I should stop seeing Kit. The thought of his transition was too painful. I was really going to miss him.

But I owed him an explanation. Might as well get that over and done with. Besides which, maybe he would make me laugh?

He was really good at that. And I could really use a laugh.

I let Coach know I would skip fencing practice. She was very understanding. Everyone was. I'd actually been looking forward to practice: I was very much in the mood to stab people. Sadly, when I was in that mood, I fenced horribly, all technique out the window. Wild stabbing is typically not good saber technique.

✦

Camille opened the door before I'd even knocked. I'd have to get used to superexcellent vampire hearing.

I couldn't help thinking that once Cathy transitioned, I'd never be able to surprise her again.

"Come in, my dear," Camille said in her austere way, shutting the door behind me.

The endearment surprised me. I wondered if she felt sorry for me after what had happened.

I walked into a room full of vampires. It would be a lie if I didn't mention that my first instinct was to run a million miles away.

Turns out their teeth really do gleam, and when you

see that many of them together, that gleam is very bright indeed. And terrifying.

Marie-Therese waved in an airy I-am-queen kind of way. I tried not to think about what Kit had said about her voting to eat him and waved back. Minty was contemplating her remarkably long nails and remarking that she was missing out on her bridge party for this.

Francis nodded at me gravely, an action I mirrored back at him, though possibly my nod was even graver than his. Albert was looking at Kit, who was sitting by himself, facing the rest of his shade. I smiled at him, and Kit returned the smile, even if his smile was shaky.

And who could blame him, when his family meetings looked like this? I'd be intimidated too.

The treacherous pinpricks returned behind my eyes. I was going to miss him.

I shuffled into the chair Camille indicated next to her.

I wondered what Kit could possibly have to tell them, and why he had wanted me here.

"Right," Kit said, clearing his throat. "You're all here. So, um, I have something I want to say to all of you."

"We rather gathered that," Francis said dryly.

I was sorry I was sitting out of kicking range of Francis, but Kit lifted his chin at the words.

"Right then, thank you, Francis." He swallowed. "I've been thinking about this a lot lately, and obviously, you're the ones it most concerns. You're my shade. So I—I have to let you know. I had to tell you, as soon as I was sure."

They were all watching him, with those clear, unblinking eyes, a ring of natural predators.

Kit looked scared out of his mind.

"I'm not going to transition," he said.

There was an immediate stir, a hissing and several voices raised in exclamation. Kit was breathing hard, his eyes wide and showing a lot of white, but he managed to get enough breath to speak over the noise.

"Not immediately," he said. "I'm not saying I won't ever transition, but I am saying—that I want to wait and see. I'm not saying that I definitely will transition, either. I've been realizing lately," he said, glancing at me and then away, "that there's a lot I don't know about being human. As in pretty much everything. There are so many human things I've never done. Never thought about, even. I don't think I can become a vampire unless I've lived as a human first. I need to know what I'm giving up before I take the risk of dying or worse. Before I do something I can't take back."

He didn't look at me again, but I knew we were both thinking of Dr. Saunders.

"Old age," Minty said in a crisp, cold voice. "Becoming a vampire means giving up old age. I for one was not sad to miss that little part of human experience. Skin losing its elasticity, sagging toward the ground, teeth falling out—"

"Pain," Albert agreed in a sonorous voice. "Searing,

agonizing pain. When you get hit by a bus, young man, you will not be able to merely push the bus aside and continue on your way, you will *suffer*."

I barely heard the litany of objections. I was staring at Kit. He was shaking as he listened to them.

Albert stood up. "Of course, vampires can suffer too," he said, eyeing Kit coldly. "We can suffer disappointment."

Kit flinched back as if Albert had hit him.

Albert left the room, Minty beside him, murmuring something about ingratitude.

I sneaked a look at Camille. She was sitting very stiffly in her chair. Her profile looked like something carved out of ice.

I wondered if she was disappointed in Kit too.

I'd been wrong again. Kit hadn't been looking at them as a ring of predators, but still and always as his family, having something huge and life-altering to tell them, hoping it wouldn't change how they felt about him.

"You seemed perfectly happy to become a vampire before," Marie-Therese murmured. "As we always planned."

"I know," Kit said. "I wanted you all to be glad you took me in. I wanted to be like you. I did. I still do. But I don't know how to be sure about it anymore. I couldn't do it now. I'd always wonder."

"What you missed?" Marie-Therese asked, with an arch look at me.

I glared at her.

"Laughter," Francis said. I turned to look at him. "He would miss laughter. I think we all know that. You laugh all the time, Kit. You are very human," Francis said with a minuscule smile. "It is nothing to be ashamed of."

I almost fell off my chair. *Francis* was encouraging Kit to stay human? I swear, if he had been sitting closer I would have hugged him.

"Thank you," Kit said after a moment. "Thank you all, actually. You did take me in. I'll always be grateful. I'm sorry if you're disappointed in me, but you'll always be my shade, and I love you. And I have something more to say. Maybe one day I will change, but right now," he said, glancing at me again, "I really want to give this being human thing a shot. I want the full human experience. So I've enrolled at Craunston High. I'll be a junior."

Francis stiffened, clearly outraged by this slight against Kit's obviously superior homeschooling. A few other vampires looked indignant as well, reminding me of parents looking at unfair report cards.

Kit's mouth twisted, wry and hopeful.

"They said we were too far into the year for me to start as a senior. Even though they were impressed by my test results on account of my *excellent* tutoring. Apparently the extra year gives me a better shot at getting into a good college. I've missed a lot of extracurricular things, you see. Though I hear my waltzing will be great for college applications." He smiled properly, and

Francis managed to smile back.

The mention of waltzing seemed to signal the end of the meeting. A couple of other vampires left, shutting doors emphatically, giving Kit looks that made his shoulders hunch. A couple more stepped up to him and whispered to him seriously, like he'd decided to pass up Yale and go backpacking around the Amazon, all "think about your future, young man," and that wasn't so bad. That was how family behaved.

Camille kept her seat until she was the only vampire left in the room. Then and only then did she rise and glide over to Kit, graceful as a swan. She put her hands on both his shoulders.

I crossed my fingers and wished as hard as I could for her to understand.

"You have made me very happy today," said Camille in her cool, emotionless voice. She stood looking up into her son's face. "But there is nothing new in that, is there? No matter what you decide, no matter how long you live or I do, you will remain the great joy of my life."

I realized she had known what Kit was going to say all along. Of course she had. She was his mom.

✦

And me? What was I?

I was beaming. I could have danced the whole way home. Instead I walked hand in hand with Kit.

"I'm so glad," I told him again.

"I didn't do it for you," he said. "I mean," he added

hastily, "you were a big part of my decision. You showed me what I'd been missing. That there was more to humanity than what I'd seen through the eyes of my shade. Camille and Francis kept telling me that, but it took meeting you, and hearing you laugh, to make me see. Thank you."

He squeezed my hand as he said it, and I stopped and turned to face him. It was not long after dusk, so the streets of the Shade were mostly empty.

"I'm glad," I said, looking up at his eyes and wishing once again that I was as tall as my sister or even my little brother. I went up onto my tiptoes, he leaned down, and we kissed.

Kit's breath on my face was warm, so were his lips, and his arms holding me tight. I could feel the heat of his body pressed to mine, smell the oh-so-human smell of him, feel both our hearts beating faster, the blood racing through our veins.

I pulled away briefly. "Welcome to Team Human," I said.

Kit laughed. It was a glorious sound.

CHAPTER FORTY-ONE

Crossing the Bridge

I had passed by the New Whitby Center for Transition a hundred times without ever thinking much about it. It was like any other government building, big and irrelevant and the subject of grown-up discussions.

I vaguely remembered Mom and Dad talking about it when it was built, a few years back. Saying that it was an awful lot of money to spend when not so many people transition these days, and how the New Whitby council always listened too much to Geoffrey Travers, just because he'd been on the council for a hundred twenty-five years.

Then Mom made a joke about how no other vampire would accept the position, and Dad said that he thought Travers had been wearing the same waistcoat for at least a hundred of those years. The conversation had moved on to other things.

The new building, a Rubik's cube of steel framework and smoked glass, had risen on the south bank of the Bathory River.

Cathy would have preferred to become a vampire in the arms of Francis's shade, in their beautiful old house. (She wouldn't have wanted to transition in Kit's room, which had a drum kit and posters taped to every available surface, including the mirror, and was the opposite of beautiful.) She would have worn an elegant white dress and the lights would have been down low, if she'd had it her way.

But Cathy had already been given enough exceptions by being allowed to transition young. The media would have a field day with a seventeen-year-old girl who was transitioned in any way that wasn't completely by the book, especially a seventeen-year-old girl who had been involved in the Saunders zombie case.

Especially if the transition was unsuccessful.

I didn't want to think about that.

The transition room was a bit like a hospital room and a bit like a prison: The walls were so thick, it was like we were all in a huge white concrete bathtub. One of the walls was reinforced sliding glass opening onto a balcony almost as big as the room itself.

The transitioning expert assigned to us was a red-haired vampire. Vampire pallor on top of normal redhead pallor meant her skin almost glowed, and her hair looked scarlet in contrast.

I'd been thinking about the thing I didn't want to think about and so totally missed her name. I was mentally calling her Dr. Vampire.

"You may experience a feeling of claustrophobia," said Dr. Vampire to Cathy in that good, professional voice: infinitely kind and totally distant. "You may become distressed because you perceive temperatures differently. We find that in some cases the transitionee will want to go outside immediately. With the balcony we can relocate you to the cool open air instantly if you so desire."

Cathy nodded, her eyes huge and nervous.

It made me think of the way she'd looked on our very first day of kindergarten, small and serious and anxious to get this right.

Except that it didn't remind me of that, not really: I only imagined it did. I didn't really remember our first day of school.

All I knew was that I'd been there on her first day of school. It had been my first day of school too. I was not going with her on this journey.

I was terrified I didn't have enough memories of Cathy. There had been years' and years' worth, but I couldn't remember what color her dress had been on that first day or where our families had taken us on our first vacation together. What had been the name of that band we were going to form? I'd forgotten too much.

Today could be the last day. These might be all the memories of Cathy I would ever have. They weren't enough.

Valerie Beauvier was sitting in a chair, staring at Cathy with tears in her eyes. It made me furious to see Cathy's mom giving herself tragic airs, when she'd signed off on the papers. When all of this was her fault.

I curled my hands into fists, my nails biting into my palms, and told myself to stop blaming other people.

This was Cathy's decision. She wasn't being forced like Dr. Saunders. She wanted this, and I had to find a way to respect that.

Somehow.

Kit and Camille were here, both standing by the wall. Kit looked awkward. I wondered if it was because he didn't know Cathy very well or if he was thinking about how this could have been his transition. Cathy said she was glad to have members of what would (if all went well) be her shade with her.

I suspected she wanted Kit there for me, for moral support. In case . . .

I wasn't going to think about it.

Francis was sitting by Cathy's bedside, her hands in both of his. He was wearing a black silk shirt that made his hair look silver and her hospital gown look paler.

He'd dressed for the transitioning.

I could almost hate him for that, but Cathy had wanted a tableau as well. Scene setting must be a couple's hobby for them, like some people play tennis doubles.

"My darling," said Francis, "if you need more time, I will understand. We don't have to do this today."

His voice was the usual Francis voice, cool and composed, but Cathy smiled as if she heard something else in it. She reached out and rested her palm against his cheek.

"This is no time for nerves, beloved."

Francis bowed his head and stood up, walking over to the glass doors and through to the balcony.

"So, Cathy," Kit said, "when you have your first drink of blood, do you want to have it in a champagne glass to celebrate?"

Dr. Vampire gave Kit a tolerant look. "She will be given it in the regulation packet."

"I'll sneak you a straw," Kit said. "And maybe a pink umbrella."

Cathy smiled, and I was glad that somebody could be there to make her smile a little, help her relax, but I couldn't do it. I bolted out onto the balcony.

Oh, excellent. Special alone time with Francis.

The balcony had a high, reinforced glass wall, taller than my head. New Whitby at night was spread out before me, a glittering carpet with a pattern I knew by heart. There was the Shade, and there was my neighborhood, and there was our school.

Down below our feet, the Bathory River ran, moonlight and movement changing it every moment. First silver, then darkness.

"When I asked her if she might consider becoming a vampire," Francis said, "I did not give her a date. I would have been happy to wait until she completed university, until she had—" He swallowed. "She is so young. We have been together for such a very short time." He straightened a little, which was when I noticed he had been the Francis version of slumped before. "But it's her decision."

I'd been all ready to yell at him for putting that option in front of her, my romantic Cathy, but him saying that made me close my mouth.

It was her decision. Francis hadn't wanted to push her into it.

I couldn't act like he was my friend. I couldn't act like I had any sort of positive feelings toward him at all. I couldn't even say that I wouldn't blame him if something went wrong.

But he stood here staring out into the night, and I thought there was a chance he was feeling a little of the same desperate fear as me.

"We both love her," I said, and put my hand on his arm.

Francis didn't draw away, not until Cathy murmured our names. Then we both left the balcony and went back to her bed. I took her mom's place by Cathy's side, and Valerie Beauvier went over to her chair to weep again. Kit put an awkward, comforting hand on her shoulder. Camille looked disturbed by the excessive human display of emotion, but Kit stood by Ms. Beauvier and Camille stood by him.

I made an effort and met Cathy's eyes. She was crying too, silent tears that slipped down her cheeks and sparkled on her lashes.

"I love you, Mel," she said. "You're my best friend. It won't matter if I live to be a thousand years old, or—" Cathy stopped. "It won't matter," she went on, softer now. "You'll always be the best."

"You're pretty okay too," I whispered back. "I mean, not perfect, but I'd give you a solid B."

Cathy smiled through her tears. "You know I always make A's."

I stooped down and kissed her on one wet cheek. "I love you," I murmured, in her ear so nobody else could hear, and then because it was her decision, I stepped back from the bed.

Francis took out a linen handkerchief from his breast pocket—of course he did, classic Francis—and began to tenderly dry her tears, but Cathy checked him and took it gently from his hand.

She dried her own tears, carefully, taking her time.

No matter what happened next, how well things went, this was the last time Cathy would ever cry.

"Are you ready to begin the procedure, Ms. Beauvier?" asked Dr. Vampire. For a second I thought she was speaking to Cathy's mom, but then Cathy nodded. "And you, Mr. Duvarney?"

Francis nodded.

Dr. Vampire cast a discreet glance at the Zombie Disposal Unit, lined at the back of the room with their nets and weapons.

She said, "You may begin."

I backed up, into the open door. I felt the night air run down the back of my shirt and shuddered.

Francis took Cathy's face between his palms and looked at her for a long moment. Then he let her go.

Cathy tilted her head back, baring her throat, and Francis brushed a long strand of dark hair from her neck.

He sat there on the bed, looking at her neck, and I saw his fangs.

His teeth glittered, sharp and thin as stiletto knives. Francis the soft-spoken, Francis the perfect gentleman, crouched over my best friend like a hungry animal.

Cathy lay trusting and still in his arms.

I backed up another step. I couldn't run to her, I couldn't tear her away. It was her decision.

Francis bit in.

I only saw it for an instant, those sharp teeth breaking her skin, the swift scarlet welling of blood, and the way Cathy's body jerked in a spasm of pain.

I whirled around and looked out at the city. I couldn't bear it.

New Whitby glittered. The river rushed by. And my best friend was dying behind me.

I took deep, shaky breaths, and I heard someone

approaching. Kit's arms went around my waist and he said, in my ear: "Hold on."

He was warm and solid at my back. I tried to fix my blurry eyesight on something, and looked at the Remembrance Bridge, a wide stone bridge with columns on either end, bearing the names of humans and vampires who had died in World War I.

I fixed my eyes on the bridge, solid and real. The river had been running under it for a hundred years. I wasn't going to cry.

I took in one more deep breath and pulled gently away from Kit.

I looked through the open door.

Cathy lay so still on the bed. There was blood on her mouth, blood on her neck, blood on the sheets.

She looked dead.

The ZDU moved to surround Cathy's bed, making sure no human was too close to her. Francis stood at the foot of the bed.

I held on to the glass door and thought, with a conviction I hadn't been able to muster before, Yes, her decision, yes, be a vampire. Don't laugh, don't cry, don't ever see the sun again.

It wouldn't have been my choice, but it wasn't my choice.

Please let her get what she wants, I thought.

It didn't matter if I agreed or disagreed with my best friend. What mattered was keeping my best friend.

I could see her, past the guards. Her chest did not rise and fall. It wouldn't ever again.

If she didn't move, she was dead.

If she did move—I thought of Dr. Saunders and knew there were worse things.

She moved. I grabbed Kit's hand and held it hard.

I saw her eyes open.

I saw her head move and lift. I couldn't see well enough with all those bodies in the way; I couldn't tell.

Then I heard her. Clear as a bell in that clinical white room, with the doctor and the guards around her, Cathy said: "Francis."

I turned around again, this time because I was crying. The lights of New Whitby blurred, forming a new pattern, and I cried and cried because I was so happy.

Then Cathy said, "Mel," and I turned to look at her.

She was watching me. She looked like Cathy and yet not like Cathy, eyes a little too brilliant in a face that was a little too pale. She looked like a new Cathy.

She held out her hand to me, and I crossed the room to her bed.

CHAPTER FORTY-TWO

Prelude to a Win

Of course, Cathy wanted to finish school. Ty joked that even if she'd become a zombie, she probably would have wanted to finish school.

Ty's zombie jokes never went over well, and we had all warned him that if he made them in front of Anna, he would regret it.

Naturally, Francis the chivalrous had to accompany her. Besides which, he was still writing his magnum opus. I had seen his and Cathy's office/library, the walls lined with shelves full of gold-spined volumes, both their desks piled high with paper. Francis seemed to be adjusting to Cathy's addition of a computer. Kit swore he'd even seen him watching online videos of hilarious monkeys.

Cathy seemed to be enjoying her role as cowriter and researcher.

I was happy for them. Just as long as nobody expected me to read any of it.

On this particular fine winter day—with actual sun!—we'd decided to play Ty's new invention of snow baseball at lunch. (Remarkably like regular baseball except played in the snow with an orange ball.) We were all going a little stir crazy. February is always the worst. Short days, long cold nights. It did mean hanging with Cathy outdoors was easier. I asked her to join us for baseball, but she didn't seem eager to leave the library and don her hazmat suit.

It was still weird for me, having to leave Cathy inside.

"I don't mind," Cathy told me in her new voice, cooler and somehow hushed, as if being undead meant you were always at the library. (Cathy did love libraries.) "Really, it will give us a chance to put our notes in order."

"Oh, is that what they're calling it these days," I said, waggling my eyebrows.

From across the room, I could see Francis was scandalized. These special moments with him always made my day.

Cathy's mouth, lips a paler rose than they had been, turned up at the corners about half as much as they would have before.

There was a pang in my chest, knowing that once she might even have laughed. But it was worth a lot, to have her here and smiling at me.

"All right, you two crazy kids," I said. "Can't hang

around. My team's going to get creamed without me. See you in Local History?"

"After that, back to the library for study period," Cathy said sternly. "There's much more research to do."

Ever since I'd first expressed a desire to look into the police force as a future career, Cathy had been making me research every detail of it, finding out which were the best courses, Police Science or Law Enforcement or Criminal Justice, and which were the best colleges. Or should I go straight to the police academy? Was that even possible?

It was nice to discuss it with Cathy. The police mission statement felt right as nothing else had felt right.

If you want happiness for a lifetime, help somebody. Protect and serve.

"Sure, sure," I said, pausing at the door to give Cathy a little wave.

She and Francis bent over their books, dark and fair heads close together, serious and absorbed, protected from the sun by smoked glass.

Even undead, Cathy was still dragging me to the library. Stuff like that allowed me to pretend things hadn't changed that much.

She seemed happy, I thought, as I ran through the shadowed corridors, then into the gym and across it, heading for the door. I hoped she would never regret it, not if she lived to be a thousand years old.

If she did live to be a thousand years old, though, I hoped she'd at least take a break from Francis and date an alien. I imagined Francis's reaction to being dumped for an alien, and I came out into the bright but still chilly sunlight laughing.

Kit looked up at my laugh from where he stood at second base.

"Get your butt over here!" he yelled.

I sauntered over. "I'm sorry, what was that?"

"Darling, we implore you to rescue us from ignominious defeat with your superior athletic skills," drawled Kit, doing his best Francis impression. "So get your butt over here."

"Oh, well, when you put it like that," I said, and jumped at him.

He caught me neatly, my legs around his waist, and spun me around for a brief kiss. It was kind of a handy way to work through the height difference.

I grinned up at him, the kiss still sending sparks through my blood, and he grinned back, his curls lit up against the sky.

"You guys want to play ball or you want to fool around?" Anna called, tossing her blazing hair.

We hadn't been sure Anna would come back to school, not with her mother getting fired and given community service.

They said it was the lightest possible sentence, considering she had kept a zombie so close to schoolkids. We had all been a few basement walls away from disaster.

Principal Saunders had been a hairbreadth away from

disaster herself. She'd fed Dr. Saunders with her own blood, but she'd cut herself and let it drip into a cup she gave him. She could have been bitten countless times. Anna had almost been orphaned. I shivered thinking about it.

But the court had determined that Principal Saunders had been of unsound mind, given the traumatic experience of walking in on her husband's forced and unsuccessful transitioning. She was getting counseling now, at the center where Dr. Saunders used to work, and she'd been chosen as a group leader for some of the sessions. Anna said helping other people was helping her mom more than anything: Principal Saunders was looking into a new career as a counselor.

They were both doing much better than we had expected. It made me hope Cathy was right, that I hadn't been such a bad friend to Anna after all.

"Fooling around later," I said, waggling my fingers at Kit as I backed off. "Victory now!"

This evening, we were going on our first official double date. Kit refused to go on double dates with Francis: He maintained it was creepy and would call him Uncle Francis all day whenever it was suggested.

We were going on our double date with Ty and Jon the soccer player.

Turned out Ty had not so much been trying to fix Anna up on a date with Jon as trying to date Jon himself. Whoops.

We'd all been staggering around after the discovery of Anna's dad and Cathy's transitioning, so Ty's revelation that he might want to date guys as well as girls had been received by us all in a way he found disappointingly low-key.

However, I very much enjoyed discussing how Francis's beauty had awakened Ty to this realization. Such improper conversation made Francis so, so hilariously scandalized.

"Victory?" yelled Anna, who can be very competitive. (It's one of the things we have in common. Friends should have stuff in common.) "Check your team's score, Mel."

I jogged over to the plate and took the bat when Ty tossed it to me. Ty gave me a look of mute supplication, and I winked at him. When I turned, I saw more looks: Anna's of challenge, and Kit's of cheerful expectation, bouncing on his heels, ready to run.

Across the grounds at a window, I saw a shadow moving, and I grinned. I wasn't going to lose with my best friend watching.

The sun was warm on my hair, my blood already racing. I swung the bat experimentally and couldn't stop the smile splitting my face.

"I don't need to know the score," I said. "I like my team's chances."

ACKNOWLEDGMENTS

Team Human sprang out of our shared love of vampire stories and long discussions about what kinds of vampires we'd write about if we were ever to do so. We had many vampire questions we wanted to answer. Were vampires actually icy cold or were they room temperature and just felt cold to us non–room temperature types? Somehow it became a dare, and before we knew it we were writing a vampire book together. Best. Fun. Ever.

As we started writing, we gave each other reading lists to round out our vampire education. Both had read *Carmilla*, *Varney the Vampire*, and, of course, *Dracula*, not to mention Anne Rice. But Sarah had not read Suzy McKee Charnas's *The Vampire Tapestry* or Tanith Lee's *Sabella*, and Justine had never read L. J. Smith's *The*

Vampire Diaries. That had to be corrected! The ensuing discussions shaped *Team Human* in a plethora of ways. Without those books and our youthful vampire obsession this book would not exist.

We'd like to thank our agents, Jill Grinberg and Kristin Nelson, and everyone at their agencies who found this book such a good home.

Our editors—Anne Hoppe at HarperCollins and Jodie Webster at Allen & Unwin—have been marvelous, and have improved the book in a thousand different ways. The gorgeousness that graces the front cover of our book is thanks to our art director, Amy Ryan, and to Joel Tippie, among many wonderful people—we love our cover and appreciate your work so much! And the final touches were added to our book by our lovely copyeditor, Renée Cafiero.

Our first reader, Scott Westerfeld, who knows a thing or two about vampires, had lots of wonderfully useful suggestions to make. He also gave us the fabulous title.

Ordinarily, we would thank all our writer friends. But we kept this book a secret, which made it even more fun. But thank you, wonderful YA writer friends. You know who you are.

Justine would like to thank Jan Larbalestier and John and Niki Bern for all their support. And, of course, Sarah Rees Brennan, without whom this would never have happened. It's been a blast, SRB. Thank you. Let's write another one!

Sarah would like to thank Pat Rees, for giving her *Interview with the Vampire* when she was nine (thanks, Mum!), and Genevieve Rees Brennan, for reminding her to go see *New Moon* by asking for a Team Jacob T-shirt. She'd also like to thank Natasha Walsh, for putting up with her making loud phone calls to Australia at one a.m., and most of all, Justine Larbalestier—for taking said loud phone calls, plotting out novels even though it's traumatic, and single-handedly changing my mind about cowriting being a bad idea to cowriting being the most fantastic idea ever. And like all good ideas, it bears repeating. . . .